THE COUPLE ACROSS THE STREET

STREET

ANITA WALLER

Boldwood

First published in Great Britain in 2023 by Boldwood Books Ltd.

Cover Design by Head Design Ltd.

Cover Photography: Shutterstock

The moral right of Anita Waller to be identified as the author of this work has been asserted in accordance with the Copyright, Designs and Patents Act 1988.

This book is a work of fiction and, except in the case of historical fact, any resemblance to actual persons, living or dead, is purely coincidental.

Every effort has been made to obtain the necessary permissions with reference to copyright material, both illustrative and quoted. We apologise for any omissions in this respect and will be pleased to make the appropriate acknowledgements in any future edition.

A CIP catalogue record for this book is available from the British Library.

Paperback ISBN 978-1-80415-327-7

Large Print ISBN 978-1-80415-328-4

Hardback ISBN 978-1-80415-326-0

Ebook ISBN 978-1-80415-329-1

Kindle ISBN 978-1-80415-330-7

Audio CD ISBN 978-1-80415-321-5

MP3 CD ISBN 978-1-80415-322-2

Digital audio download ISBN 978-1-80415-323-9

Boldwood Books Ltd
23 Bowerdean Street
London SW6 3TN
www.boldwoodbooks.com

PREVIOUSLY PUBLISHED WORKS

Psychological thrillers

Beautiful published August 2015
Angel published May 2016
34 Days published October 2016
Strategy published August 2017
Captor published February 2018
Game Players published May 2018
Malignant published October 2018
Liars published May 2020, co-written with Patricia Dixon
Gamble published May 2020
Nine Lives published April 2021
One Hot Summer published August 2022
The Family at No.12 published November 2022

Supernatural

Winterscroft published February 2017

Kat and Mouse series

Murder Undeniable published December 2018
Murder Unexpected published February 2019
Murder Unearthed published July 2019
Murder Untimely published October 2019
Epitaph published August 2020
Murder Unjoyful published November 2020

The Connection Trilogy

Blood Red published August 2021
Code Blue published November 2021
Mortal Green published March 2022

For our little collection of great-grandchildren,
Lily Grace Taylor, Elle Isla Taylor, William Louis Kitchen.
We love you so much.

Murder is always a mistake. One should never do anything that one cannot talk about after dinner.

— OSCAR WILDE, 1854 – 1900

Through violence, you may murder the hater, but you do not murder the hate.

— MARTIN LUTHER KING JNR, 1929 – 1968

PROLOGUE
JULY 2003

There was a silence in the hospital side room that was like no other. It was marred occasionally by the slight snuffle from Eloise Grantham as she had, despite wanting to stay awake, slipped into a troubled sleep; she needed the child in the bed to open his eyes, to begin his journey back to health, to prove that the awful car smash wouldn't take his life.

Both the nurse and the grandmother missed the first visible signs of awakening from the young boy. Josiah Grantham's eyes twitched before opening, then flickered, then closed again. It was enough for the moment.

* * *

Eloise's head dropped to one side and she woke with a start, guilt enveloping her as she realised she had slept. Her eyes travelled instantly to her grandson, this most precious child, and saw that she had missed nothing. He was still, but today, hopefully today, he would start to exit the awful tunnel he seemed to be in. Eloise needed him to come back to her, to show her that she hadn't lost a very precious part of her.

She reached to the foot of the bed and unhooked the medical chart. Josiah John Grantham, date of birth 25 December 1999, parent Kirsty Grantham. She gently stroked her fingers across his name. It had been a difficult Christmas, that one six years earlier, but the tiny baby placed in her arms at the end of Christmas Day had made the half-cooked turkey worth all the effort.

How she and Kirsty had laughed as they had tried to lift the turkey, now surrounded by potatoes as they began their journey of being roasted, but the extra weight had proved their undoing. As Kirsty had bent to help slide the roasting tin back into the oven, her waters had broken. And this wonderful boy lying in the bed had arrived with ten minutes of Christmas Day still to enjoy.

No daddy to share the joy of the moment; in fact, no daddy ever admitted to exist. And in that moment of Eloise holding her grandchild for the first time, it hadn't mattered. She and Kirsty would be enough for this wondrous being.

And now there was currently no Kirsty to hold her boy, lost inside a coma that everyone hoped would end. Eloise clung to the hope extended by the doctors that this child would surface when his body was ready, just as his mother hopefully would, but she was so scared. Scared she would lose both of them.

She reached out to grasp his hand, the one that didn't have a cannula inserted in it, and she prayed. As she had prayed ever since the police had called to tell her of the accident on the M1.

Kirsty, unconscious in the Northern General Hospital, her child in a similar condition in the children's hospital, and all because Kirsty had wanted to take him to Meadowhall to see a movie.

Between visits to her daughter in one hospital and her vigils at Jed's bedside in the children's hospital, the details of the smash had slowly emerged. A tyre blow-out in a Jeep that had been over-taking Kirsty's car at ninety miles an hour had caused the Jeep to veer towards her, flip her own much smaller Fiesta over for it to be hit by a white van that simply couldn't stop in time to avoid the car – the car carrying everything that Eloise loved in the world. Kirsty had died at the scene but had been resuscitated by skilled para-medics; six-year-old Jed had been strapped into the back seat. He'd suffered a head injury, some spectacular bruising and a broken arm, all mendable if he would only wake up and begin his climb back to being the wonderful child she had loved from the moment of his birth.

* * *

The second time he opened his eyes she whispered his name, and gently squeezed his fingers. He squeezed back but didn't speak, just closed his eyes once more, hiding away the bright blue that was so dear to his grandmother. Half an hour later he opened his eyes again, and the nurse held a sippy cup to his lips. After the drink that moistened his lips and throat, he spoke.

'Granny,' he said.

Jed's climb back to health had begun.

1

Clare Staines was feeling muddled. Her mind was struggling to cope with this unusual (for her) feeling, and really it had been mainly caused by Aunty Freda. Aunty Freda had lost her husband some fifteen years earlier and he was all she talked about, all Freda thought about; she loved him still and would quite obviously grieve for him for the rest of her life. Now a reluctant and doddery seventy years of age, she had been fifty-three when he'd died – Clare's age now. And Clare was pretty sure Aunty Freda had never felt any sort of muddlement about her love for the late Uncle Joe. She had been steadfast, dusted his photograph frames every two days, and went to simply sit and chat to him at his graveside at least once every week. She had loved him then, and she loved him still.

Clare had lost John, her own much-loved husband, eight months earlier, in January of 2022, to cancer. The muddle in her mind was caused by the fact that she thought she was over it. Her life had changed and she had welcomed the alterations to her routine. In fact, she didn't appear to have any routine; that had gone by the wayside.

She shouldn't feel like this. She should be visiting his grave every week and plying him with roses, talking to him, telling him what was going on in their lives, hers and the lives of their two daughters. Saying over and over again how much she loved and missed him. In other words, she felt she should be emulating Aunty Freda.

She did for the first couple of months. She grieved; she coped sporadically, not wholly. It had been a month since she last took John some flowers, and they weren't exactly roses, just a hurriedly picked bunch of assorted blooms from the garden; whatever looked quite fresh, really. Did she tell him she had started a yoga class? She didn't think she had. Or had made tentative enquiries about the creative writing group that met at the village hall every month? She didn't think she'd actually told him anything.

She had intended to talk to him about the progress of the purchase of Grace and Megan's new home, cementing their affiliation even further, but knowing how she hadn't really been able to discuss the relationship between the two women while he'd been alive caused her to think twice about mentioning it now, at his graveside.

She remembered taking his old flowers to the rubbish container, filling the metal vase with fresh water and carrying it back to the grave, then arranging the fresh flowers so they looked nice – but she couldn't remember speaking about anything at all.

Not a word of conversation had left her mouth. Did she say goodbye as she left? Did she make her usual promise to see him soon? Did she, at any point, say 'I love you'? Did she finger kiss the very new, white marble headstone, as she always did? The questions rattled around her brain as she realised she remembered very little about her last visit; it had felt almost as if it was expected of her to turn up routinely with flowers and say all the right things. Except, she had said nothing.

This couldn't be right. She couldn't be over him as quickly as this. They'd known each other since infant school, been married for thirty-three years – Clare felt she simply couldn't have got over his cruel death so soon. Wasn't he the love of her life? And why did these feelings of guilt keep washing over her every time she thought about doing something she knew she would enjoy doing? John had always been a little controlling, and now suddenly the chains seemed to have been removed, and she was feeling guilty because of that? Surely not.

Sara and Grace would be horrified if they knew how her mind was working. They adored their father, as did Clare, which made it all the more peculiar that she was having these feelings now – or not having feelings, if Clare really thought about it with any depth. She really was muddled.

She actually felt quite angry towards John because she wasn't normally a muddled person. She was convinced that this, in some way, was his fault as well as Aunty Freda's. Clare was usually quite composed, knew what she wanted from life, and she didn't like this troublesome state of her mind. She couldn't talk to the girls about it; they just wouldn't understand. They would be hurt and she would let nothing on earth hurt her girls.

* * *

Clare's closest and best friend was Vicki Dolan, but she wasn't even sure she could tell her about this unsettlement. Vic wasn't happy with Rob, her own dearly beloved who had, for the last two or three years, dropped down the rankings in Vic's life. No, Clare really couldn't burden her with stories of her muddle. Vic had enough to worry about. She had muddled feelings of her own.

When John's cancer was first diagnosed in October 2020, Clare and John had taken the decision to keep it from the girls, temporarily at least, partly because Sara was due to marry Greg two weeks after and partly because Grace, along with Megan King, her partner, had booked a holiday and were due to fly to the States three days after her sister's wedding.

Vic was Clare's rock, her support system. Clare knew she had to tell someone, so one night, three days before the wedding, she broke down at Vic's kitchen table. They talked and talked and talked, none of it making much sense because once the words 'eighteen months maximum' had been said, nothing seemed to make sense. John rang while they were talking; he knew just from the pain in his wife's voice what was keeping her out so late.

'Stay as long as you need, sweetheart,' he had said softly. 'I love you.'

It was about a month after this that they finally told Sara and Greg, Grace and Megan. Their reactions were quite dissimilar; Sara, their ever-practical Sara, immediately began researching to see if anything could be done to halt, reverse, wipe out this horrific thing that was happening to her father, and her younger sister fell apart.

Grace felt anger, sorrow, uncertainty – every emotion that could possibly be conjured up, she conjured it up. Megan was her mainstay, her proverbial tower of strength, guiding her at every turn in the road, whether it be good or bad.

Clare remembered Sara screaming at the computer screen one night while she was searching online.

'What do you mean palliative care? This is fucking 2021. There should be a fucking cure!' She had turned to Clare with a haunted look in her eyes. 'I'm sorry, Mum. Sorry for the language...' and they'd sobbed together, understanding all too well the frustration behind her words. Clare thought that was the evening when the enormity of it all had hit them the hardest.

As they watched John deteriorate, there was a subtle shift in the girls. Grace grew stronger, more focused on helping her mother cope with the day-to-day problems, and Sara slowly withdrew into herself.

The unhappiness in their lives had been hidden from John, but he wasn't a stupid man. He knew. He recognised the heartache in his daughters, and the eventual acceptance in his wife that she would be widowed at fifty-three, and there was nothing anyone could do about it.

* * *

When John died in the hospice on 23 January, they became a three-sided unit. The church was packed for his funeral but the three women banded together, totally united in their grief. Greg and Megan stood by, waiting to console them when it all became too much to bear on their own. The loss of this man, the strength holding their home and lives together, was such an immense thing. The combined love of that triangular unit made their family stronger, their closeness closer.

The wake had been a gathering of their friends, along with many golfing acquaintances, work colleagues from John's office, and family, such as it was. Everyone was in shock that he had gone at such a young age, and that had been what almost everyone had said to the grieving triumvirate of Clare, Sara and Grace. And they all seemed to follow up with *if you need anything at any time, just shout out.*

But Clare had found a strength she'd suspected was there, but had never really been pushed into using, because she'd depended on John. He had been her strength, the decision maker, the organiser of their finances and the person to whom they all turned to resolve any of life's problems, large or small. John Staines, an extraordinary man, a ruler, a man of strength, a much-loved family member who had left them too early.

And now Clare was muddled.

2

SEPTEMBER 2022

The family home was quite large really, Clare mused. It boasted five bedrooms, three bathrooms, two reception rooms, a huge kitchen with separate utility room, a conservatory, a massive garden and a feeling inside Clare that she was beginning to think and sound like an estate agent.

The house was where she began her muddled phase; Clare Staines, widow of John Staines, mother of Sara Carter and Grace Staines, outwardly quite confident and sociable, but muddled.

It was while she was standing in the conservatory a week or so earlier, wondering whether to give the lawn its last cut of the year or whether to leave it another week, when she realised she actually liked living there on her own. She enjoyed her own space, enjoyed the freedom of being able to do what she wanted when she wanted. John would have said cut the lawn now, don't wait another week. It will probably be raining and too wet in a week's time. And she would have got the lawnmower out immediately, then would have ended up giving it a second 'last cut of the year' because she had done it too early. In the end, she decided the last cut would be the second week in October, then the grass was on its own until March the following year.

Clare rather liked this new person, this decisive, somewhat cavalier Clare.

And she knew she was going to remove John. Today she would pack up the last of his clothes and take them to the hospice charity shop and then she would return home and... oh, she didn't know, just do something! She was going to make this house hers, not theirs.

Was this muddlement purely a feeling of liberation? She didn't think so; it felt as if it was more than that. It was more a sensation of change, of taking control maybe. Possibly it was time to stop thinking *I am muddled*, and start thinking *I am changing, I am growing into myself.* Financially, she had no worries; the house was paid for and John had been a shrewd provider. She didn't need to work, but the time had come to decide if she might *want* to work. She wanted to take some courses, maybe painting, maybe sewing, maybe a creative writing course, maybe even a plastering course! She wanted to rid herself of the overpowering presence of her husband. There! She'd said it! Admittedly, it was only to herself and not out loud, but she felt truly exhilarated.

Clare's hands were shaking with the excitement of acknowledging that John was gone and she wasn't totally miserable about it. She could remember his face – there were many photographs dotted around the house reminding her of him daily. She couldn't really hear his voice any more though. She could accept her thoughts, store them inwardly, but nobody, not even Vic, must know of this total abandonment of her previous life. Outward appearances would remain the same; she would live in the same house, live in the same body. Her mind was going to fly.

* * *

'Mom!' Grace's voice came from the hall and Clare shouted down to tell her she was in the bedroom. Clare heard her daughter's footsteps as she ran up the stairs.

Grace stared around in astonishment. 'Why... what?'

'I'm clearing Dad's things out, sweetheart. It has to be done, and other people might benefit from his clothes.'

'No,' she said, 'you can't. It's too early... You can't! Let me ring Sara, she'll tell you...'

Clare went to her and held her. Grace was rigid with shock. That was the defining moment that confirmed something really was out of kilter with Clare. Clearly their daughters hadn't yet come to terms with John's death, so why had she suddenly dismissed it, and him, from her life?

'Let's go downstairs. I'll make us a cup of tea.'

Clare led Grace out of the bedroom, away from the various piles of her father's clothes, and softly closed the door behind them. From now on, she would have to be more careful about what she did with anything relating to her husband, would have to accept that the girls were still unable to move on.

Grace's expression was almost mutinous as she sat at the kitchen table. Her mother passed her a tin of biscuits along with a mug of tea.

'Help yourself,' she said quietly, 'and we can talk.'

'There's nothing to talk about,' Grace snapped. 'You have enough room here to store his things if it upsets you so much to have them near you.'

Clare sighed. 'It's not about that. We have to let go. This is just my way of handling things and I have to do it. The hospice people were absolutely wonderful with Dad, as you know, so I'm taking everything to their charity shop. It's one way we can do something for them to say thank you, but it's also allowing me to begin a long journey of learning to live without the only man I've ever loved. I have to do this, Grace, and now is the right time.'

Grace took a sip of her tea and raised her eyes to meet Clare's. 'I know. I'm such a cow. It was just the shock of seeing all his clothes...'

Clare stood up and went round the table to where Grace sat. She put her arms around her and bent to kiss the top of her daughter's head.

Grace sighed, such a deep, deep sigh.

'I'm not sure I can help you,' she said and Clare smiled at her.

'I don't need your help; I'm quite capable of sorting things. Now, let's talk about the new apartment you've been to see.'

Grace and Megan had been together for three years, living in a tiny little house they rented from Megan's parents. It had taken John some time to accept their relationship. He had eventually come to like Megan but even at the end, Clare didn't think he really understood that Grace had made her choice just as much as Sara had with Greg.

And now they were about to take the next step by sealing a deal on a new apartment overlooking the river in the city centre.

'We complete on Friday,' she said. 'That's really what I came to see you about. We're going to see it again tomorrow, measure windows and floors and such, so Megan thought you might like to come with us.'

'I'd absolutely love to,' Clare said, relieved that for the moment Grace's mind seemed to have diverted itself from the issue of John's effects. 'I'm going to be having a bit of a clear out here, so if there's anything you want...'

Clare looked at Grace's face and knew she'd done it again.

'What?' Grace said. 'What are you doing, Mum? Are you trying to get rid of Dad altogether?'

Clare's mind guiltily jumped back to the fleeting thoughts of only minutes earlier when she had acknowledged that that was exactly what she was doing. She gently touched her daughter's hand.

'Grace, my love, one person living alone does not need the clutter and suchlike that two people need. I may even decide to move from here eventually. It's a massive house and much better suited to a family. But all of that's in the future. For now, I feel I need to step aside from the grief, the months of knowing your Dad was going to leave me. I need some peace and a little bit of me time. And the things you can have for the apartment are nothing to do with Dad dying anyway; they are simply surplus to requirements.'

Grace nodded but Clare didn't know whether it was in agreement with what she had said, or whether it was just a nod.

A car horn hooted outside and she jumped up. 'That's Megan. She said she would call here first before going home. Is that okay?'

Clare looked at her in surprise. 'Why on earth do you need to ask? Megan is just as welcome here as you are.'

Grace gave a small apologetic shrug of her shoulders. 'Dad...'

And Clare's brain cells temporarily froze. She had thought John's attitude towards Grace and Megan's partnership had been known only to her.

'I am not your father.' The words came out much harsher than she really intended and Grace looked at her, her blue eyes wide open. 'As long as you are happy, I don't care who you are with. For goodness' sake, Grace, I could shake you.'

'That would be child abuse.' She grinned.

'You'd better believe it,' she retorted, relieved to be back to their usual banter.

* * *

It was only after the girls had left that Clare decided the time had come to look at John's office. He had always done quite a bit of work from home and had spent a small fortune turning one of the bedrooms into his office. It was, however, a beautiful room as a result. The walls were lined with bookshelves and these were filled not only with the law books necessary for his work as a solicitor but also many works of fiction, both modern and old. Since his death, she had been in to dust a couple of times but she now wanted to look at it from a more practical point of view.

The first thing Clare needed to do was contact one of the new partners at Staines Solicitors and ask them if they wanted John's legal books; once the books were gone she could re-evaluate the available space and design it to fit her own needs, the needs she had never been allowed to have when John was alive. She knew it would never have occurred to him that she might want to do something other than look after him and their daughters. The provider provided, and his feeling was that his wife should be grateful she had such an easy life.

Clare went down to the garage and brought up several cardboard boxes. She made the phone call to David Barker, the new owner of John's practice, and arranged for someone to call round and collect the books the following day. She packed them into six boxes, trying to even out the weight, then tugged them down into the hall. Clare felt nothing as she looked at them, stacked as tidily as she could manage. David had said they would be invaluable to the new young solicitor they'd just brought in, so the only feeling she had about them was thankfulness that they would be of use. She tried to picture John using them but couldn't.

She really couldn't.

Shaking her head, she went back into the office and just stood. Enough had been done for one day; Clare was already nursing a hefty bruise on one arm from trying to get the heaviest box downstairs and she decided to leave everything just as it was for now. It was something of a shock to realise how empty the room looked, and yet all she had removed were his books.

She ran the palm of her hand along the polished surface of John's desk and decided it would have to be moved. She needed to accommodate a sewing machine yet still retain the desk for general things such as paying bills and suchlike. It would be a pleasure to use the desk; it was an early Victorian, highly polished item of furniture, that she and John had seen one day while having a stroll through the antiques quarter looking for a card table. John had managed to get it reduced by £100, and the previous owners agreed to deliver it. John had loved working at it, said it suited him much more than the more modern one he used at work.

The room boasted two windows on one long wall, quite high, and the desk would fit nicely underneath one of them, while the other would take a work surface to hold her machine. She felt quite excited by the prospect of redesigning the room; the empty bookshelves would soon be refilled. She could picture bolts of fabric, boxes of thread stored in a colour coded way, books of every description. All of John's fiction books could remain in situ until she sorted through which ones she had read, then they could go to the charity shop.

Despite feeling that she had done enough for one day, she retrieved a can of spray polish and a duster from the utility room and quickly cleaned the shelves. The room now smelt much fresher and Clare finally went to bed with her head full of plans. Muddled plans of course.

3

SEPTEMBER 2022

Clare felt pleased as she waved goodbye to Andy, the young man sent from David's firm the following morning. It had only taken a few minutes to load the boxes of books into his car. They'd made a huge pile in the hallway and she knew if they stayed there any longer, she would get another round of sorrowful expressions and chastisement from the girls if either of them dropped by. What they didn't see...

David rang later to say how pleased he was with them and they were already in place on their office bookshelves. He thanked Clare and said the business would be donating to cancer research as she would take no money for the books. They had made polite chit-chat, wished each other well for the future and Clare came away from the call feeling that the final link to John had been severed.

She had really and truly loved him; they'd met at infant school, as a lot of youngsters of their generation did, and grew together. She'd never looked at another man – oh, who was she kidding, she lusted after David Beckham, tattoos and all – and they had a good life. Their daughters, of course, made it complete;

if their son had lived beyond his allotted two days on this earth, life would have been blissful. Daniel had been a full-term baby, just not meant for this world. They had held him while he simply faded away on that awful day just before Christmas 1999; they were even close enough to weather that storm.

After Clare's exertions with the books, she napped for an hour on the sofa in her new room and dreamt of John, the dream no doubt brought on by the offloading of his things; the dream wasn't clear when she awoke and she quickly dismissed it. After getting her brain into gear, she took a really good look around. She decided to ask Grace and Megan for help with moving the desk when they called to collect her for the proposed apartment visit – everything else she could manage for herself. Once the desk was in its permanent place under the left-hand window, the room would be ready for worktables and other such items. She would design the room around the desk.

She was feeling quite elated and pleased with herself but then she heard the front door open and knew Grace and Megan had arrived. Her heart sank – she hoped there would be no more recriminations. She could hear their excited chatter as they went through to the kitchen and she called for them to come upstairs and join her.

They stood just inside the doorway and surveyed the empty room.

'I want to put the desk under the window,' she said. 'I know your dad liked it in the middle of the room but that was because he was always on the move, using books from the shelves and stuff. I need the centre of the room clear, so can I borrow you two and have help moving it, please?'

Grace looked miserable, but they came to stand by her and the three of them began the mammoth job of moving the desk. It was heavy and they dragged rather than carried it. Clare loved how it looked – so much better in front of that massive window – and she would be able to see outside when she was sitting at it. Even Grace grudgingly agreed it looked good. Megan playfully punched her on the arm.

'Shut up, misery. I'm on your mum's side with this. She needs this room to work for her. What else do you have planned for it, Clare?'

'I need a couple of flat surfaces, one for my sewing machine and one for cutting out on. I need a big cupboard for storage and that will get me started. I can add things as and when.'

Grace looked around her. 'It's a lovely room.'

'It certainly is, and that's why I'm going to use it. Your dad loved to be in here, and I'm sure I'll be the same. He put a lot of thought and money into this room to make it special, and there's no reason I shouldn't benefit from that now.'

'Do you miss him, Mum?'

'That's a silly question, Grace. You know I do. But at some point we have to live again. He's never coming back; he'll live on in my heart and I'll carry on thinking about him every day of my life. And in here, his special room, he'll always be with me.'

Lies.

Both Grace and Megan hugged her, so she must have sounded convincing. They went downstairs together and she chose to follow them to their new apartment in her own car, rather than clamber into the back of their tiny little Aygo.

They parked side by side and the three women walked over to the edge of the car park and looked down onto the river. Clare stayed a moment longer than the girls, watching some ducks swimming by, and thought how lovely the view would be on a gloriously hot summer's day. Today wasn't that day. It was quite cool and she hurried to catch Grace and Megan up before they reached the lift.

The apartment wasn't huge, but it had two bedrooms and a beautifully proportioned open-plan living area. They walked through the door and immediately the tape measures were produced. Clare had the responsibility of writing all the measurements down and she insisted they use both metric and feet and inches. They laughed at her, but she'd been caught out before with measurements that made no sense to the English brain!

'So, you complete on Friday?'

Grace nodded. 'We certainly do. It's why they let us have a key. And we can't wait.'

'Well, don't forget my offer. If you're short of anything, I'm sure I'll have got it.' Clare thought about the tiny property they were currently living in. 'Have you enough furniture for here?'

'We're bringing our sofa – I know it will look a bit lost in all this space, but we'll get a new one eventually. We have kitchen chairs for visitors.' Megan laughed. 'They're used to it.'

They were clearly very happy and so together it made Clare feel quite envious; she handed Grace a cheque.

She looked at it, and then at her mother. 'Why? I mean... we can't take this, Mum!'

'Why not? It's your inheritance. You'll have it one day, so why not now when you need it? And before you say anything, I have another one here' – Clare waved a similar piece of paper – 'for Sara and Greg for exactly the same amount.'

Grace handed it to Megan, and Megan's eyes widened. 'Clare...'

'Megan King, don't go all soppy on me. When I married John, his parents were already dead, but my parents gave us £150. It was a lifeline, because we had nothing. John was a very junior solicitor and I worked in a shop, so money was short. I remember that feeling, and that's why I'm helping you out now.'

Grace took Megan's hand. 'We can have a new suite, a sofa with matching chairs, or even a corner unit. Oh my God, Megan, we'll be able to sit down properly!'

The expressions on their faces made Clare laugh.

'Just remember, whatever you have from me now won't be here when I'm gone.'

'You're going nowhere.' Grace walked across and kissed Clare.

They had thought that about her father, but Clare said nothing.

They finished taking the measurements and agreed to meet up in the Marks & Spencer's café on Fargate for something to eat, and maybe some shopping.

* * *

It was a good lunch; they chatted, talked about a concerted trip to IKEA in both cars so that Clare's larger vehicle could carry any major purchases they were likely to make, and then she left them, after making a joke about their car not having a boot large enough to fit all their Marks & Spencer bags inside it, never mind a big blue IKEA bag.

* * *

Clare arrived home, collected her mail from the mailbox on the back of the door, and headed for the kitchen. She made herself a pot of coffee and sat down at the kitchen table, feeling marginally relieved that Grace appeared to be coming round from the sight of her mother folding up her father's clothes ready for the charity shop. It had been a happy day, and Clare hugged that thought to herself, feeling so much better than she had after the fallout with Grace.

There was a light tap at the kitchen door, and then she heard the immortal words, 'It's me.' Fortunately, years of hearing the phrase told her it was Vic, and she stood to unlock the door. Vic shivered as she entered the kitchen.

'Bloody freezing out there. Thought it was supposed to be autumnal, September,' she grumbled.

'No, it's not bloody freezing. It's not even classed as cold if you put on a jacket, numpty.'

'But I'm only crossing from my house to yours!'

'Okay. I give in.' She flashed a smile at her friend. 'Coffee?'

'If it's too early for gin, I'll settle for coffee.'

'It is. And I might need to hear what's wrong with you before you get the gin inside you.'

'How did you know something was wrong?'

'I can tell. I've known you for God knows how many years now, and I've always been able to tell when something's wrong. I'm assuming it's Rob?'

Vic's nod was barely discernible. 'I've told him I'm leaving.'

'What? What happened to the plan to make him leave so that you could stay in the house?' She knew that a look of concern was clear on her face.

Vic hooked her long auburn hair behind her right ear and turned her head slightly. 'He did this.'

The bruise was evident, despite the layer of make-up Vic had applied.

Clare felt lost for words. She reached out a hand and held back Vic's hair, looking closely.

'The skin isn't broken. Why did he do this?'

'Because I said I'm leaving. He's convinced it's to move in with another man; he can't seem to understand that I simply don't like him. He makes me unhappy, we never talk, and we have no shared interests at all. I've found a little flat to rent until I get some money from the house, and then I'm off. It never occurred to me he'd be violent; I didn't think he'd got that much energy, if I'm brutally honest. It's mainly the horrible things he says. He's so nasty, never has a decent word to say, and I've had enough. I'll give up the house to get some semblance of happiness and relief into my life. I went to see the flat yesterday, paid the deposit and it's mine now. I told them I needed to move quickly, but when I said that it was really because I didn't want to change my mind. But last night he hit me hard enough to knock me to the ground, and I knew there was no going back.'

'Where is he now?'

'At work. I'd like to be gone by the time he comes home tonight, but I didn't want to just disappear; I had to tell you, to let you know my side of things before he comes barrelling round here tonight to see what you know.'

'Then don't tell me. I'm better at acting dumb if I know nothing. I expect texts every hour on the hour to let me know you're okay, and as soon as he's accepted you're gone, you can tell me where you are. Okay?'

She poured the coffee and handed the mug to Vic. 'You want something in it?'

Vic shook her head. 'No, I need a clear head. The gin was only a joke. I rang in at work this morning and told them I'm not well, and I'll be back as soon as I can, but I'll go in and tell them the truth once I can think straight.' She sighed. 'This is massive, Clare. I'm scared, but I'm feeling lighter for doing this. The flat is nice, just one bedroom, but it's all I need for the moment.'

Vic sipped at her coffee, gathering her thoughts. 'And there's a car park in a courtyard area round the back, so even my car is hidden from view. I'll be fine, I know I will. He frightened me, Clare. It was so unexpected, and I didn't even have time to get out of the way of his fist.' The tears started to rain down her face, and Clare pushed some tissues across.

'This happened last night? You should have come here straight away.'

'I daren't, I didn't want him going for you as well. He was in a right old temper, believe me.'

'I've got a baseball bat...'

Vic snorted as she erupted with laughter, and wiped her eyes in an attempt to recover from her misery. 'I'd forgotten about that. You're right, it would have helped. You still keep it by the front door?'

'I do, but only because I've never thought to put it away.' John was often away so she'd followed his instructions to put it there because she would often be in the house on her own. 'I'll chuck it in the bin tomorrow; I never really wanted it anyway.'

Vic drained her mug and stood. 'I knew you'd make me feel better. I'm going to get in my car and go. I've loaded it to the hilt with stuff, bedding and towels, the immediate things I'll need, and I'll get out of the way before Rob comes home. Let me know if he comes looking for me, will you?'

Clare nodded. 'If he turns up here, I'll make damn sure he knows I've seen your face and its new addition of a bruise.'

Vic leaned to kiss her friend's cheek. 'Thanks, pardner. I'll be in touch later. And when I'm settled and sorted, I'll tell you where I am. Then I can make you a gin-less coffee.'

4

SEPTEMBER 2022

Clare stood at the window until she saw Vic's car disappear from view, then walked slowly upstairs. She wanted to get the office sorted quickly, but needed measurements for the table she planned to buy that would become her cutting out surface, whatever it may be that she was cutting out.

Clare had always enjoyed crafting; it had been her escape from the housewifely role she knew John wanted from her. Having the girls had been a blessing for him. It had meant she had to stay home to look after them, and he got all his home comforts. His promotion shortly after their wedding had seen their income double almost overnight, and from that time onwards he had tried to get her to become the housewife he wanted. She'd fought his plans until she became pregnant with Sara, but then gave in to the inevitable. She had taken to crafting, to fill in the endless hours.

She taught herself to crochet, became adept at knitting Aran jumpers, and went to various craft classes. She had loved the patchwork class, but John had complained at the fabric everywhere, and so she had let that hobby drift away. But now, contemplating the desk up in the office room, she considered resurrecting her undoubted talents in that activity.

She opened the office door and drank in the feel and the smell of it, brought on by consecutive days of polishing the shelves. She walked across to the window that would cast natural light on whatever was eventually put in place to be her workstation, and looked out at the front garden.

She fancied having a little bistro set out there – John had said nobody sat in their front gardens, even if it did get sun most of the day. It simply wasn't done; it was too public. People sat in their back gardens. And so they'd bought a comfortable dining/seating set for the rear patio. But why waste sunshine? She felt she could sit quite happily in the front, and if it literally was a small table and two chairs, she could move them to wherever she wanted them to be, either in full glorious heat, or in the shade if it got too fully gloriously hot. As she stared out of the window, she mentally planned a trip to a garden centre, credit card in hand and ready to be used.

She could feel John in this room, despite the removal of his books and the rearranged furniture. But she couldn't *hear* him any longer. Or had she simply stopped listening?

The length of wall available to her was a little over eight feet, and Clare gave it some thought, realising that if she had two four feet long tables side by side, she would get a good length, but she could also move them to give her a large square if she needed it. She sellotaped two large pieces of *The Guardian* into the sizes of the table she had seen online, and placed them on the floor, moving them around into various configurations.

Finally, with both sides of her brain in agreement, she opened up her laptop and placed the order for two tables, sitting at the beautiful antique desk which she knew would look a little incongruous beside the modern collapsible tables, but she didn't care. She didn't for one minute imagine she would come across antique cutting-out tables in her lifetime, so she sat back happily in the comfort of John's leather desk chair, and smiled. She would enjoy the reality of shopping for her own chair to use for crafting – it wasn't something she could order online; she had to physically sit in one, she decided.

It was while she was enjoying the slight rocking motion of the comfortable chair, happily musing and considering the stupidity of not cancelling John's newspapers, that she heard the banging on the front door. She stood and peered through the window, knowing exactly who she would see down on her front path.

Clare opened the window and called down to Rob that she would be down in a minute.

* * *

She opened the front door, and Rob pushed past her. 'Where is she?' His voice was strident, demanding.

'Getting the bruise on the side of her face photographed ready for the divorce court,' Clare said, moving a little closer to the baseball bat.

'What? What the fuck are you talking about?'

'Don't swear in my home, Rob.'

'Don't swear? Is that all you can say? Where the hell is my wife?'

'I have no idea. She was here a couple of hours ago, but I asked her not to tell me where she was going so I didn't weaken and be tempted to tell you when you started blubbering and falling apart.'

'That'll be the day.' The words came out almost in a snarl.

'I don't doubt,' Clare said quietly, 'but I'll never tell you where she is, so I'd like you to leave my home now. Don't make me call the police...'

He stared at her for what seemed a lifetime, then turned and walked out. Clare locked the door quickly, then glanced through the small hall window to check he had actually gone. She could see him crossing the road to his own home. As she turned away, her eyes fell on the baseball bat, the butt of so many jokes by her and her girls after John's insistence that it remain in the hall. She decided to leave it exactly where it was.

She quickly messaged Vic to tell her Rob was on a mini rampage trying to find her, and not to worry. Vic just as quickly responded, saying she loved her little flat but it wasn't very clean so she was busy scrubbing everything. She thanked Clare for her support and sent three kisses.

Clare smiled, wondering why all of this had taken so long to erupt; Vic had been so unhappy, since long before John's diagnosis, and yet she'd waited for the blow from Rob's fist before doing anything. Maybe, she thought, this wasn't the first time; the flat was ready and waiting for her, and she didn't think that could have happened in less than a day. It pointed to an earlier blow that she hadn't mentioned, maybe because she needed to think things through before making her move.

The move had certainly been made now, and Clare knew it wouldn't be the last visit from Rob; he would try to prevent his wife from lodging a formal complaint, or even seeing a solicitor, with that bruise on the side of her head.

Clare headed back to the office, gathered up the newspapers lying on the floor, and closed her laptop. She picked it up to take downstairs with her, then replaced it on the desk. This was where it lived now; the desk surface didn't look quite so naked and unloved with the computer on it, and she needed to get used to treating the room in the way it was intended: a work room.

* * *

Clare knew Rob had upset her more than she had initially thought when she realised she really didn't want anything to eat. She checked all her doors were locked, moved into the lounge with a pot of tea, and picked up her Kindle.

An hour later the teapot was empty, and she had read a few electronic pages before abandoning the activity when the little piece of technology advised her the battery was low.

The sun had dipped fairly low, and she unlocked the patio doors and stepped out into the rear garden. The roses they had planted to border the patio wafted across on the night air, and she knew she had been right to insist on highly perfumed varieties only. John had wanted a range of different colours, but she had stuck to her guns; the end result was a glorious mix of different rose scents.

She walked the length of the garden, stopping to smell the lavender, the perfect complement to the roses, and did a little dead-heading of some of the flowers. Clare loved her garden, and was seriously considering letting the small vegetable area go back to a second lawned section – she smiled to herself as she considered the possibility of one day having a sand pit and a swing set on it, if only one of her daughters ever got around to producing a grandchild for her.

She stood and looked at the sad-looking vegetable plot and made the decision. She'd organise some turf to be delivered, and make the garden a little easier to work. And then wait patiently for a grandchild to arrive to play on it.

She reached the far end of the garden where the pergola

caught the last rays of the dying sun, and sat for a moment, looking back up the garden. She was pleased with what she saw, very pleased, and added gardening to the list of everything she would now be doing to combat the muddle in her mind.

The last time she had sat where she was now sitting, John had still been alive. She had helped him down to the pergola area because his legs had become very unsteady. They had talked of their daughters, delicately skirting round the subject of Grace and her 'friend', Megan. The word 'friend' had been used in two different ways; from Grace, it had meant 'friend who was so much more than a friend', whereas the word coming from John showed a sense of derision, almost disbelief that his daughter seemingly preferred another girl to a man. Clare knew he would be horrified at their present plans of buying the flat together, and she briefly wondered just how far that bigotry would have extended, if he had lived. So many times she had kept quiet, so many times she had wanted to yell at him to move into the present century, but his illness overrode everything, and she'd let it go. She'd let it go knowing he would be dead soon, and she could hide his nastiness from Grace.

As the dark descended, the new garden lights began to flicker on in different areas and she waited for the rest to come on, loving it when they all lit up the space. Some took longer than others, but within about quarter of an hour they were all glowing, and would do so for a few hours until their solar batteries needed the sunshine to recharge them. She stood and moved back to the patio doors, still drinking in the scents of the garden, and bending down to touch the occasional light that hadn't yet been triggered into life.

She stopped on the patio and looked backwards – totally beautiful, a bit like a mini Blackpool, she thought with a grin. John would have hated it.

She stepped inside, locked the doors behind her, and closed the vertical blinds. She poured a glass of wine, welcoming and soothing, and she nibbled on a breadstick as she picked up her now fully charged Kindle. She still didn't feel hungry, but figured drinking wine changed things, and she might just need something to line her stomach other than a glass of Prosecco.

She settled on the sofa, made herself comfortable and began to read. She didn't feel the thud on her nose as the Kindle fell onto it, but brushed it off in her sleep as a minor irritation; the next time she woke it was five in the morning, and she was desperate for a wee.

It was an early start to another gloriously sunny day.

5

SEPTEMBER 2022

Waking so early had created a hefty kick-start to her energy levels, and after a quick breakfast and two cups of coffee, Clare headed for the office, armed with a tape measure in case she changed her plans, a notepad and a pencil, and a bucket loaded with cleaning materials. With the blinds due the following day – something else ticked off her to-do list – she wanted to clean the windows.

She began by double-checking her figures for the tables she wanted to install as her work units, although with their delivery due that afternoon she knew it was too late to change anything.

She did a quick sketch in her notebook, noting down lengths and the configuration of the intended furniture, and briefly wondered about getting a joiner in to fit doors on the bookshelves. It would certainly keep the dust from any fabrics stored on the shelves while adding protection to books that didn't necessarily need to be on display. She would go through John's paperwork and find the name of the nice chap he'd had in to do the original work, then ring him – she thought his name was Ben – explain what she wanted and see if he could fit her into his schedule.

Half an hour later, the windows were gleaming, along with the mirror. She sat in John's chair, not feeling anything. There was no sense of him pervading the atmosphere, and she put it all down to the reconfiguration of the furniture. The desk, this wondrous antique piece of furniture, had been in the middle of the room throughout John's ownership of it, but now it was hers and in a different place, underneath the left window, with a view of the front garden.

Sorting through the three drawers in the right-hand pedestal was the obvious place to start. All of an equal size, meticulous files were kept by John of their finances, his stocks and shares, and anything else she was likely to need to know. However, the top item in the drawer was nothing of an official nature: it was three Christmas cards – one from her, one from Grace and Megan and one from Sara and Greg. She felt a lump in her throat, and read through the family's words, all upbeat despite knowing they would never send him another one.

She stacked the paperwork into a pile, realising she needed to keep it all but not necessarily in the top drawer, then sprayed polish into the interior to give it a satisfying clean. She opened the middle drawer which contained very little. She added his last diary to the pile destined for the bottom drawer, hoping Ben's name and phone number would be somewhere in it, sorted through the other bits of notes and comments about cases he was involved with and started a fresh pile of paperwork for shredding. She cleaned out the drawer and moved on to the bottom one which contained two bottles – one whisky, one brandy – a brandy glass and a whisky tumbler.

She carried the contents downstairs, quickly washed the glasses and put the drinks in the drinks cabinet, next to other alcohol that would probably never be drunk now. Before returning upstairs she made a huge mugful of coffee, taking with her a coaster from the lounge. Heaven forbid that she ever dare leave a ring on the desk to mar its perfection, she thought, smiling to herself.

With the bottom drawer cleaned, she picked up the pile of paperwork that was for saving and placed it all inside, then popped into her bedroom for one of the Marks & Spencer carrier bags from the previous day. She dumped all the paper for shredding inside that bag, then turned her attention to the left-hand pedestal.

Once again, the drawers were perfectly matched and she couldn't help but take in the beauty of the piece of furniture. It had cost a small fortune, but when she had mildly remonstrated about it, John had said, 'Well, when I'm dead and gone, you can sell it for even more than I paid for it. It's an investment, Clare.'

They hadn't known his prophetic words would come true all too quickly, and he would only have the pleasure of sitting at his desk for a mere five years or so.

There was very little in the top drawer on the left-hand side – new notebooks, pens and pencils, his fountain pen, which he preferred using instead of ballpoint pens – the tools of his trade. She took everything out, cleaned out the drawer and replaced it all. The bottom two drawers held nothing except scraps of paper, mainly with doodles that John had drawn while speaking to clients. They'd always laughed about this quirk with him, but he'd always insisted it helped him to concentrate. Some of the drawings were very good, and brought a smile to her face. She picked out three of the better ones. She had some idea in her mind of framing the three pictures, and her and the girls having one each.

The rest she tipped into the carrier bag, before putting it on the landing along with John's old shredder, and returning to finish cleaning the desk. With all drawers clean and moving smoothly – she'd had to run a candle along the little used bottom left-hand one to facilitate this – she turned her attention to the outside of the desk. It had a small hutch, with six tiny drawers. They contained nothing at all, but she took them out one by one, sprayed and polished them, then slid them back in. She struggled to get the bottom right one back in, so removed it and rubbed the candle along both top edges before trying again. It still didn't go in easily, so she removed it once again and stuck her hand inside the aperture, this time without a duster in it. She felt the small sliver of wood on the left of the opening, and leaned her head on the desk to see inside.

'Oh,' she said, talking to herself, 'what the hell is that?' She pushed her hand back inside, and touched the tiny piece of wood, then pulled on it. It moved, and she heard the tiniest of noises. It came from under the desk. She pushed back the chair so that she could see what was happening.

A small drawer had appeared in the leg aperture of the desk, and she could see something white in it. She eased it out carefully, then placed what seemed to be an envelope on the desk before flicking the duster around inside the previously hidden drawer. There was nothing else in there. She pressed the drawer back into place, then felt for the small protuberance that had caused the drawer to open. It was now flat against the leg of the desk, and completely invisible to the naked eye.

She replaced the hutch drawer before going any further, marvelling at the idea. A secret drawer. She'd heard about desks having them, but John had never said his had one. Maybe he hadn't known, and this envelope had been inside since before John had bought it. He would have been thrilled to discover it for himself, if that was the case.

The desk simply needed its work surface polishing, and all was good. Then she would allow herself the small pleasure of inspecting the envelope and its contents.

She sprayed and polished, settled herself comfortably in the chair, then saw the stamp with Queen Elizabeth's head on it, and the posting date of 15 June 2004, addressed to Mr John Staines.

6

SEPTEMBER 2022

With a posting date of 2004, the envelope was definitely no antique, a mere eighteen years old and in pristine condition. The postmark showed it had been posted in Sheffield. It hadn't been opened with a letter-opener, as was John's normal habit; simply an easing of the sealed flap had sufficed. The address was his business address, not his home one, and Clare felt an icy trickle run down her back. It was obviously a card of some sort, and she shook off the unease and decided stupidity wasn't called for. All the answers were in her hands.

Clare held it for a moment longer, initially wondering why she couldn't remember seeing it before, then she eased her fingers inside and pulled out the contents. She smiled when she saw it was a Father's Day card, and wondered which one of the girls had taken the time and trouble to post it to his office – she guessed Sara, who would have been ten years old in 2004, and probably at the stage where she would have wanted to do something different from her baby sister.

The front of the card proclaimed, 'Happy Father's Day Daddy', and showed a small picture of a man driving a sports car. Clare smiled. Definitely a Sara-type card; she had always actively encouraged John to buy a sports car instead of the more family-sized vehicles he preferred. John had clearly saved this; it meant something special to him. His first Father's Day card bought by Sara on her own?

Clare opened it. There was a photograph inside.

It showed a little boy sitting at a table with a large birthday cake in front of him. The cake was in the shape of a four and had four candles on it.

Clare placed the photograph and the card on the desk surface, and pushed back the chair. She felt sick. This card was nothing to do with either Sara or Grace. What secrets had John been keeping? And did she really want to know? Her muddled state appeared to be getting worse with each day that passed.

Clare left the picture and card on the desk, unable to touch them, and walked from the room. She opened the landing window, and leaned her head against it, taking in deep breaths of the fresh air. She wished she hadn't found the card; now she knew, she would have to discover more. And she also wished she hadn't taken the two bottles of alcohol downstairs; she could certainly use a brandy right now.

She waited there, with her head against the windowpane, until her heart rate had slowed down, then returned to the desk. She slid the photograph across until it was perfectly positioned in front of her. Now she was certain she didn't know the child. She picked up the picture and turned it over, drawing in her breath as she began to read.

Jed, fourth birthday party, 25.12.03

And that was it. No further information on the photograph.

She pulled the card in front of her, pushing the picture to one side. The card said more.

It was written in cursive, an adult hand, because the little boy was still too young to be writing messages, though he had attempted to add his name. Jed, in large letters, and very wobbly ones at that. The adult, probably his mother, had written,

I love you and miss you, Daddy.
Have a lovely Father's Day,
From your little boy

In the space underneath her words, the little one had written,

JED.

The worst moment came with the message on the facing page.

John – he wrote his own name! Love always, K. xxx

Clare reached for the empty bucket she had carried upstairs, and was violently sick. Jed. The name rang around her brain, as she wondered who he was, where he was... Who could K be apart from his mother?

Who was this child born on Christmas Day 1999? And then she froze. Daniel had been born just six days earlier on 19 December, the baby who had been too precious to live. It now seemed that while they were sharing their grief at losing their two-day-old child, John had been celebrating the birth of another son. Clare couldn't come up with any other explanation, though she also couldn't comprehend how this could have been kept a secret for so long. Did this child, this Jed, know of his father's death? Did he even know who his father was? The passage of time, the possibility that the love mentioned in the words on the card had died and K had chosen not to allow Jed to have contact with his father... all of this ran through Clare's mind as she debated what to do. She could never unknow this now.

And what of Sara and Grace? In future years, when their mother was no longer there to protect and guide them, would they stumble across this secret of their father's? Perhaps Jed would track them down. It was getting all too easy to find DNA matches on genealogy sites, and he could turn up one day and blow their comfortable lives wide open.

Clare took the bucket to the bathroom, emptied it and cleaned it, then carried the cleaning materials and her empty coffee mug downstairs. Work was done with for today. She needed to think.

She returned to the office and put the picture and the card back into the envelope, after first opening the secret drawer and checking that she hadn't missed anything else inside. She felt surprised by how easy it was to open now she knew it was there, and yet if you didn't, it was totally secure. It must have been the duster that had caught the edge of the lever that released the mechanism, making it difficult to replace the drawer that hid all the clever stuff. It now ran smoothly, and she felt sure her daughters would never find it... unless they felt like giving the desk a damn good clean. Should she destroy the card and photo? Would that be the obvious thing to do?

But deep down she knew she couldn't do that. Jed was, according to the card, their half-brother, and one day that picture may be needed. Best leave it where it had lived for five years, and probably in a similar place at his workplace for almost fifteen years prior to that.

* * *

The tables arrived just before two, and she dragged them one by one up the stairs and into the office. Once they were in place, she lifted her sewing machine and placed it at the end of the table on the right, the closest point to the wall socket. She connected it, and pulled a small piece of material out of the box of remnants she had placed on one of the shelves. She fed it under the presser foot, and pushed the button. The machine instantly whirred into life, and for the first time in a few hours, she smiled. She then collected the small Victorian dining chair that lived on the landing, and placed it in front of the machine, a temporary bit of comfort until she could go and choose a proper typist's chair for herself.

Settling easily, she changed a couple of the stitches and continued to sew lines across the scarlet fabric, then released the foot. She took out the tiny remnant and inspected it – all good. No missed stitches, tension perfect – it seemed such a long time since she had used it. She switched off the machine light, replaced the cover, and stood, leaving the chair where it was for the moment – she might want to use it again before her new chair was in situ.

Her eyes strayed to the desk, and then she deliberately turned her back on it. Maybe she would have to find a different place to hide the card, somewhere where it wouldn't constantly be in her mind, easily accessible.

Her thoughts drifted to John, and his inability to climb the stairs for that last month of his life. He had slept downstairs, hardly able to walk, never mind climb up to their bedroom, and she had been by his side for the whole of that time.

Would he have been thinking about the hidden drawer? About the card that could cause a whole heap of issues? He must have felt so frustrated by his lack of mobility, and he surely would have prayed that the little drawer would never be found.

Clare headed back downstairs. Her muddled state was growing by the day, but one thing was for sure. John had committed an unforgivable act by having an affair with whoever K was, but she strongly suspected he had also abandoned a child. The affair was unforgivable, but the child situation was downright cruelty.

Could she ignore it? *Should* she ignore it? Clare had no idea, and needed time to think. She felt a small sense of gratitude that the only real information she had was the name Jed, and that his mother's name began with K. None of that was enough to send her off on some hare-brained scheme to track down the boy – adult now – and offer apologies on behalf of the man she had loved most of her life.

Learning about Jed had brought back the memories of losing Daniel, of his tiny heart, damaged during his time in her womb, and unable to beat after a mere two days of life. It had been a dreadful Christmas; the quietest one they had ever had. Sara and Grace had understood the enormity of what their parents were going through and had opened their gifts before heading up to Sara's room to play. Christmas lunch had been a sombre one, and in the afternoon she had taken herself off to bed, staying there until Boxing Day.

And clearly on that Christmas Day, Jed was making his own successful entry into the world. One child out, one child in.

Clare stood at the lounge window, staring out at a world her little boy had never known, and wiped away a tear. John's ashes had been buried in the grave that held Daniel's tiny body – she had said no to cremation of her son – and she decided that one day soon, hopefully during the following week, she would take flowers to the grave along with cleaning materials. The flowers would be for Daniel. The scathing words of contempt would be for John.

She noticed Rob's car driving past, then kept watching to see whether he would come by again. He opened the driver's door and slammed it shut, his temper evident in the way he handled himself. He didn't go into the house; he began to cross the road towards her home.

She moved into the hallway, placed the baseball bat where she could grab it if it was needed, and waited for him to hammer on the door. She left the door chain in place and opened the door slightly.

'Where the fuck is she?' He wasn't shouting, but his tone reflected a degree of menace.

'Well, to use your words, Rob, how the fuck should I know? Because of you, I seem to have lost my best mate. If I don't hear from her in the next day or two, I'm reporting her missing to the police, so get ready for that.'

And she slammed the door shut.

She'd just about had enough of the men in her life, and she wasn't taking any shit from any more of the male sex. She watched as he headed across the road, looking back once towards her. She hoped he genuinely believed she hadn't been in touch with Vic.

7

Grace and Megan had ordered a huge bunch of flowers to be delivered to Clare, and they arrived on the stroke of nine, Friday morning. Clare hadn't enjoyed her night's sleep; her mind had been riotous, one minute deciding she should tell the girls about the unknown Jed, the next deciding they must never find out and that she would keep their good memories of their father intact. As a result, she had slept very little.

She was staggering down the stairs feeling the need for a huge mug of coffee when the doorbell pealed.

She expected it to be Rob, so once again moved the baseball bat and kept the door on the chain. But as she peered out, it was a lady smiling at her, waving the huge bouquet of flowers, and apologising for getting her out of bed.

Clare removed the chain, recognising the bouquet was much too big to go through the opening created by keeping the chain in place, and thanked the woman.

'Enjoy your day,' the woman said, and handed the flowers over. Clare thanked her again, pushing her hair behind her ears and trying to appear a bit more respectable than she felt. Carrying the bouquet through to the kitchen, she laid it on the side, while attempting to get her brain into gear and think where the biggest vase was likely hidden.

With the flowers suitably arranged between two vases, having been unable to locate the hiding place of her really huge vase, she eventually made herself a coffee and popped a slice of bread in the toaster. She sent a swift text to the girls to thank them for what she termed a greenhouse of flowers, and added six little heart emojis.

Would Vic be available for a chat? She considered the issue. It wasn't something she'd usually do. Vic had been unable to have children, and Rob had been opposed to adoption as a way of having a family, so Clare had always steered away from talking over serious issues concerning her girls, just in case it caused any sort of upset to her friend, but this was something completely different. This was John's child, a child they didn't know about. A problem she had never envisaged, ever.

Her thoughts during the night had almost convinced her that she needed to know more; she didn't want to be caught unawares if John's son ever arrived on her doorstep.

She sipped at her coffee, then messaged Vic.

* * *

An hour later, the two women were inside Costa, enjoying a large latte and an even larger lemon muffin each, squashing any feelings of guilt over calorie counts.

Vic was clearly unsettled and kept glancing around her.

'Stop worrying. I saw him head off to work as I took in my bouquet this morning, and he hasn't returned home since. He can hardly do anything in the middle of Costa anyway.'

Vic tried to make light of it. 'He might want my muffin.'

'He can't have it; he can buy his own muffin and I hope it chokes him.'

'I couldn't be that lucky,' Vic said, disconsolately. 'So, what did you want to talk about?'

'A Father's Day card.'

Vic gave a short bark of laughter. 'Well, that's one thing I don't have to think about. It's not Father's Day, anyway, is it?'

'No, and your reaction just then was one of the reasons I hesitated about messaging you, but I really need to talk to somebody who knows me and my family well, and will understand.'

A frown flashed across Vic's face. 'Clare, you're worrying me. I hope you know you can talk to me about anything, just as I've burdened you with my current problems. I'm well over the issue of not having a family of my own, and I hope Sara and Grace know I class them as my adopted daughters... so is it some problem with them?'

'Not at the moment, but unless I do something to head things off, it could become one.' She broke off a piece of her muffin and popped it into her mouth.

Vic stared at Clare, waiting for her to continue. 'Well?'

'Let's finish our buns, then I've got something to show you. I don't want to get finger marks on anything.'

'God, you're an infuriating woman, Clare Staines,' Vic grumbled. 'Just tell me.'

'I can start with what's led up to what I'm going to show you. You know the antique desk John bought at some extortionate price?'

Vic nodded.

'Well, it turns out it's got a hidden drawer. I only found it because I did a really thorough clean of it, and threw out any stuff I didn't need. I think the duster snagged on the release lever for the small drawer, and it partially opened it.'

'Just tell me he stashed a million pounds in it.'

'It's quite a tiny drawer.' Clare smiled. 'I don't think a million would fit! No, inside was an envelope, which I initially thought was going to be really old, and at that point I considered the fact that John probably didn't know about it. It's really well hidden. I was looking forward to a bit of detective work, finding out who had owned the desk before John, maybe. Unfortunately, that's not the case. The envelope was dated 2004, and addressed to John. At his office. It was a Father's Day card.'

'Tell me it was from the girls...'

Clare shook her head. 'No. I'm saying nothing more until you've actually seen what I have to show you, so finish the muffin and I'll get it out of my bag. I won't say anything. I'd like your first impressions to be your own without any input from me.'

Vic nearly choked as she stuffed the last of the muffin down her throat at warp speed, then grabbed a tissue to wipe her hands. 'Okay, I'm done,' she said, swallowing some coffee.

Clare handed her bag to her friend. 'It's in the zipped up part. Take it out carefully, while I finish this.' She waved the remnants of her own muffin at her.

Vic opened the zipper and peeked inside; Clare had put the envelope in a polythene sandwich bag, so she pulled it out carefully, then slowly removed it from the plastic. She eased out the card, and stared at it.

'Look inside,' Clare urged.

She held the photograph in her hand, Jed's smiling face staring up at her.

Clare remained silent, waiting for Vic to assimilate what she was seeing. Finally, she lifted her head.

'He even fucking looks like John.'

Clare choked on the coffee she was trying to swallow. She

gasped. 'Well, of all the things I thought you would say, that didn't cross my mind.'

'Oh, come on, Clare. Look at his eyes, his chin. He's John's double. What did you think I would say?'

'I thought you'd notice the date of birth first.'

Vic turned the photograph over, and Clare waited, watching as the penny dropped with her friend.

There was a loud gasp, followed by equally audible words. 'The absolute bastard.'

Vic lifted her eyes and looked at Clare. 'He never said a word? His floozie gave birth to a kid in the same week that you... you lost Daniel? And he never said anything about kid number two? My God, Clare, this makes Rob look like an angel by comparison.'

Clare tried – unsuccessfully – to stem her tears. She picked up a napkin and dabbed at her eyes, then felt Vic's hands touch hers.

'I'm so sorry, Clare. You didn't need to hear me ranting on. What do you want me to do?'

'I don't know. I needed you to know, but apart from that I'm at a loss. All I have is his Christian name, and the knowledge that her name begins with K. Do I look for him? Do I pretend this never happened, put it back in that little drawer again, and hope it never surfaces, ever? I can't talk to the girls – they idolised John – but one day, when I'm long gone, it may come to light and I won't be here to protect them. To explain.'

Vic frowned. 'Could this K be someone from the office? Katherine, Katie, Katya, Kim, Kirsty, Kathy, Kerry... Do any of those names ring a bell? Think back to your pregnancy, and see if he mentioned anyone with a name beginning with K.'

'I was awake half the night trying to link a name to K. It's why I looked a wreck when the flower delivery arrived this morning. Oh, I forgot to mention – Grace and Megan sent an enormous bunch of flowers to say thank you for a gift. My eyes had hardly opened.

I'd actually got my hand on the baseball bat in case it was Rob, but that's when I spotted his car going past as he went to work.'

'Bugger Rob. I've blocked him on my phone, so he can't bombard me with texts any more. This' – she tapped the card – 'is more important. Those girls of yours don't deserve a bombshell like this landing on their heads. So tell me what we're going to do.'

Clare shrugged. 'The one thing we know is he's called Jed, and he was born on Christmas Day, 1999. He's safely into his twenties now and must be building an identity in the world.'

'He's not necessarily called Jed on his birth certificate. What's that programme you and John have watched a million times?'

'Nine, not a million.'

'Nine times of watching *The West Wing* and I know you know every word. Me and Rob quote it a lot too, which is why it came to me. President Josiah Bartlet, Jed to his friends. John loved that series. That's possibly where the Jed comes from.'

'Maybe you're right. That's potentially two names to choose from, Jed and Josiah.' Clare paused, realisation sinking in. 'He named his second son after his favourite show. I know it's silly but... it hurts. He never suggested it when we were choosing Daniel's name...'

'He can't hurt you any more, he's dead.' Vic raised her hand to cover her mouth. 'Oh God, I'm sorry, Clare, I know you love him...'

'Loved,' Clare said quietly. 'I've almost forgotten him. I'm happier now I'm on my own, and I'm struggling to keep that from the girls because you know how much they adored him. I can't understand how he could risk losing them by having this affair, because, believe me, if I'd known about it, he would have been gone from our lives.'

Vic stared at her. 'It's a good job we've met up. I suspect you desperately needed to talk things through with someone.'

'I knew I had to discuss it with you. And now you know, but all

I've succeeded in doing is giving the two of us the problem. I know you, Vic, you'll not let this drop. Somehow, we've got to find Jed, find his mother, and work out what to do after that. I think once we make contact, the girls will have to be told immediately, because they'll never forgive me, or their father, for not telling them everything earlier.'

Vic stood. 'I'll get us another coffee. This was never going to be a one-coffee discussion, was it?'

8

FRIDAY 9 SEPTEMBER 2022

Clare felt as if she was on some sort of Secret Service mission. She followed Vic's car as they drove back to her new flat, parking it alongside with almost a sense of liberation. It was clear that Vic was paranoid about Rob finding out where she lived, and that paranoia had now passed on to her. Once they were hidden in the car park around the back of Vic's new home, Clare breathed a sigh of relief.

They walked across the car park quickly and Clare found herself relaxing once they were inside the building, after using Vic's key fob to gain entry. Vic would be safe and secure in this place.

A flat tour didn't take long – the general living area was an open-plan lounge and kitchen area, and the bedroom had an en suite bathroom that was tiny but adequate.

'This is a bit different to your last place.' Clare laughed.

'It is. I'm safe here. There's nobody to knock me about. Oh, I know it's tiny, but it's only the first part of my escape bid. I'm going to see a solicitor later in the week, get things moving, and Rob'll either have to buy me out of the house, or sell it and we get half each. Then I can look around for something more permanent, and hopefully in a year's time everything will be different for me.'

'You might need a job...'

'I might indeed. I've had some thoughts about it. My Etsy shop is a nice little earner, and I can easily make two journals a week plus the digitals I create, but little is the main word there, and Etsy take their share. I'm considering expanding, but that's going to mean getting more of my stuff from Rob's; I couldn't get much of it in the car when I left. I have this idea of opening a shop not just to sell my goods, but to sell other artisan stuff for other local artists and makers which I can take a cut from. Handmade With Love, that's the shop's name. Like it?'

'Love it. And you know I'll help. But you need to divorce first. You got anything written down about this shop?'

'I have. I didn't intend talking about this yet, but my head's all over the place so I thought I'd try and calm it by getting stuff planned out. And maybe in a week or so, when Rob's back into his proper routine of working nine to five, I can pop back and fill up my car with the die-cutter and the other machines I need, and anything else I can fit in.'

'We have two cars between us,' Clare said softly.

Vic's eyes glazed with unshed tears, and she smiled. 'Thank you. You're an amazing friend.'

* * *

Clare pulled up to the end of the car park, ready to go out into the traffic. She waited until the road was perfectly clear of all cars before exiting – Vic's paranoia had definitely transferred to her. She didn't want to be the one who inadvertently led Rob to his wife. His anger had been palpable, and she would hate it to escalate further.

She called in at Grace and Megan's new place on the way home to see if they wanted a takeaway with her, and found them painting a wall in the lounge a moss green.

'That's nice,' she said, thinking how good it would look in her office on the wall opposite the windows.

'We like it. Didn't after the first couple of brush strokes, but we really do now we're onto the second coat. You want to make us all a drink, Mum?'

Clare walked across to the kettle and switched it on, marvelling at the fact that it had water in. When her girls lived at home nobody ever thought to top up the kettle.

'Our suite's coming tomorrow, so we want to get this finished,' Grace explained, as she picked up more paint on her roller.

'Can I do anything?' Clare asked.

'Buy us a takeaway?'

'That's actually why I called. I thought you might be too tired to do anything else. You're both off work next week?'

'We are. This place will look like a palace by Friday, then we can return to being slobs for the rest of our lives. It's actually pretty clean, and we could have just put the cream all the way round in here, because it only took one coat on the other three walls, but we wanted some colour. The other rooms have one coat of the cream until we decide what we really want but we decided to freshen it all up for now.'

Clare looked at them. 'You're happy?'

'Very. Discussing a wedding, in fact.'

Clare gave a small laugh. 'I'm surprised it's taken you this long.'

'Dad...'

'I know.' Clare spoke quietly. 'You don't have to explain. But I'm not your dad, and neither are Sara and Greg. We'll support you all the way.' She glanced at her watch. 'What time do you want to eat?'

'Chinese.' Megan said the word, and Grace laughed.

'That's not what I asked.'

'Whenever it arrives,' Megan said. 'We've five more minutes on this wall, then that's it for today. And Chinese. Menus are in the top drawer in the kitchen.'

* * *

Thoughts of Chinese takeaways were far from Greg's mind as he arrived home from work. The warm smell of home-cooked food wafted around the house and he walked through to the kitchen. Sara ignored him while she lifted the cottage pie out of the oven, and placed it on the side.

Greg kissed the back of her neck. 'That looks good.'

'It is. We had exactly the same last week. I made two, and froze one.'

Greg laughed loudly. 'You're such a housewife, Sara Carter. What's happened to this nightclubbing, cocktail drinking girl I first met?'

'You married her,' was Sara's dry response, 'and turned her into a slave to your every whim.'

He nodded. 'And it was a damn good idea. What do you want to drink, wench?'

'Water. We're going over to Grace and Megan's new place after this, so I'll drive.'

'I'll drive,' he said. 'Don't want you complaining I've turned you into a chauffeur as well. Gin and tonic?'

She shook her head. 'No, I'll stick to water. Then if you want a drink at Grace's, you can have one. I don't doubt they'll want to open the bottle of champagne we've got for them.'

Greg's eyes lit up. 'Have we?'

'We have.' She served up the meal, and placed it on the kitchen table. 'And I've got something to tell you before we head off out.'

'I hope it's that we've won the lottery,' he said, pulling out the chair and sitting down.

She laughed at him. 'You have to actually buy a ticket to win that. It's a similar sort of thing though,' she said, sitting down opposite him and reaching across the table to clutch his hand. 'You're going to be a daddy.'

* * *

The champagne was received with enthusiasm, and Megan apologised for the lack of flutes. 'We only have wine glasses, but I'm sure it will taste just the same.' She reached up to the kitchen cupboard, and heard Sara call out to say she wanted water in her glass. Megan frowned, then realised.

So did Grace and Clare. All three turned to look at Sara.

'What?' she blustered. 'What? If a girl doesn't like champagne, then she doesn't have to drink it.'

'But you do like champagne,' her mother said. 'You have something to tell us, Sara?'

Greg dropped his head, trying to hide his laughter. The conversation in the car had been about waiting another couple of weeks before telling anyone, when Sara would be twelve weeks pregnant and feeling better about it.

Sara looked at Greg for support, but he merely shrugged and smiled.

'Sod it,' Sara said. 'Look at his face. How can I keep it quiet? We're pregnant. Baby Carter is due around the end of March, I think.'

Grace squealed. Megan cheered. Clare raised her arms above her head and yelled.

Sara looked around her. 'You're pleased then?'

'My darling girl,' Clare said, 'this has been the most wonderful day. These two moving in here, and now your amazing news. I think you realise we couldn't be any happier. Now let's have that drink; we've a couple of toasts to make.'

* * *

Sara drove home feeling really happy with just a little bit of nausea thrown in. It had been a bout of sickness that had sent her to her calendar to check when she'd last had a period, and she realised it had been quite some time. A pregnancy test had confirmed the reason for the nauseous feeling she'd been experiencing frequently. Her first thought had been that her father would have been delighted at the news.

Greg treated her as if she were made of glass, and helped her out of the car. He held her hand as they walked up the garden path to the front door, then took her into the lounge and settled her on the sofa before locking up for the night.

He returned to sit beside her and handed her a glass of milk. 'Here, you have to take care of yourself now, eat properly and suchlike. And I promise that we'll have this baby together – while you're not having alcohol, I'll be the same. Anything you need, just ask; I'll even go shopping with you for any baby stuff we'll be buying.'

Sara looked at the white liquid in the Father Christmas glass. 'So where's your glass of milk?'

He stared at her. 'Everything I've just said I meant.' He stood and returned a minute later with a glass with a Christmas elf painted on it. The glass held milk. 'See? And you know I'd never drink this under normal circumstances. Cheers!' He drank half of it and placed the glass on the coffee table.

'I want to see that glass empty before we go to bed.' She grinned at him. Maybe having this baby was going to be fun.

They chatted for half an hour, drinking milk and eating biscuits, before standing up and heading upstairs. It was only after getting into bed that Sara spoke of her mother.

'There's something on Mum's mind, and it's nothing to do with Baby Carter. She's over the moon we're finally going to present her with the grandbaby she's longed for, but after the initial announcement she was really quiet. She said anything to you?'

'No. It seems ages since we had a chat, though. I'm sure she knows if there are any issues, either with the house or anything else, that I'm there for her. I've always felt as if Clare was more of a mum to me than my own mum was, and I've told her that lots of times. Maybe it's this thing with Vic leaving Rob. It must be playing on her mind. She's coming round a bit from your dad dying, but now she's plunged straight into supporting her best mate. Let's invite her over for Sunday lunch, see if she says anything.'

Sara turned to Greg and held him tight. 'You're a lovely feller, Greg. Thank you. I'll ring her tomorrow and see what she says. Maybe Vic can come with her; it seems they've seen each other today, so that's a little bit of normality for her. And I'm pretty sure Rob isn't likely to turn up here looking for her.'

'You never really liked him, did you?'

'No, he was always a bit moody, always more for Grace than for me until he found out Grace and Megan were an item, then he really started to ignore both of us, not just me. Vic's been unhappy for so long, I don't know how she's put up with him for all these years.'

'Ring your mum tomorrow and invite them both. Let's play agony aunt with the two of them, maybe somebody will slip up and explain why your mum isn't her normal self.'

9

WEDNESDAY 13 APRIL 2022

The sun was struggling to disperse the clouds. The long road that wound through the cemetery was quiet, still damp from the overnight rain, as the funeral cortège wound its way towards the crematorium. The hearse, with a single wreath of white roses atop the oak coffin, was followed by two large black cars and around eight or nine private cars, all travelling to pay their final respects to Kirsty Grantham.

In the first car, the atmosphere was tense. Jed stilled blamed his grandmother, Eloise, for keeping the diagnosis that his mother's cancer was terminal from him; if he had been told the true state of affairs, he would have returned to the home they had all shared before he changed his job, in order to spend as much time as possible with his mother before death claimed her.

He felt they had both lied to him. He rang his mother at least twice a week, and she had mentioned malignant melanoma, but she had reassured him that the operation to remove it had been successful, and she was simply taking time off work to recuperate from what had been a pretty major operation. She had spoken of lymph nodes having to be removed and tested, of full body scans, and still he had thought it was simply a matter of time before she was declared free of cancer.

He had believed her. Why wouldn't he? She didn't normally lie to him, unless you counted lying by omission. All the years of hiding the identity of his father felt like lying. And how many times had he thought to himself that maybe he could try to trace his father, make contact, spend future time with him if they formed some sort of bond.

He stared out of the car window as it moved slowly up the drive, not wanting to communicate with Eloise. They had exchanged many harsh words over the last two weeks as he blamed her for not giving him the time he needed to say a proper goodbye to his mother. He now intended to stay in Sheffield; his boss had been very helpful in arranging for his transfer, especially after he'd explained how fragile his grandmother was in her later years. There was no fragility, and at seventy years of age she could have many more years in front of her. He would make sure they weren't happy years. He had every intention of being a thorn in her side for the rest of her life. She was now his lodger, after all. His mother had explained her will; although leaving the house to him, she had made the proviso about Eloise a hard fact. He would make sure his grandmother was always aware she could be evicted at a moment's notice; even if he knew it would only ever be just words, she didn't. It had been a smart move on Kirsty's part to buy the council house she shared with her mother, and an even smarter move to ask Eloise to care for Jed so that she could return to work after his birth. Kirsty had both a full-time carer for her child and a full-time career for herself.

And now, Jed had a granny he used to adore, Eloise had a safe and secure home for as long as she needed one, and Kirsty had upset several apple carts by dying.

He brushed away the tears with an angry sweep of his hand,

and Eloise reached across the chasm that was between them on the back seat to clutch that same hand. He pulled it away from her, then sat forward as the hearse in front, carrying his mother on her final journey, drew to a halt outside the main doors of the Hutcliffe Wood Crematorium. He took a deep breath and waited for the funeral director to signal the start of the activities he had been dreading.

Jed would be pleasant, let everyone see how upset he was at losing the woman who had given him life; he would be a dignified and loving son, and if necessary, a dignified and loving grandson. For one day.

* * *

The coffin was carried inside to a Rod Stewart song, 'Tonight's the Night', following the detailed instructions for the funeral left by Kirsty. Jed wondered why. He knew she loved Stewart's music, always had, and he had been brought up listening to the rocker's words over and over again, but why this song? Had it been special to her? Or had it simply been that she liked it?

There was a degree of shuffling as people filled up the room, and the service began. Jed had wanted to speak, to say something about the mother he had loved with all his heart, but he knew he would only get about three words out before falling apart, so in collaboration with his Uncle Tim, his mother's cousin, they had put together some simple thoughts which Tim had shared with the mourners.

There was a period of reflection during the service, a time set aside to think about his mother, during which her chosen song, Barry Manilow's, 'Even Now', played. He listened closely to the words and knew that his mother had loved his father. The song told him she did. He had wrongly assumed, at one point in his life, that she had possibly been raped, but the choice of that particular song told him otherwise. Barry Manilow may have been singing, but the words were directly from his father.

The tears fell heavier and he bowed his head as the vicar began to pray.

'...and forgive us our trespasses as we forgive those who trespass against us. And lead us not into temptation, but deliver us from evil. For thine is the Kingdom, the power and the glory, for ever and ever, amen.' Jed spoke the words almost to himself, wiping tears from his eyes. He felt Eloise sag against him, and for the first time he offered her some comfort by putting his arm around her.

And then it was over, the tune Kirsty had chosen to be played as her exit line being 'We'll Meet Again'. He felt the warmth of her surround him; he knew she would be laughing at this final song. She had intended it clearly to be taken as a joke, but he hoped it was true.

He and Eloise walked across to the coffin and touched it one last time, each placing a red rose on top of the lid, and they exited, the strains of the song causing everyone to follow, singing the words.

* * *

It had been a good service. Everyone told Jed it had been excellent, wonderful music, and he explained several times that his mother had organised everything herself.

The wake went well, everyone talking to him about his mother, being surprised by his decision to return to the city of his birth, and even more surprised as he revealed the house was owned entirely by his mother, and therefore he now owned it.

He wasn't surprised to find out, after speaking to his mother's close friend, Tanya Lawford, that her will stipulated that Eloise had a home for life. Tanya, a solicitor, had drawn up Kirsty's will, and she confirmed what Jed already knew.

'It's so good that our lovely Kirsty thought to put it in writing that you inherit the house, with the added condition that Eloise can remain there for the rest of her life of course.'

Jed squashed the anger rising in him. 'Mum told me. But I would never have asked Granny to leave. Is there anything else I should know about?'

'I can give you the full details if you can find time to come into the office. Shall we say one day next week? There are a couple of small donations to be made, and she's left a letter for you.'

Tanya spotted Eloise looking at her, and waved the older woman over.

'Eloise, can you join me, along with Jed, next week for an hour? I just want to go through the will with both of you present. Shall we say Tuesday, at ten o'clock?'

* * *

The wake ambled along for a further hour, then everyone started drifting away. Jed was hugged over and over again, with everyone telling him what a wonderful person his mother had been, and how much she had loved him.

The day drew to an end, and finally Eloise and Jed were ferried home by their neighbour, who had wept copiously for most of the day. They left her still dabbing her eyes, and went up their own garden path, neither of them talking.

Eloise went through to the kitchen, Jed up to his bedroom, where he switched on his television and muted the sound. He'd never felt so miserable in all of his life. He thought back to the day when his grandmother had rung to break the news that things were going so very wrong with his mother. He thought of the sickness that had engulfed him, pretty much the same sort of feeling he'd been having throughout the funeral. He hadn't eaten at the wake and had carried around a half-pint glass of bitter that was still half full when he'd left the venue.

Jed had been building his career in Bristol with Taylor and Woods, a builders merchants who had depots scattered around the country, and although he, his mother and Eloise had lived in different cities for the best part of two years, he had kept in touch mainly by phone.

The phone call that had seen him travelling back to Sheffield for good within two days of receiving it had been the phone call that nobody wanted to answer. And on arriving home, the rift between him and his grandmother had been instant and vituperative.

He had verbally attacked her within seconds of walking through the front door, resulting in a shouting match between the two of them conducted in whispers. Neither of them wanted to wake the sleeping Kirsty, who was blessedly resting thanks to an increased dose of her pain medication.

And it had continued. He needed Eloise to know how much she had let him down by keeping the true state of his mother's health from him. And now he felt he could never go back to the loving relationship he had enjoyed during his childhood years of being brought up by her, by Granny. She had been the one who mended him, who stuck plasters to the various bloody wounds he had acquired after climbing trees or falling from slides – not his mother, who had returned to work within three months of giving birth.

And now he felt lost. His mother gone, his granny estranged. He was alone and back in Sheffield, having left friends of some closeness in Bristol.

He sat up, packed his pillows behind him and switched off the silent television. Decisions had to be made. He had a good, well-paid job, a mortgage-free life, a granny that it seemed he would have to learn to trust again, and above all else, somewhere in this world was a man who had fathered him.

Did Eloise know his name? If she didn't, did she know anything at all about this stranger from around twenty-five years earlier? Could she be the answer to his questions?

He'd have to swallow his anger, find a way to apologise for the way he had treated her since his return, and become an investigator.

He should go downstairs and start right now. Make her a cup of tea, milk no sugar, in a china cup with a saucer so that a biscuit could rest beside the tea, soften her up a little. And apologise. He needed her on side until he found some information, accurate information, that would take him directly to the man who had impregnated the beautiful Kirsty Grantham, and then walked away.

He stood, headed downstairs and listened for movement. He heard sobbing. Quietly opening the kitchen door, he watched her for a moment.

'Gran? I'm sorry,' he said, and walked across to hold her in his arms. 'I'm sorry,' he repeated.

Eloise wanted desperately to believe him.

10

SUN/MON 11-12 SEPTEMBER 2022

It was a day of laughter, something that Vic desperately needed. It had all seemed so clandestine when Clare collected her from her flat, with her sitting on the back seat, ready to lie flat at a minute's notice should they spot Rob's car anywhere.

They reached Greg and Sara's home where they were welcomed with hugs and kisses, and Sara wanting to know more about Vic's flat.

Vic told her as much as she could, stopping short of actually saying where it was situated. Sara understood her reasons, but having never seen any of the nasty side of Rob, she had to take Vic and Clare's words as being an accurate depiction of the man she had known for so many years.

'Well you can always run here if things get worse, Vic,' she said, recognising that the last place she could go to would be Clare's home. Much too close to where Rob was...

Sunday lunch was a triumph, and both women said a reluctant goodbye to the young couple as they left, Clare keen to get Vic indoors before daylight disappeared. She wanted to hear the door locks go on before heading back to her car.

Satisfied that Vic had emerged safely from the day trip out, Clare drove home with a lighter heart. There was a change in her friend, from the bright lively woman she had known for so many years to the downhearted and dispirited friend she had morphed into over the past week, and she had left her with instructions to call immediately if any issues arose. What she had meant was: if Rob finds out where you live and turns up on your doorstep...

It felt cool inside the house but she decided to put on her pyjamas and thick dressing gown, make a hot chocolate, sit quietly for a few minutes to think through the day, then go to bed with her Kindle. She wanted to put the desk and its contents to the back of her mind, and get a decent sleep.

Her phone rang while she was making the drink and, for a moment, she felt panic, but it was just Sara checking everything was okay and both women were safely in their homes.

'It's bothering me a bit, Mum, that he's coming across to your home and being obnoxious. Can't you have him stopped, get an injunction or something?'

Clare gave a small laugh. 'Not necessary. I've got a baseball bat and I'll use it if I have to. But I've known Rob for a long, long time, and always thought of him as being a bit weak and cowardly. I see no reason that'll change. He'll get fed up, especially when the divorce papers arrive, when he realises he can't win. Don't worry about me, Sara, I can handle myself. Night night, sweetheart, get yourself off to bed. You looked tired.'

'I'm fine. Ring if you need us, Mum. Love you.'

They disconnected and Clare rechecked everywhere was locked before climbing the stairs holding her Kindle and her hot chocolate. She stood on the landing for a few seconds staring at the office door, then shook her head and headed towards her bedroom. She'd think about things in the morning, she decided, and immerse herself in a good Stephen King book tonight. She always felt she had to marginally build up her courage to read a King novel, and tonight she'd reached the right level of bravery. It must be all that talk about the baseball bat, she thought.

Fifteen minutes later, the blank Kindle was open by her side, the last of the hot chocolate was turning to cold chocolate and she was asleep.

* * *

The next morning, Clare put on the small television in the kitchen to see what further news there was about the death of the Queen. Elizabeth had been taken in the hearse from Balmoral the previous day, and as Clare watched the news, she felt a small prickle of tears. A wonderful woman, and now a man had taken over her role. It had been a strange few days, unexpected despite the great age the Queen had reached. Only two days before her death she had been pictured welcoming the new prime minister; it was definitely shocking that two days would see such a massive change.

Clare took her slice of toast and cafetière to the kitchen table, and pulled her post towards her. Two junk envelopes and an invitation to a wedding in Florida between old friends who had finally decided to tie the proverbial knot after twelve years of living together. She put the junk mail to one side to go into the recycling, and popped the invitation in the pocket of her dressing gown. She would reply in the negative, and send a cheque; thank goodness she'd discovered the cheque book when clearing out the desk. And a Father's Day card...

She washed the few dishes that had accumulated since returning from Sara's, then headed upstairs. The card was back in the secret drawer, and she removed it. She put it to one side, dealt with the rejected wedding invitation and wrote a cheque, stuck the last stamp in the book on it and felt a sense of satisfaction that it had been sorted. After John's death, nothing had happened in a rush; her mind had gone into shutdown, but now she realised it was better to deal with everything immediately, or issues seemed to go into temporary oblivion until somebody reminded her. Hence the speedy response to the wedding invitation.

In the spirit of doing things immediately, she placed a small note into her mobile phone holder that said *buy stamps*, then sat quietly for a moment before pulling the card towards her. Could there possibly be some sort of clue in the photograph that she hadn't spotted through her tears and anger?

The child, Jed, was sitting at what appeared to be a kitchen table. There was a birthday cake shaped as a number four, so it was easy to date the picture. Christmas Day 2003. According to the envelope, it had been sent to John at work in June 2004. Was this his only Father's Day card? Or simply a final one?

Other possibilities began to open up to her, the more her mind began to whirl. Had the child not survived? Did he not reach his fifth birthday? Or more simply, had K, his mother, decided to cut off communications after this card was sent?

In the background of the picture was a small Christmas tree. It had decorations that seemed to be made of paper, and probably handmade by Jed and K. She could imagine the two of them sitting at that table, glue sticks at the ready, kiddie scissors wielded, and glitter ready to be sprinkled.

She smiled as she thought of the Christmases with her own girls – glitter everywhere, and they had loved it. Had Jed enjoyed it? She found herself experiencing a change in her mood. It wasn't the boy's fault that his mother and his father had had an affair; he was the innocent one in it.

The candles on the cake were alight, and they reflected in his eyes. She couldn't tell what colour they were, but he was obviously excited and happy. His name was written in blue icing.

Clare assumed K had taken the photograph; there was nobody else in the picture, and no clues as to anything beyond the date the picture was taken.

She sighed. Detective work completed on the photo, she pulled the card and envelope towards her. The envelope told her nothing other than John's name and the address of his office, plus the date it was posted from Sheffield. This suggested that the sender had lived in Sheffield at that time, but she knew it meant nothing now. A lot could have happened in almost twenty years.

The card was also information free; it added nothing to anything she had already learnt.

She pushed her chair back. What to do next? How could you track down a Jed, or Josiah, born on Christmas Day 1999?

'Idiot,' she said aloud. 'Of course you can! *The Star* always puts pictures of Christmas Day babies.'

She felt a small glimmer of hope that she could at least get a full name for him. She switched on her laptop and entered the words *Sheffield Star*.

It was a complex website, and she tried everything to find pictures of Christmas Day babies from 1999, to no avail. She suspected they were there somewhere, but her limited capabilities with technology were leading her nowhere.

What felt even more disheartening was that the only person she could ask to help her was Vic, and Vic was about on a par with her when it came to technology. They could be trusted to safely clear Amazon of their stock, send emails and chat with Facebook friends, but that was about the sum total of their skills. Their combined skills.

She rang Vic, checked how she was before moving on to the

issue she was really concerned with, and explained her thoughts in detail.

'You're asking me to help with something on a computer?' Vic's laughter was good to hear, but not helpful.

'I merely thought you might be able to come up with an answer, as you're my best friend and would want to help with this. As any best friend would, of course.'

'Oh, of course.' Again, Vic laughed.

'Vicki Tarran Dolan, stop laughing at me! I need help. Now think.'

'It seems pretty obvious to me that going online for a picture from *The Star* dating back to 1999 might be a lot of hard work, but doesn't the Central Library have microfiche things? I seem to remember going there with school and being shown how to use them. It should be fairly easy because you have a specific date. It's not as though you have to plough through every day of 1999. I reckon the Boxing Day edition or the day after should be enough. And I just know you're going to want me to go with you.'

'We can't go yet. They've closed lots of places down because of the Queen, lots of Council-connected places anyway, so I can't follow up on this until after the funeral next Monday. So, in the meantime, keep thinking. See if you can come up with some other brainwave. And I have to take you with me; I've never even seen a microfiche thing. And after we could always go to Ego for lunch. My treat.'

There was a pause. 'It's really got to you, this Father's Day card, hasn't it?'

There was silence for a moment. 'It's more than that,' Clare said. 'I feel as if it's made a complete mockery of our lives together. We met when I was five, and have been the best of friends ever since. But now I find out there's a massive secret he'd been keeping for twenty odd years. And you know the most important thing? He's not around any more to pay the price.'

'Oh no, Clare. You sound so down. And I can't come to you to comfort you, cheer you up or anything. Bloody Rob's got a lot to answer for. Look, we'll meet up as soon as the libraries are open again, and we won't stop till you have answers. You'll have to be prepared for stuff you'll not be happy to know, but I'll be with you.'

'Vic, you're a star. You watching the funeral next Monday?'

'Definitely. You coming over here?'

'Can do. Take care, and keep your head down.'

They disconnected and Clare frowned. She may not be able to use *The Star*'s website, but she could google microfiche and see what she could find out about that. She had a week to get herself organised.

11

30 JUNE 2022

Jed posted the DNA test, and walked home. He had no idea if it would help but he had heard reports that there was a possibility of connecting with others with familial DNA. Anything was worth a try when you were starting with a completely flat plane and no information at all from which to build upwards, outwards or even downwards.

It had been a busy Monday, and as assistant manager filling in for a manager on holiday in the Algarve, he had taken on the full managerial role for two weeks. It had proved testing; an attempted burglary on the second night had resulted in Jed being called into work at midnight by the police. Nothing had been taken, the thieves probably scared off by the cacophony of alarms that connected directly to the police headquarters, but the damage to the premises' doors and windows was extensive.

Five days further on, and with all repairs and replacements completed, Jed felt he could think about other things apart from work. Hence the posting of the DNA test, sent with a short silent prayer asking for a positive outcome.

Although things were still a little uncomfortable between

Eloise and himself, he was at last beginning to see that it was his mother who had expressly forbidden Eloise to contact him and tell him the true state of her health. Kirsty had known that the deep love that bound her and Jed was a detriment as she approached the end of her life. He would be distraught and she needed to head towards her final days at peace, her pain under control, but in the end Eloise had rung him and told him what was happening.

They had discussed it several times since Kirsty's passing, until finally he could see both sides. Slowly they were recovering their closeness, and slowly he was talking to Eloise about the absentee father.

She initially said she knew nothing.

'Mum didn't have a boyfriend?' He kept his tone as subdued as possible, careful not to antagonise her. After all, she was the only person who might have some knowledge of who had been in her daughter's life all those years earlier.

'If she did, I never met him. She never spoke of one special person. Kirsty was a bubbly person, as you know. She chatted to everybody; I never knew her to argue with anyone, fall out with anyone. She had lots of friends, male and female.'

'Do you remember their names?'

'Oh, for goodness' sake, Jed! It's getting on for twenty-five years since she had those friends; I can't remember any of them.'

Jed backed off. He would bide his time. Knowing his grandmother as well as he did, Jed knew she would mull things over, and it would only take one little item of remembrance to lead him in the right direction.

Why hadn't his mother had his father's name added to the birth certificate?

And with that thought, he suddenly knew his initial feelings on the matter had been correct; felt it deep inside him. This was no rape situation, as he had previously assumed. This was a married man. The world was full of married men, able to get away with having an affair, while hiding it from wifey at home.

If Jed had any say in his future, that wifey at home was due for a shock. He was quite surprised by the sudden wave of determination that threatened to overwhelm him. Could this situation lead to a discovery of half brothers and sisters? Having siblings during his own childhood would have completed his life, but his mother had never borne another child. Had she ever wanted one? Perhaps having him had put her off for the rest of her days. It made sense that the man who had impregnated her was someone she had loved and continued to love for the rest of her life – she had never had a man friend to his knowledge. And she hadn't gone down the abortion route either. Her child had been loved, just as the father had been.

Jed hadn't been a bad kid. He had studied hard, left school with good grades and had been approached by his current employers, Taylor and Woods, following a careers' evening at school. They had been impressed by his leaving report, his folder of work, and ultimately he had gone to the company for a more formal and in-depth interview. He knew, as he'd left the building later that day, that this would suit him down to the ground. They had offered him day release to continue targeted studies, plus regular bonuses, and a large ladder to climb within the company.

Since joining them he had moved around various branches and he had been in Bristol when the call came through from Eloise to say things weren't good for his mother.

He had now made a permanent move back to Sheffield, and was only one step down from being manager of the flagship branch. And the company had been particularly supportive, especially when he explained he had an old and infirm grandmother he needed to look after.

They had created a sideways move to Tool Hire Manager for the Branch Assistant Manager, and shoe-horned Jed in as Assistant Manager, Sheffield branch. His new position made him happy. As did the increase in pay.

The old and infirm grandmother would have created holy hell if she'd known the excuse he'd used to put the transfer on the cards.

* * *

Eloise poured the tea into the china cup with the dainty violets on, picked it up and sipped. Thoughtfully.

Would it cause harm to Jed if he did track down his father? She had been perfectly honest with him when she said she didn't know his name, but if pushed, she could hazard a guess. She hadn't been strictly truthful when she'd told him that she couldn't remember anyone from 1999 who Kirsty used to go out with – she could recall a couple of faces. And maybe even a couple of names. And no doubt something would show up if she ever brought the box down from the attic that contained all the memorabilia from Jed's birth. The congratulation cards, the tiny wrist bracelet with his name and weight on, the appointment card for all Kirsty's ante-natal visits; all of this and much more was in the box at the far end of the attic. A box that Jed would know nothing about until her own death; then he could explore the entire house without her attempts to steer him away from the attic with tales of spiders as big as her hand.

The card that she suspected came from Jed's father bore no name, just a simple kiss. But Kirsty had known, and Kirsty had smiled, both at her tiny son cradled in her arms and the card with the kiss.

It was very obvious to Eloise that the parents of baby Josiah

John Grantham had an understanding. She assumed that the middle name was the name of his father, but she didn't have to guess where the name Josiah came from. How many times had they watched *The West Wing*? The series had started in the September of 1999, with three months of the pregnancy still to go through. President Josiah Edward Bartlet, Jed to his wife and his friends. And how many times had Kirsty giggled about calling the baby Jed because she wanted an unusual name? They had spent the last three months with Eloise favouring the name Sam after Rob Lowe's character in the series, and she had assumed it was all a game until she heard Kirsty tell the delivery midwife the name Josiah, before the woman wrote it on his wrist band. After Jed's birth, Kirsty had purchased the newly finished series on DVD and they had settled in to watch all the episodes all over again. It was a series on continuous loop as far as the two women were concerned. Jed had watched it intermittently, partly because he had been named from the series and partly because it always seemed to be on, but he had never fully taken to it, not like his mum and his granny.

Eloise felt suitably grateful that Jed had never realised the name Jed came from an amalgamation of the J in Josiah and the Ed in Edward. If he ever realised that, he would then start to wonder where his very plain name of John came from...

It gave her some comfort to watch the series now Kirsty had gone, but she made sure never to have it showing when Jed was in the house. He was a bright lad, and could very easily start joining up the dots with the slightest of clues. She wanted him to be a Josiah and not a John. Everything was safer that way.

Eloise poured a second cup of tea from the teapot, but decided she'd left it a little too long. It was no longer very warm, and definitely stewed.

'Come on, woman,' she grumbled aloud, 'you're a Yorkshire

lass. We don't drink stewed tea ever. Get your act together.' She carried the teapot, cup and saucer over to the sink, clicked on the kettle once again and prepared to make a second pot. This time she'd drink it all, and stop letting her thoughts and worries take over her valuable tea-drinking time. All she needed to do was switch off from thinking about whatever routes her beloved grandson might be taking in his quest to find his father.

She was pouring her first cup of tea from the fresh brew when she heard the front door open.

'Granny?'

'In the kitchen, Jed,' she responded. 'I've just mashed if you want a cuppa.'

'Certainly do,' he said and bent down to kiss the top of her head.

She felt mildly surprised by the action, but took it as a good sign of returning to their closeness of earlier years.

'You're home early,' she said.

He nodded. 'I know it seems as though I am, but this is my true finishing time. I've just been doing such a lot of overtime following the break-in; I'd almost forgotten I actually only work until five.' He grinned. 'So I thought I'd come and see if my favourite person would like to go out to eat tonight, save us going through the usual rigmarole of not knowing what we fancy for our meal. I've messed you about too much with not knowing what time I was coming home, so I've booked us a table at The Vicarage for seven o'clock. You up for that?'

'Could be if you twist my arm,' she said, a smile lighting up her face. 'In fact, don't bother with the arm-twisting. If we're going to The Vicarage I need to spend an hour getting ready.' She pushed the teapot towards Jed. 'Here, you finish this. I'll be ready by half past six. That okay? It's a few years since we've been there; I'm going to enjoy this. I was thinking of a tuna sandwich or something, but I'm not now.'

'Yeah, half six is fine. Give me a shout when you've finished in the bathroom and I'll have a quick shower. And there's no rush; I know wrinkly old ladies take a long time to get ready so they look beautiful.'

'I'll give you wrinkly old ladies, young man.' Eloise picked up the wet dishcloth, took careful aim and threw it. 'Bingo,' she said. 'I was going to offer to do the driving so you could have a drink, but forget that now, pal. Bring on the Nuits-Saint-Georges.'

She turned to leave the kitchen, trying hard not to laugh.

'Okay, I'm sorry,' he called after her, removing the wet cloth from his head as she headed down the hallway.

She turned back and, standing in the kitchen doorway, she said, '2018.' He groaned.

12

TUESDAY 13 SEPTEMBER 2022

Grace slowly awoke and coughed to ease the slight soreness in her throat. It felt cold in the bedroom, and she rolled over, prepared to snuggle up to Megan who she knew would be warm, because Megan was always warm. Except there was no Megan in her part of the bed.

She sat up and shivered. It really was a chilly morning in this little corner of South Yorkshire, and she swung her legs out of bed, prepared to investigate why sleepyhead Megan was first up.

She wrapped herself in a fluffy dressing gown and walked down the hallway, listening for sounds of activity that would indicate which room her partner – make that fiancée – was in. The click of the kettle switching off as it reached boiling point gave her a clue, and she headed towards the kitchen door.

Megan was just lifting the kettle as Grace walked through. 'Coffee?'

Grace looked at her. 'Yes please. Do you know what time it is?'

'Morning, I believe. Alexa, what time is it?'

The disembodied voice told them it was seven o'clock.

'Stop being clever and... and awake! Why are we up at this time? I thought we'd taken a week's holiday from work?'

'We have but not to laze around.' Megan smiled at the expression on Grace's face. 'We've a new home that we need to make ours. And we've a week to do it in, because I thought next Sunday we might ask people round for drinks and desserts, let them see the place in all its glory. But at the moment, there's not much glory.'

'Oh, God.' Grace slumped down on a mismatched kitchen chair donated from a friend who had discovered they only had three chairs to go around the four sides of their kitchen table. 'Does this face look as though it's ready for work at seven o'clock in the morning?'

'Porridge or toast?'

Grace realised nothing was going to deflect Megan, so she picked up the coffee now sitting in front of her. 'Best make it toast. I can eat that with one hand, while painting a wall with the other.'

'Now, now, little miss sarcasm.' Megan grinned at the usually pleasant love of her life. 'Just picture it forward to the end of the week and it will all be different in here.' She put the bread into the toaster.

'Have we actually got some paint?'

'Kind of. We've got tester pots.'

'So we don't even know what colour we want?'

'We know we want blue; it's in my notes.' She moved her notebook towards her. 'I've got five blues, so tell me which you prefer.'

Grace opened the book and on five different pages she saw assorted blue shades. 'I thought the idea with tester pots was to paint little bits on the wall.'

'I thought we could narrow it down first – five different blues on the wall will only confuse us. And you look pretty confused already. So, tell me which two you prefer.'

There was silence while Grace flicked backwards and forwards through the paint swatches, unable to believe she was choosing paint at such an ungodly hour. The toaster popped and Megan stood to butter it. She smiled as she thought Grace looked ready to go back to bed, instead of heading out into the crispness of the morning to buy their paint choice. She handed her the plate holding her toast. 'Well?'

'Thank you,' she said absently.

'I meant, well... have you decided?'

'Two and five, I think. Which do you prefer?'

'Two and four, so as we're both agreed on two I'll put a bit on the wall to make sure we really like it, then when you're awake we'll nip down to B&Q and buy some. There's other stuff we need to get as well. We need a new shower screen; the one that's in is a bit wobbly. Think we'll get a shower screen in the Aygo?'

'I'm not even convinced the Aygo is big enough to carry a tin of paint. We could look at shower screens on Amazon?' Grace finished her toast and took a gulp of her coffee. 'I'm starting to come round now. I'll go for a shower and try to avoid dislodging the shower screen until we get a new one, however it gets here. We could do a swap with Mum and borrow her car for the day while we get all the bigger stuff we need?'

'Your mum hates our Aygo.'

'She doesn't really. She calls it 'arry. 'Arry Aygo.'

Megan laughed. 'I do love her. She always makes me smile. And I do believe she's finally accepting she'll not see your dad again. Something's changed inside her, and we need to show her some support, not battle her as you did a few days ago. She's not the sort to put a shawl around her shoulders and wear a mob cap to show she's widowed and therefore her life is over. She'll never move on fully, but she needs to start trying and I think organising that office to fit her needs is a brilliant beginning.'

'Okay, I get you.' Grace sipped at the coffee, her eyes clouded over as she listened to Megan speak. 'You're a wise old bird, Megan King. I'll back off, be more supportive.'

'Not so much of the old bird please. Now, go and have that shower – not much point in getting up early if we don't make full use of the day. I'll paint a bit of the wall with the one we both like, and it will have dried to its finished colour by the time you've woken up properly. And watch the screen; don't make it collapse altogether – not yet anyway.'

With a final agreement on the blue paint, they were inside B&Q as soon as the doors opened at eight. Megan had brought her note-book, and they had a long walk around the massive store, filling up a trolley as they went. Their intention to paint their walls – as it was the quickest way to inject their personalities into their new home – went out of the window when they spotted a wallpaper they fell in love with that would be perfect for the headboard wall in their bedroom. They put two rolls in the trolley, then returned to the paint section to choose a pale blue for the three remaining walls to complement the background colour of the wallpaper.

They loaded the car after laying down the back seats, and decided to head over to see Clare before returning home. 'She'll have buns and coffee,' Megan explained. 'We've only got the coffee.'

'I love you for your smartness,' Grace said, glad she now felt fully awake after her early morning start. 'I'll text her and tell her we're on our way. It's not even nine o'clock yet, and she might still be in bed.'

* * *

Clare was showered, alive and eating her Weetabix when the text came through, so she put on a fresh pot of coffee, and as she heard the little car arrive she went to meet them at the door.

Megan and Grace were disembarking, Grace having to extricate herself from a curtain pole that was balanced precariously across her shoulder. Rob pulled out from his driveway and left for work, but not without first putting up a finger in salute as he drove past the three of them.

Megan saw the finger, and was furious. 'Who the hell does he think he is? No wonder Vic's gone.'

Clare smiled. 'I'm learning to live with it. He's never going to be in my fan club, obviously. Lock the car; I'd hate anybody to pinch your curtain pole.'

'It would make life a lot easier if they did,' Grace said. 'I should have offered to drive, not be the unfortunate passenger. Perhaps I'll drive on the way home.'

* * *

The two girls, with Grace now fully awake, chatted about their plans, everything they had bought, and their inability to carry a shower screen.

'Why didn't you ring? I would have met you there. It will go in my car.'

Megan sighed. 'Clare, there's something you should know about us. We're not that smart. We did consider asking you to swap cars for the day, but never thought for a minute of asking you to meet us to ferry the screen home. We'll leave the bathroom till the end, so perhaps when you've got a spare couple of minutes you can go and collect one for us?' She took out her phone. 'This is it. I took a screenshot of it on their website so we can check the measurements are okay for our place, but I'm sure they are.' She sent the picture to Clare's phone, and Clare promised to collect it the following day.

It was a pleasant hour, and Clare realised just how much she was missing company. She loved time out, time to think things through, to plan, but she loved her daughters more. Grace and Megan had arrived at a timely moment when she was trying to work out what to tackle first: buying her new office chair, or tidying the bottom end of the garden.

Whatever she did, it had to be something to take her mind off the card in the secret drawer.

'So, you busy, Clare?' Megan asked.

'Megan, I have a full social calendar. I am always busy... No, I have absolutely nothing at all that's a definite plan. You need a hand?'

'You have mucky clothes as well as the smart stuff you're wearing right now?'

'Paint-splattered leggings and a jumper with a big hole in the elbow. That okay?'

'It is. Why not come and paint with us? We have everything for the kitchen and bedroom, so while we're tackling the kitchen, maybe you could make a start in the bedroom? Please...'

'Please, Mum,' Grace added. 'And can you bring your own stepladders?'

* * *

Vic arrived later with her own version of paint-splattered leggings and a holey jumper, and by the end of the day the only thing left to do was put up the wallpaper in the bedroom. The four women laughed and joked throughout the day, and although it was quite exhausting work, everyone agreed it had been a most enjoyable few hours, partly because it was unplanned, and partly because the end results were stunning.

They stopped at five with the delivery of pizzas, and the girls decided to use the pale blue left from the bedroom to paint the small amount of bare wall in the bathroom. It would look good against the white wall tiles, and Clare promised she would go first thing to B&Q to pick up the shower screen, having now removed the wobbly one altogether.

Clare was home by half past seven and immediately checked in that Vic had also got home safe. How she wished she could offer her best friend a sanctuary with her, but she lived much too close to the man that had been the cause of all this uproar in her life.

Vic reassured her that everything was okay, and they chatted about the good day they had shared. 'Is Rob home?' Vic asked as a final word.

'He is, so you can collapse in safety now. You still want to collect your stuff tomorrow?'

'Yes. Will you be back home for eleven?'

'I'm sure I will. In fact, I'll text as soon as I'm home, and you can come over here as soon as you can. And I'll make sure Rob is well out of the way. We'll get all your stuff, don't worry.'

13

Wednesday morning brought clear skies, an autumnal feel in the air, and an early start for Clare.

She was down at the DIY store as soon as it opened, and soon had the shower screen in the back of her car. She collected a McDonald's breakfast and drove back home feeling really pleased with her early morning jaunt. She was home by 8.45, and as she climbed out of her car, she saw Rob unlocking his garage to get his own car out. She presumed he was about to leave for work, and she smiled inside. When the man returned home, he would find out he wasn't going to win this battle.

The plan was for Vic to arrive around half past ten, they would load up both cars with everything Vic wanted to take with her, then be on their way by noon. But first, Clare had to eat her McDonald's breakfast and deliver the shower screen.

* * *

Rob went back inside the house to collect his briefcase, annoyed that the sight of the tart across the road had caused so much anger in him. He was convinced she had persuaded Vic to up sticks and walk away from him, and one day he'd make damn sure she paid for that. Her and her bloody daughters – the coven, as he always called them. They'd warped Vic's mind, he knew that for a fact. How the fuck was he supposed to get her back home if the tart wouldn't tell him where she had moved to? And she had a key to his home, he remembered. Tonight, he decided, he would go across the road and demand she give it back.

He slipped a scarf around his neck; the autumnal feel to the morning had taken him by surprise when he'd gone out to bring the car out of the garage. Winter was on the way, and it made the memories of the forty-degree heat from those couple of days in summer now seem a little sad.

He closed the door to the lounge then headed towards the front door, which he'd left open as he'd popped back inside.

He was aware of a shadow, a movement, behind him, and pain exploded inside his head.

Clare heard the throaty roar of Rob's exhaust, and she knew his car was probably gone for the day. She finished her hash brown, and picked up the flat white. She grabbed her car keys, sent a swift text to Grace to say she was on her way, and headed out to her car, taking the coffee with her.

She checked across the road – Rob's car had definitely gone. That was the first obstacle over and done with. She shivered as she climbed into her car, and turned the heater up a notch. The day really had an autumnal bite to it, and she felt a touch of sadness. It had been a good summer, and she knew the nip in the air heralded the start of much colder days to follow.

Grace was waiting in the car park when Clare arrived and they carried the shower screen up to the flat. Megan was nursing a hot drink and laughed with delight.

'This will make such a difference; the old one is in the council skip in the car park. Thank you for collecting this for us, Clare. I'll go and have a shower now, and risk the water puddling on the floor, as I stink. It might be a cold morning, but it sure makes you work up a sweat on the morning run. We'll fit the screen later.'

Clare kissed them both. 'I have to rush off. I'm helping Vic move all her stuff out today. Rob's already gone to work so at the moment we're safe. Ring if you need anything, and take care in the shower, Megan.'

She left them to whatever plans they had and went back down to the car park, keen to get home. Her shoulders were aching, and earlier, as she'd driven her car to the DIY store, she'd noticed a slight tremble in her hands. Stress, she had decided, from the constant lifting and lowering of her arms while painting the bedroom walls for the girls, and moving her own furniture around in the office.

Megan and Grace had appeared equally distracted and tired, and Clare considered the possibility of a girlie weekend. She'd ask Vic later, and give Sara a ring that night, get something organised for maybe mid-October if everybody could get a Friday and a Monday off work. Megan and Grace had definitely shown signs of burn-out, after the previous busy day.

* * *

There was no sign of Vic's car over the road at her house, so Clare parked hers outside her own home, waiting outside for Vic to arrive to see what she wanted to do. She glanced at her watch. Vic was a little late, but that was Vic. She never arrived anywhere on time.

Ten minutes later, Vic turned the corner at the bottom the road and pulled up with a screech outside her former home. She ran across to Clare who was leaning against her car, waiting for instructions.

'You're late, Dolan.'

'Sorry. I had something to do.' There was no smile.

Clare stared at her.

'Something wrong, Vic? Look, come in and we'll have a quick coffee before we start.'

Clare unlocked her front door, and a silent Vic followed her inside. Clare switched on the kettle and grabbed two mugs. She spooned the instant coffee into them, figuring it was quicker than putting on the percolator.

After she'd made the drinks, she sat down at the kitchen table, pushing Vic's cup across to her. 'Want to talk?'

'Nothing much to say. He knows where I live. I nipped out to get some milk and a few bits and bobs from Asda about eight-ish, and when I got back home there was a note stuck in my letter box. Only a bit of paper torn out of a pad, but it said *I know where you live.*'

Clare thought for a moment. 'He's not been out before eight this morning, so it must have been yesterday when he left it. I saw him get his car out of the garage earlier, then I heard him drive off to work. All at his usual time.'

Vic shuddered. 'If I hadn't gone out to Grace and Megan's, I would have been there when he arrived. That thought fills me with dread. It's proper knocked me. What do I do now?'

'Look, we carry on as planned, but I suggest you take that bruised face of yours, which is now looking spectacularly yellow and purple, to the police. You don't have to press charges if you don't want, but you can lodge the attack with them. They'll hopefully go and have a quiet word with him. Don't let him get to you,

Vic; you've done the right thing getting away. Next time it might not be just a bruise.'

Vic sipped at her drink. 'I'm shaking. I'll be glad when we've moved all my stuff at least. No need to go back in there. I'm going to see about getting a camera to cover the door, and a couple for inside the flat. If he gets in and does hurt me, I want it on film.'

'Okay,' Clare said. 'We'll finish these drinks, then go over to move all your stuff. I'm hoping we can do everything in one trip. I don't want Rob coming back for any reason and catching us in the act. What are we clearing out?'

'It's only the small bedroom at the back. I was in the process of turning it into my workspace so most of my stuff is in there. The rest I managed to take with me on that first journey. I'm not taking the desk or the shelving unit – they'll need dismantling and they're only IKEA ones – so I'll just get new ones, but everything else I think will fit into the two cars.' She sipped again at her coffee, but Clare could see the tremor in her friend's fingers. 'You know,' Vic continued, 'this isn't me. I've never felt scared of anything or anyone in my life, but this is what he's done to me. You'll go with me to the police tomorrow?'

'Damn right I will,' Clare said and picked up her phone. 'Hold your hair back; I want a picture of this bruise before it fades any more. We need the police to see it in glorious technicolour.'

A smile flashed briefly across Vic's face, and she moved her hair so that Clare could get the shot. 'Never had so many photographs taken. You're turning into a proper David Bailey.'

'It's all evidence, Vic. We hopefully won't need them if the police manage to scare him off, but he seems like a different bloke. He's not the Rob I first met. He was lovely, and idolised you. Has he got another woman, you reckon?'

Vic laughed for the first time that day. 'No, that was your feller. I actually think he's simply got fed up with just the two of us. He always wanted kids, but said it didn't matter when they told us we wouldn't be having any by normal methods. He said the two of us was enough for him, but I think it's pretty clear now that wasn't the case.'

Clare nodded. 'You're probably right. That's why I'm asking if there's any possibility he found somebody else. He's been odd, moody and out of sorts for a couple of years or more now.'

'We'll, I've honestly never thought about it, but you're right. I should have been asking the question, maybe. He's systematically destroyed my love and we used to be so good together. He wouldn't have raised a finger never mind a fist to me, but once is enough. He'll not get the chance again. Come on, let's get on with it and really upset the bastard.' She stood and carried her mug across to the dishwasher, turned around and took Clare's mug from her hands.

'That's better. A bit of activity, and the real Vic Dolan is back. So, shall we load your car with the small stuff? We can then swap cars; you park yours on my front and we'll start to load up the bigger things in mine. Mine will hold the more solid stuff. And then, after we've loaded all the craft gubbins, take a minute to go into every room. There may be something personal you want to keep. Half of everything is yours you know.'

Vic dipped her head in acknowledgement, and the two women walked outside, both glancing right and left as they exited the front door almost on instinct. Clare knew Rob had gone to work but she couldn't escape the feeling he might jump out at them. She considered taking the baseball bat as backup, but laughed at her own stupidity. Did she really think she could bash somebody deliberately with such a weapon?

Vic fished her car keys out of her coat pocket and unlocked her car as they walked past.

Clare joined her at the car. 'I'll put the back seats down flat so we're not messing about when we have stuff in our arms,' she said, and opened both back doors. 'You go and get the house open, and make a start.'

She'd never seen Vic's car without the tartan blanket that always covered the back seat, and it looked so different without it. Vic had clearly done some forward thinking and removed it so it would be easier to make the vehicle ready for the move.

Unable to ask Vic how things worked, she used trial and error to sort out which levers needed to be pulled, placed the headrests in the passenger seat footwell, and decided where the rear seat-belts needed to be. She had just flattened the first seat when Vic careened around the corner of the house, her face ashen.

She called out Clare's name, reached out a hand towards her, then crumpled to the floor. Clare left the second of the back seats half up and half down and ran across to where Vic was lying immobile on the driveway, all the colour gone from her face, accentuating even more the depth of the bruising.

She knelt on the concrete, and shook her friend. 'God, Vic, what's wrong? Is he inside? Has he touched you?' She looked around, totally bewildered, then felt movement from Vic, followed by a deep groan.

Vic's eyes fluttered open and she leaned over and vomited. Clare held on to her, having no clue what was going on. 'Hey, come on, Vic,' she said gently. 'Let's get you back inside and cleaned up. It seems you've fainted.'

Vic turned a horrified face towards Clare. 'No! I'm not going anywhere. There's blood all over the place, and Rob's lying in the middle of it.'

14

The briefing room allocated to the Major Crimes Unit was deserted. Detective Sergeant Brendan Franks was on his third cup of tasteless coffee, considering it to be marginally better than the tasteless tea. His four-week enforced absence after a debilitating bout of Covid had left him with non-existent taste buds, and to a coffee aficionado such as himself, it was a tragedy of immense proportions.

He was taking his time reading through reports about drug related crimes that seemed to be increasing in the local Crystal Peaks area and was enjoying the quietness. He felt grateful that his offer to remain in Sheffield had been acted on, and he hadn't ended up in London with the rest of his team and most of the other teams from Moss Way police station. The Queen's funeral was a priority, and he didn't have an issue with that, he simply hoped the criminals didn't realise just how thin on the ground the police staffing was. He currently had a team of one, his DC Rosie Waters, and her attendance at court in a case that was long overdue for a hearing was needed this morning.

As a result of Rosie's absence, the entire place felt a bit like the

Marie Celeste must have appeared to the first people to board it. He had watched a couple of squad cars leave the car park, but it seemed to him that it was merely a token to show that they were fully manned, and criminals beware. The truth was far from that.

He stood in an effort to stretch his stiff limbs, and took his cup back to the small kitchen area to rinse it out. He couldn't face another one, and decided that lunchtime would see him go out of the office and maybe treat himself to a Costa meal.

With these thoughts in his head, he returned from the kitchen to see Rosie sitting at his desk, and a large Starbucks coffee on it, waiting just for him. An equally large one was in front of her.

She looked up at him. 'Don't ask. Bloody criminals these days don't know whether they're coming or going. Everybody's sitting there twiddling thumbs, reading Kindles and such like, waiting to be called, and he changes his plea to guilty. I got out as fast as I could in case he changed his mind again, and picked up a couple of drinks before heading back here. Anything come in?'

Bren shook his head. 'Not even a phone call. I've finally got round to reading this report about the increase in drug related crimes in this area, and it's not good reading. Have a look at it when you've got some time, and we'll have a general discussion with the full team when they get back, about different areas to target. I'll bring the boss in on it as well, because I feel we need to make some changes.'

She gave a deep sigh. 'You know, when you've got three kids of your own, it's scary reading. I know I don't have to worry yet – at the moment their drug of choice is Calpol – but one day they'll be able to think for themselves, and the syringe they use then, if they so choose, won't be the Calpol syringe.'

Bren removed the top from his coffee, and sipped at it. 'As you know, I can't actually taste this, but taste buds working or not, it's hell of a lot better than the stuff we get from that kitchen. Thank you, you may just have saved my life. You didn't hang around to hear what the sentence was this morning then?'

She shook her head. 'No, he's going to get at least three years, so I figured we'd not have him to worry about for quite some time. Have you done the report on that lady we went to see yesterday about the two dogs next door to her?'

'I have. I've passed it on. We're not dog experts, but I do think one, if not both, are on the banned list. We've set the ball rolling, and I did understand her concerns, I must admit. I was a bit worried to hear two children live in the house with the dogs, so I've pushed it through on a priority stream. There's probably nobody there to deal with it though, they'll all be in bloody London.'

Rosie picked up her coffee. 'Okay, I'm going to write up this morning's foray into the court world, see what's in my inbox, then we'll discuss what happens next. Yes?'

'Yes. Isn't it strange not hearing phones ringing?'

She laughed. 'Don't knock it. For the third day running we could actually finish on time. Gets a bit boring though doesn't it...'

The phone rang on Bren's desk and they both stared at it. 'It heard us,' she whispered theatrically. 'That's spooky.'

'Rosie, it's not spooky, it's normal.' He picked up the receiver. 'DS Franks.'

She watched as his face changed, and knew it wasn't worth going to her own desk. 'Okay. Send the address to my mobile, and DC Waters and I will leave immediately.'

He stood. 'Nine-nine-nine call. Unconfirmed suspicious death, Owlthorpe. We're three minutes or so away; let's try to get there before anybody destroys the scene, shall we?'

15

The body was lying half in the hallway and half in the kitchen, and to Clare's untrained eye, all the blood seemed to be around the head area. She made Vic sit on the stairs, and she went to check for signs of life.

She knew it was a waste of time, but if there was even a glimmer of a thready pulse she had to try to save him. She could feel nothing. He was totally unmoving, still warm but cooling. She pulled her mobile phone from her jeans pocket and was soon connected to someone who was trying to help.

'You're sure there is no pulse?'

'Positive. And I think there's only me and his wife here. I can't hear anything from upstairs. His wife was first in the house and found him, and she came outside to tell me and fainted. I'm watching her very carefully; I've sat her on the bottom stair facing the front door so she can't see this mess. I've only been as far as Rob's neck to check him, then I've come back out to the hallway. Please – get somebody here quickly just in case I'm wrong.'

'We have a paramedic en route. He'll be with you in two minutes, Mrs Staines. Are you okay?'

'I am, but I'm concerned about my friend. She looks grey.'

'They'll look after her but their priority will be to establish what the situation is with Mr Dolan. Please stay with Mrs Dolan.'

Clare heard the sirens and breathed a sigh of relief.

'They've just pulled into the driveway,' Clare said to the operator. 'And it looks as though there's a police car following them.'

'Then I'll leave you in their capable hands. Thank you, Mrs Staines.' And she disconnected.

* * *

The paramedics took in the scene at a glance. Their concerns were for Rob; they had no interest in who had done what, why and when.

When the two police officers turned up, they showed their warrant cards, and one of them, DC Rosie Waters, led Clare and Vic out to the police car. She helped Vic into the back seat, then turned to Clare.

'Please get in as well, Mrs Staines. We'll have a little chat while my DS checks in with the paramedics. We'll all know more when he's spoken to them. I understand you were the one who found your husband, Mrs Dolan?'

Vic nodded. Speech seemed impossible.

Rosie turned to Clare. 'I think Mrs Dolan needs a minute or two to take things in. You were with Mrs Dolan?'

'Yes. Mr and Mrs Dolan have recently separated, and I was here to help Vic take some stuff, her crafting equipment mainly, to her new home. She entered the house first, and I stayed on the drive to ready the car. We'd planned on using my Toyota for the bulky stuff. She stumbled round the corner, kind of held out her arms towards me, and fainted. I left the car with its doors wide open' – Clare glanced back towards Vic's car – 'and ran towards her. I had no idea what was wrong, and I was starting to think about pulling her onto her side when she groaned, then projectile vomited onto the drive. She started to talk about lots of blood, so I brought her inside, sat her on the stairs and went to see what had happened to Rob, check if I could help him. I realised I couldn't, but I felt for his pulse. It was obvious he was beyond help, so I backed away and rang 999. Then I stayed with Vic until you and the paramedics arrived.'

'Thank you. Is it okay if I call you Clare and Vic?'

Both women nodded.

'Thank you. We're obviously going to have to talk in more depth, but when did either of you last see Mr Dolan?'

'About five days ago when he did this,' Vic mumbled. She turned her face to reveal the bruise and tucked her hair behind her ear.

'And in my case, it was just before nine this morning,' Clare said. 'I saw him unlock the garage and pull the car out onto the drive. He always put his car into the garage overnight, never left it out. I didn't see him go to work, but I thought I heard him leave. His car has a really throaty exhaust. I assumed he'd gone to work; nothing was any different today to the rest of his days. He goes to work just before nine, comes home just after five. It's why I went as close as I did to check him, because it didn't make sense. His car isn't here.'

'It's not in the garage?'

'I definitely heard it being driven down the road, and prior to that I definitely saw him bring it out of the garage, but I went into my kitchen to finish my breakfast, so what happened in between I've no idea. If he's not returned it to the garage, and he's dead on the floor in the kitchen, who has his car?'

Clare could tell that Rosie was feeling uncomfortable. Clare was asking all the right questions, but they were questions *she* should be asking *them*.

'Okay,' she said gently, 'I do understand the shock of finding your husband, Mrs Dolan, but I'm going to have to take you to the station and take statements from both of you about what you saw, what you remember, anything you noticed such as the noisy exhaust... Oh, we have reinforcements arriving.'

Two further police cars pulled up, parking on the road; the driveway was full.

'Are you feeling better, Mrs Dolan? Do you need medical help?' Rosie leaned towards Vic, who was starting to look marginally better.

'You'll be pleased to know I don't feel so sick,' Vic said, 'but I would like to know what's going on. The only person Rob has hurt is me, and even that was out of character. He'd never touched me in anger before and we've been together many years. I just didn't intend to give him a second chance to hit me, so I left. So whatever has happened, it's nothing to do with our separation, it's something else. He wasn't happy I'd gone, and he's been bothering Clare to try and find out where I'm staying, but it doesn't make sense that he's dead. It feels wrong.' She dropped her head. 'It's so confusing.'

Rosie listened carefully. She could see puzzled faces, and knew they had either been knocked sideways by what they had found, or they were supremely brilliant at acting. These ladies were smart, intelligent human beings, trying to work out what this devastation in their lives might mean. The biggest puzzle of all, and one that she guessed was about to be voiced by Bren, was who the hell had driven Rob Dolan's car away from his home, and where was it now?

* * *

Clare looked at Rosie. 'So I'll ask again: who drove Rob's car away this morning? Because it was definitely his car, I hear that same noise every single morning. And where have they driven it to, and why?'

'Exactly what I was thinking,' Vic said. 'Give me a minute to recall the registration, and you can put it through ANPR to check if it can be found.'

Rosie hid her smile. *Everyone's an armchair detective these days,* she thought. *Far too much* Vera *and* Midsomer Murders *on TV.*

* * *

Grace and Megan were waiting to collect Clare and Vic from the reception area at Moss Way police station. Grace was in tears as the two women walked out together, and she hugged them both.

'I'm so sorry, Vic, I know you'd split up but you were with Rob so many years. Have they been able to tell you anything?'

'Not really. I'll be meeting a Family Liaison Officer later and I suppose they'll keep me informed through them. They think he died very shortly after bringing the car out of the garage, and although they've not said this, it seems like the killer took his car. He was killed in the house, and that's another mystery. If it was a random killing purely to steal the car, how come it happened in the house, with the car ready and waiting to go on the driveway? He'd already started it, as usual. The keys were in it. They could have just made off with the car. They didn't need to kill him. It makes no sense at all.'

They reached the little Aygo parked in the nearby Asda car park, but even seeing the car didn't raise the usual jokes as they climbed into it. Grace drove them back to her mother's home, where they could see crime scene tape surrounding the house that was almost directly across the road, as well crime scene tape around Vic's car.

Vic sighed. 'I guess I might need a taxi to get me home then.'

'No you won't.' Clare's voice was firm. 'You'll stay here tonight. I'm not going to let you be on your own. We'll figure out tomorrow what happens next. I don't think we're actually suspects, but I'm not sure where we stand with our cars. At least mine hasn't got crime scene tape round it so I'm assuming they don't want to check that, and it sounds like it's been quite some time since Rob was last in yours, Vic, so they're going to find nothing to help them. My God, please don't say we might have to borrow the Aygo!'

Clare's words lightened the atmosphere, and when Sara and Greg arrived, their faces reflecting their anxiety, they decided to order in takeaways yet again, and try to avoid talking about the events of the day. Effectively, they all wanted to keep Vic's mind off what she'd seen as she'd walked into her house. Seeing your husband with a crater in his head and copious amounts of blood pooling around him was a first, and they all knew it would be heart-breaking for Vic when she tried to close her eyes to go to sleep.

Clare was determined to be with her best friend, supporting her every step of the way.

* * *

Eventually Clare's house settled down for the night. Sara and Greg left first because Greg had an early start the following morning, and within fifteen minutes of them leaving, Grace and Megan said goodnight too.

Clare and Vic decided to have ten minutes down the garden, enjoying all the lights, the night perfume of the roses, the lavenders, and anything else down there that tickled their olfactory senses.

Vic was quiet. She had joined in with the chatter while Clare's family had been there, but once there was just the two of them, the bravado disappeared.

'He's dead, Clare.'

Clare put her arm around Vic's shoulders and hugged her. 'I know, and I want you to stay here as long as you need to. It's good we gave the police this address as your place of residence until we tell them otherwise, because they'll want to talk to you again and I can be there to support you. Cry when you want to, but don't be afraid to laugh as well. And when you're ready, we'll talk the whole thing through, because there's stuff that doesn't make a lot of sense about this. Did anybody else know he'd hit you?'

'I haven't told anyone. It's possible people have seen the bruise, but they would only be guessing how I'd got it. I told you all: he wasn't killed because he walloped me; he must have upset somebody else. And I reckon it's totally unconnected with what he did to me. I'm going to have to talk to the people he works with... worked with... and explain as much as I know. We had to watch John die over many months, but we knew it would happen sooner rather than later. This doesn't feel right at all, this is bloody awful. A copper on duty outside my home, it's all wrong. God, Clare, what have I done to deserve this? And as far as I'm concerned that absolutely awful part, and one that shook me to the core, was when they told me not to leave the locality at all without notifying them of where I was going.'

'I don't know what you've done to deserve it, Vic, but I hope they find something out to make sense of it soon. We'll get through it together.'

16

27 AUGUST 2022

Jed felt as if he'd been granted the freedom of the city. Eloise had just been collected in a taxi for transfer to the city centre, where she would be helped onto a coach that would take her to Sandown on the Isle of Wight for five days.

He had bought her the holiday as a birthday gift, and she had been delighted. He'd given her a big sloppy kiss, wished her bon voyage and waved her off with a huge smile.

The smile had disappeared as the taxi turned the corner at the end of the road. He hadn't told her he'd also booked a week's break from work. He needed to be able to devote time to discovering the name of his father, and he couldn't do anything with Eloise in the house. He would now be able to go into his mother's bedroom and look in every nook and cranny. There had to be something somewhere that would offer a glimmer of a clue as to who the unknown man was.

He'd take a drink upstairs with him, then begin the search. He stared at the kettle for a moment then opened the fridge and took out a beer. He glanced at his watch. Just after twelve. Sun over the yardarm and all that. He opened the can and took a long sip, not bothering with a glass. Time to crack on. He had less than a week to solve this puzzle before Eloise returned, suntanned and talking non-stop about the island off the south coast. Far enough away from Yorkshire for him to punch the air with some feeling and shout yes, before carrying his can upstairs to the bedroom that overlooked the drive at the front of the house.

* * *

Jed walked through the door and felt immediately overwhelmed by sadness. Kirsty Grantham had been a woman of strength, a woman other people turned to when they had problems, and he could still feel the vibrancy of her character as if she was still alive; this room was his mother personified.

He moved across to the large bay window and pushed the curtains to one side. The dark blue velvet felt luxurious in his hands, and as he pushed them to the edge of the track, the light flooded into what had previously been a darkened room.

He guessed it was Eloise's way of grieving, keeping the room deliberately darkened. He could imagine his mother being in here and simply sitting, either on the blue velvet chair positioned perfectly in the bay so that when she had good days she could sit and watch the world pass by, or on the bed with the lighter blue bedspread. Nothing seemed to have changed since her death; she was still here. He could detect the faint fragrance of the Dolce & Gabbana Light Blue she had loved so much, and he inhaled, capturing the moment.

He sat for a moment on the chair and looked out of the window. There was no one around. Midday, and the road seemed to be deserted.

'Okay, Mum,' he whispered softly. 'Here's what we're going to do. We're going to look for anything that will tell me who my dad is, because I need to find him. And I need you to guide me.'

There was no response, but he did briefly think that if there had been some sort of sign, anything at all, he would have probably dropped his beer, legged it down the stairs and out the back door.

He sat looking out of the window until his beer can was empty, then he stood. He knew he was putting off making a start. This was his mum's domain, and although he couldn't see any other way of searching for the information he needed, it did feel as if he was intruding into her life. Without her permission.

He stood by her bed and did a full 360-degree turn, taking in as much as he could of the room. He realised that though he had been in his mother's bedroom many times over the years, he had never really looked at it.

There was only one wardrobe, but it was a large oak one, with a huge drawer at the bottom. There was a matching chest of drawers, two bedside tables and a television on the wall. The room was neat, with very little dust; he guessed Eloise took good care of it.

Where to begin? He figured he should start small and work up towards the massive wardrobe. The bedside tables.

He moved the one that had been the receptacle for his mother's medication away from the wall and checked behind it. He hadn't a clue what he was looking for – a diary, a letter, a notepad – and he also had no idea if it would be easy to find or well-hidden. He didn't underestimate how difficult this job was going to be.

He slid open the top drawer of the three. It was tidy and he took out his phone to take a shot of how it looked. He was guessing Eloise had disposed of all the remaining medication after Kirsty's death, and tidied the contents that were still in the drawers. He had to be careful to leave it all exactly as it was. There was a small notepad, personalised to Kirsty with her name etched in gold on the front, which he carefully opened. Nothing. She hadn't even written so much as one word in it.

There was a pen, a manicure set, half a packet of indigestion tablets and a small pack of tissues. He placed them carefully back inside the drawer then checked against the photo he had taken. It all seemed to be the same.

The second and third drawers revealed nothing at all. He pulled them fully out, but his phone flashlight revealed no hidden items.

The other bedside table proved to be completely empty. He felt mildly disheartened, but had he really expected to find his father's name within the first five minutes?

The chest of drawers was tall, and held five deep drawers. The bottom two contained fresh bedding, but the top three had been emptied of Kirsty's clothes. He knew she had kept her nighties and pyjamas here because in her later moments, he'd passed her a clean nightie one evening, at her request. He had chosen a Minnie Mouse one, and she had laughed. How they had loved Minnie and Mickey...

She had confessed to not having enough strength to pull open, then close, the heavy drawer, and even then, he hadn't considered that death was inevitable and drawing ever nearer.

Jed was starting to feel bursts of anger once more towards Eloise. His mother seemed to have disappeared. Her clothes had either been thrown away or sent to charity shops; not even her books were left. She had always had a large collection of books, but even the bookshelf had disappeared from the bedroom. He knew she loved the ease of her Kindle, but she also loved the feel, the smell, of a proper book. Had Eloise simply moved them to her own bedroom? Or had she passed them on?

He was beginning to realise that instead of drowning in his sorrow, and making the transition to his new job in Sheffield, he should maybe have kept a closer eye on what was happening in this house. Had something unknowingly been given away that possibly contained the key to his father's identity?

Jed removed the lining paper from the top three drawers in the chest of drawers. It smelled faintly of lavender and he checked underneath each piece, but there was nothing.

It slowly dawned on him that maybe he had left it a bit late to find anything here. It had clearly been emptied, possibly while he was at work to spare his feelings. Eloise would have known it would upset him to see his mother's belongings being removed from the house; he hoped that that was the reason, and not just a way of disposing of any clues to his father.

He checked the wardrobe. It was empty of everything except coat hangers that clanged together as he opened the doors. He stared. It had once been packed tightly with beautiful dresses, workwear, winter and summer coats... all gone.

The large bottom drawer that they had laughingly called the coffin still held three blankets that they used to put in the car for picnics. They had always loved their picnic days, and he lifted out the woolly throws, carefully stroking them. The memories almost overwhelmed him. It had been so long since those wonderful times.

He had moved on. It wasn't Kirsty's fault they no longer shared trips to the coast, or exploration days in Sherwood Forest – it was all about his leaving school and starting work. And acquiring his own car, therefore being able to go for a quick spin on his own just for the hell of it, to Bridlington, or Filey, or Scarborough, places close enough to have visited with his mother before he became an adult himself.

He wondered if she had missed the fun times as she watched him mature into an adult and leave behind the childhood once shared with her.

He replaced the blankets in the drawer, once again referring to the photograph to check it all looked exactly the same.

He returned to the window and sat once more on the blue velvet chair. When his mother had sat here, towards the end, it had made her look so fragile, but it meant she could see a little of the world going on around her, and he tried hard to feel close to her as he looked out at what she had enjoyed.

He made sure the chair was in its earlier alignment, then closed the curtains to what he hoped was the right width, allowing the correct amount of sunshine to filter through. He hadn't thought to take a photograph before opening them.

Standing in the doorway, he took a long look around the room. He didn't think he'd missed anything – there wasn't actually much of anything in it. His answers simply weren't in this room, but something must be somewhere. Eloise had always hedged away from saying anything, and he didn't like to push her too hard. It was clear the subject of his illegitimate birth and lack of a father upset her, but it was just as clear how much she loved Kirsty, and him. He suspected she thought she was protecting him by steering clear of the subject, but one day, hopefully soon, he would know. He would track down this man.

Somewhere, there was something. Had he paid maintenance? The thought hit him like a sledgehammer. He knew his mother had done internet banking – the solicitor had sorted out all the monies, and handed him a final statement for the amount he had inherited, alongside deeds to the house and Kirsty's instructions to always take care of Eloise and give her a home for the rest of her life. His mind was now whirring. He had gone paperless several years earlier, and he guessed his mother was the same. She had always used her phone...

So where was the bloody phone? Definitely not in this room. Would Eloise have tossed it into the 'everything drawer' in the kitchen? Would she have thought it would never be needed again, a final link to the daughter she had loved with all her heart, its battery as dead as she was?

Jed carefully closed the door behind him and ran downstairs. He needed to scout through that drawer, through the sandwich bags, the spare screws, kept because they might be useful one day, through all the odds and sods that didn't have another place. He needed his mother's phone. And he could hazard a guess at her code to unlock it – 251299.

17

The drawer was a mess. Jed grinned as he looked inside it. It was definitely the family joke, the everything drawer. Because it held everything. If you found something and you didn't know where it belonged, it went in this drawer until somebody, needing it one day, would reclaim it, the drawer giving up its treasure.

As it did with Kirsty's phone.

It was dead, so he connected it to his iPhone charger and opened it up. He put in 251299, and just as in life, in death his mother didn't let him down. The phone flared into life.

He began with her contacts list; there were surprisingly few people on it when he compared it to his own. He took screenshots of everything, then forwarded them to his own phone. He opened up her photo file and was pleasantly surprised by the way they were organised into albums. There were very few pictures that didn't belong in any of the designated categories. He spent some time looking at them carefully to see if there were any strangers he didn't recognise, but it was only office parties that showed him people he didn't know.

He clicked onto her banking app. It was set for facial recognition, and he had no idea what her manual login would be – banks required at least two login details, and he couldn't even begin to guess beyond 251299. Besides, he needed to go back several years to check for maintenance payments; he doubted he would see anything on the app that far back. He closed it down.

A quick glance at the time showed him the afternoon was getting on; his empty stomach confirmed it by giving a gentle rumble, and he decided to make a sandwich and a drink.

He grabbed a notebook from his briefcase as he went past it, and put it on the kitchen table. He could get some thoughts down on paper while he was eating, and then the following day could be devoted completely to searching. He would start with the top of the house and work down from there.

* * *

Sunshine woke Jed shortly after six on that late August morning, and he lay for a few minutes wondering whether to try to nod off again, or whether to get up. He sat up and rubbed his eyes, then stretched. An early start then, he decided.

Today would be a trip into the land of the giant spiders – the attic. He knew Eloise hated it, and only put stuff up there that she didn't want to throw away but likewise didn't want to use again. He thought about the boxes of Lego, his early train sets, small tricycles that had served him well until the first stabilisers were removed and he had discovered two-wheel cycling, and boxes and boxes of 'stuff' that he knew he would have to search through to satisfy himself that there was nothing in them that could be a clue to the father he was seeking.

He settled for a cereal breakfast, taking it out onto the patio to eat it. The cafetière was empty by the time he returned everything to the kitchen, and he collected the double step ladder from the shed, a clever ladder that opened up on a hinge to twice its length, then locked into place. It was their only access to the loft – the thought, *was this deliberately difficult to stop anyone from going up there*, flashed briefly across his mind.

He carried the ladder to the landing, then leaned it against the wall so that he could climb up and fling open the loft hatch. He tried to remember where the light switch was, a thought coupled with a fervent hope that the bulb hadn't blown, but all was good. The switch was immediately to the right and glory be, the light bulb gave instant illumination.

He paused for a moment, surveying the scene. It was a reasonably tidy place, this alleged haven for arachnoids the size of a dinner plate, but he rather thought, and hoped, that snippet about spiders was all a figment of his grandmother's imagination.

The floor of the loft had been boarded out, but he had no memory of this ever having been done during his lifetime, so he hoped it hadn't deteriorated and was stable. It would be difficult to explain away a gaping hole in a bedroom ceiling from where he had fallen through, and possible breakages of limbs.

A grin flashed across his face at the thought of what the ensuing conversation with his grandmother would be, and he stepped carefully up into the loft space. It was a huge area, with almost half of it completely empty. Spiders forgotten, he tested the floor gingerly, but it seemed to be solid. His trainers made no sound as he walked across the floor towards the start of the contents of what he was now beginning to think of as a magical room, containing possible answers to all his queries. Or at least to his one major query: *who is my dad*.

He did a very short video of the space, in case he moved anything out of its original position, then walked over to where everything was. The first items were two huge holdalls, the first of which he unzipped. Kirsty's clothes. He said an audible, 'Sorry,

Gran.' She had clearly not sent them anywhere. He gently looked through everything, but both bags only held clothing and shoes. He zipped them closed, and moved on.

The first cardboard box was sellotaped closed, so he peeled it back carefully, aware it would need to look the same once he finished looking. Inside were around a dozen jigsaws, all large ones, which he took out to look at, lost in the memories of seeing them as completed pictures. His grandmother and his mother had loved doing them together, working on them after he had gone to bed. It had been good to inspect what they had completed when he got up for school.

He had loved the Paris picture, alive with the vibrancy of France's capital city; the Eiffel Tower in its lit-up state absolutely glowed from the picture. It suddenly occurred to him that he had never actually seen either woman take a jigsaw to pieces after it was completed. Strange. And yet here they all were, packed away never to be seen again.

There were two more boxes with jigsaws in, and he put them back in exactly the same place once he had checked out their contents. He didn't think Eloise was likely to visit the attic any time soon, but just in case, it had to look the same as she had last seen it.

A large box contained a beautiful dinner service, with a smaller box keeping safe a matching tea service. He stared at it for a while, wondering why it should be up in a dusty attic; such beauty needed to be on display, if not in everyday use.

He shrugged. Women. He would never understand them.

He discovered his toys in the far corner. A smile arrived on his face instantly as he recognised the familiar Lego boxes containing specific items to be built. The carton that brought the biggest grin was the one filled with individual tiny pieces of Lego with which he could build anything. These pieces had been spaceships, trains, cars, farms and animals – his imagination had soared with the little building blocks.

There were four small bikes. Had his grandmother saved them just in case a new baby ever arrived? He knew that would never have happened – his mother had said so, many times. And that hadn't made him particularly happy. He didn't like being an only child – he would have loved at least one sibling to bond with.

An exceptionally large box and a huge Christmas gift bag had labels on them saying 'Christmas Decs'. He knew he had to check them out, but felt deep inside this wouldn't give him anything he needed.

He dragged them a bit closer to the light as the corners of the attic were quite dim, and he took every bauble, every piece of tinsel out. When had the two women decided these pretty items were no longer needed? he wondered, carefully putting them all back in one by one to avoid any damage. By the time he was finished, his hands and face were covered in glitter, but he had seen nothing that would direct him towards the man he was seeking.

After two solid hours of looking and enjoying the memories, he was beginning to despair. Two boxes to go, both stacked together and at the back of the attic. If there was nothing in them, it was going to take a lot more investigating on his part, because he didn't know what to try next. The returned DNA results had been less than helpful, but he did concede he hadn't known what to expect anyway.

The next to last box was the one that lifted his spirits. It said 'JED' on the front in thick black marker pen, and he instinctively knew his name had been turned to the wall to prevent him accidentally spotting it. Something was hidden in the box that neither his mother nor his grandmother wanted him to see, and carefully removing the Sellotape that was sealing it revealed it to be assorted papers and cards.

He opened the final box first, just to take it out of the equation, and discovered it to be full of baby clothes. He spent some time looking through it, but there was nothing other than tiny garments inside, so he resealed it and then took the box marked JED back to the loft hatch. He took a quick photo of the layout as he stood on the top rung of the ladder, tucked the JED box under his arm, and dropped back down to the landing. He placed the box carefully at the top of the stairs, then went back to close the hatch and fold the ladders back into their original position. He left them leaning against the wall, knowing that if the JED box revealed nothing of any help, it would have to be returned to its place in the loft.

He felt dirty, and sparkly. He laughed at his own face after catching a glimpse of it in the landing mirror, so showered before heading downstairs carrying the precious box.

He placed it on the kitchen table, grabbed a beer from the fridge, and took a long drink. That effectively got rid of the dust he could taste, and he once again carefully peeled back the Sellotape holding the flaps of the box in place.

The top item was a newspaper, *The Star*, dated 27 December 1999. He lifted it out, debating whether to check it out more thoroughly or continue to remove items from the box.

The newspaper won, and he turned the pages until he saw the pictures of four tiny babies, each cradled in their mothers' arms. A much younger version of the woman he had last seen almost five months earlier stared back at him from the page.

The caption read, 'Josiah John Grantham, with his mother Kirsty Grantham, born 23.50 on Christmas Day, 1999'. The overarching banner headline said, 'A loving and warm Christmas Day welcome to the world to our newest citizens'.

He stared at it, took in the details of how he had looked, how his mother had looked, then carefully folded it back to how it was, knowing it confirmed nothing that he didn't already know.

But the tingle in his fingers told him he had to concentrate, because something in this box was important, would show him the direction to follow. He placed the newspaper to one side, then dipped his fingers inside to take out the next available item.

18

28 AUGUST 2022

Jed lifted out the next article: a plastic wallet containing paperwork. There was a photocopy of his birth certificate, a tiny armband from his stay in hospital after his birth and an appointment card with every antenatal appointment his mother had kept throughout the pregnancy, along with a couple more items pertaining to the hospital stay. He studied them carefully; he didn't want to miss any sort of clue by skim-reading the information.

Next in the box were a couple of letters, and he felt a frisson of excitement as he held them. Letters were better than official forms – more personal.

The envelopes were addressed to his mother at her home address, and postmarked during the week following Christmas. He slid the first letter out of the envelope, being careful not to damage it.

Dear Kirsty,
So very pleased to hear that all went well with the birth of your son, Josiah, and I can't wait to see you both. He's a very

lucky little boy to have a mum like you, and I'm sure he'll realise that in the many years in front of both of you.

And what a lovely date. How special is a Christmas Day baby! Was your mother with you for the birth? And what about Daddy? Does he know he has a son?

That's enough of my questions – no more prying. I know there must be a reason why you can't disclose who Josiah's father is, and I won't push it, but just know I'm always here for you. I miss you so much at work, and you do know they would have kept your job open until you could return? I'm so sorry you felt you had to leave.

Sending much love, and I have a little gift for the baby, so I'll call round to see you in the next week or so.

Take care.

Jenny xxx

Jed stared at the letter which told him absolutely nothing of help in finding his elusive father, then pulled the envelope towards him again. The sender's address was on a small sticker on the back; he made a note of it in his notebook. Jennifer Pointer. He couldn't ever remember hearing her name, and he wondered just how long the friendship lasted after his birth.

Was it significant that his mother had left her job, and not simply taken maternity leave? He drew a circle around Jenny's name, knowing he would have to contact her, find out further details from around the time of his birth.

He folded the letter carefully and slid it back into the envelope. He was guessing that, as he didn't know who Jenny was, the friendship must have been stronger in Jenny's head than it was in Kirsty's; it hadn't stood the test of time. But even so, as he didn't want Eloise knowing he was actively seeking answers while taking advantage of her disappearance for a few days, he couldn't even throw the name out casually. She would guess immediately he had been in the loft, ferreting around. This could throw their closer relationship back into the icy wastes it had been in after Kirsty's death, back when he had felt such anger inside him that Eloise hadn't kept him fully informed. Just like he was doing now with hiding his actions from his grandmother.

He pulled the second letter towards him. This too had a name and address on the back, and again it was somebody he didn't recognise... or did he? It was handwritten, not a sticker, and identified Nanette Lawton as the sender. He quickly copied the name and address into the notebook, and sat back, recalling vague memories of someone he had called Aunty Nette, although he knew she wasn't a real aunty; it was simply his mum trying to instil respect in him. That could have been short for Nanette. And if it was, she was another one who had disappeared from his mother's life, although he seemed to remember her being around in his early childhood. He pulled out the blue sheet of paper.

Hi gorgeous!

Well done you – so pleased it's over, and you're both doing well. I'll be round to see you and the little cherub as soon as you let me know you're home. I hope you're handling everything okay – tough decision you made, but I know you thought everything through.

Just know that your new job is safe and whenever you feel ready to start I'll sort you out. It's what friends are for.

You make the arrangements with your mum re the baby, and I'll employ you. Simple!

Sending all my love to you and the little Josiah,

Nette

xxx

Jed reread the letter, aware of there being an undertone to it, one he wasn't sure about. It almost seemed as if there was something hidden that Aunty Nette and his mother had shared – some knowledge. About his father?

He ran upstairs, made photocopies on his printer of the letter and both sides of the envelope, then took them back downstairs and placed them with the other letter, ready to go back in the box.

The next items he removed were cards – birth congratulations from many people. He had always thought of Kirsty as being a private person, but it seemed she had many friends and acquaintances when he was born, going by the number of cards she had saved.

He began to go through all of them, but found nothing he needed to annotate in his notebook. Everybody seemed delighted with his birth, and he took his time reading them all. He didn't know any of the names really, but he kept going. He didn't intend missing anything; slow and steady was definitely the name of this game. He picked up the next card, pale blue with a picture of a beautiful Victorian perambulator on the front and the words:

Congratulations on the birth of a son

Inside was handwritten:

J xxx

Jed paused, knowing this one was different. Without exception, all of the cards so far had contained handwritten messages wishing his mother well, but this simply said '*J xxx*'.

He held on to the card for a moment in the vague hope that he would get some sort of feeling from it, but there was nothing. J. His own name began with J. Had this been an agreement between his mother and his father? Was his name Josiah as well? Something more than a connection with *The West Wing*?

He walked across to the DVD stand and took out the box sets of the entire seven series. In one of them was a small leaflet that gave potted bios of all the characters. And there he saw President Josiah Edward Bartlet. Not Josiah *John* Bartlet as he'd guessed.

He picked up the card once more and knew what the J stood for. John, his own middle name.

His thoughts began to race and he leaned back on the kitchen chair. John had to be one of the most common names in the English language, but it was currently all he had. Deep inside he knew he was right. His father was called John. And that was why his mother had given it as a second name to him. Everything pointed to Kirsty having deeply loved this man, but they hadn't been able to be together. He was almost definitely a married man who couldn't leave his wife... Did he have children? Jed's mind was whirling.

He put the card to one side, then carried on in the same meticulous fashion, checking through all of them. Every other card was normal.

He put all the cards back inside the plastic folder, with the exception of the J one, then dipped his hand into the box. There was one plastic folder remaining, and it seemed to be all sorts of different things – photographs, bits of paper containing messages, all manner of items that had clearly meant enough to Kirsty to save them. There were payslips – her final one when she left work to have the baby, and about six or seven from the start of her new job. The one where she had worked for Aunty Nette? Her final job before becoming too ill to work hadn't been with Nette, so Kirsty had moved on. Left Nette behind?

He placed the final payslip prior to his birth on the table and flattened it. He smiled at the meagre amount – nobody would even get out of bed for such a paltry figure these days, but the company had given her a £250 bonus. Staines Solicitors had obviously felt she was worth it. Had they known she wouldn't be returning to them? He suspected not.

He looked at the payslips following her return to work after his birth, and was pleased to see her wages had improved. The payslips were headed with the name of a nursery and toddler care centre, and he felt a small thud of annoyance. She hadn't looked after him, but she had looked after other children.

It was only later, as he sat drinking a hot cup of tea, that he realised how unreasonable his thoughts had been. She'd needed to work. She had a child who required an upbringing, and that didn't happen without an income. And he certainly hadn't missed out on love – Eloise had adored him. They had lacked for nothing, due to his mother's wages from her job, and – maybe – periodic handouts from his father.

There were no further payslips, so he didn't know how long she worked with Aunty Nette. She had worked at a haulage company until the time of her terminal diagnosis, and he knew she had been there for years. Kirsty had moved on.

He continued on to the photographs; they seemed to be pictures of the various places she had worked. She had written names on the back of the group photographs, and he paid particular attention to these, feeling a massive sense of loss as he saw his mother's handwriting.

One of the photographs had a large number of people in it, all clustered around a man and a woman sitting down. It was obviously a formal affair of some sort, because Kirsty was in a stunning long red dress. All the other ladies in the picture wore similarly long dresses, and the men were in dinner suits and bow ties. Champagne appeared to be flowing freely as everybody was holding a glass as the picture was taken, and coffee cups were on the tables, indicating that the meal had already been enjoyed and cleared away. It wasn't obvious who was with who apart from the couple that seemed to be central to the gathering. The overarching impression was that everybody was enjoying the occasion; they were full of food and alcohol, and they were revelling in each other's company at a venue away from their workplace environment.

He looked at it for quite some time, stroking his mother's beautiful face, wishing it could be in real life. He longed to hold her, to hug her, even if it was just for one more time, and in this photograph, she looked happy. There was none of the pain she had felt in later years, and according to the date on the front of the picture, it was a year before his birth. He checked every other face and didn't recognise anyone, so he turned it over, overwhelmed all over again at seeing Kirsty's delicate handwriting.

She had drawn little outline figures representing where each person sat or stood on the picture, and he decided the best way was to look at a name, then flip it over to see who was who. He didn't spot the obvious difference until he actually reached it; he worked slowly to make sure he missed nothing.

The man and the woman who were sitting centrally in the picture, surrounded by their employees, were named Clare Staines and J.

19

With everything neatly back in the place it had originated from, Jed pulled his copies towards him. He felt confident his perusal of the loft contents would reveal nothing further, and nobody – Eloise – would know he had even been up there. Now he could really begin his search.

And that search would begin with a man called John Staines. He opened up his laptop, typed in the name, and discovered he was indeed a solicitor, with associates but not partners. A quite simple Staines Solicitors.

No Staines and Son, no Staines and Partners, only Staines Solicitors. It was in a central Sheffield location in the legal district, with a Paradise Square address. Jed wrote it into his notebook, although not convinced he would pay him a visit at work. That wasn't the way to go about it. This was a personal matter, and if it was possible, Jed wanted to keep it that way.

He could make it a bit more public if things changed and Staines denied paternity, but he had the information now to begin his search in earnest.

He made himself a coffee, found some biscuits, and sat on the patio to mull over the events of the day. He was uncomfortably aware that he was stirring up trouble for someone along the line: Staines' wife, any children he might have had with her, Staines himself. But he had endured all of his life not knowing anything, and surely finding out the truth should now take priority for him.

Would Staines deny it? Would it be best if he arranged to meet him away from his home or his office? He wasn't asking for a daddy to provide him with love and care, he was merely asking for knowledge, and if that upset everybody involved in Staines' world, then so be it. Jed just needed facts. Deep inside, he knew he had the truth. John was too plain a name for his outgoing mother to have chosen it without a reason, especially as she had come up with Josiah/Jed for his first name. It made sense it was the name of his father, and nowhere else in all the paperwork and pictures he had scanned through was there another John.

He would back up what he believed to be true by tracking down Aunty Nette. She would be his first stop on the journey. Because of the fact Jed could actually remember her, she must have been considerably closer to his mother than Jennifer Pointer, and would quite possibly have been in her confidence, would have known of the difficulties around naming the expected baby's father.

Jed felt frustration growing in him – he knew some, but not enough. And the things he did 'know' didn't seem to be facts, they seemed to be guesswork born of logic. He simply needed someone to say to him, 'Yes, John Staines is your father,' and he would ask for nothing more.

* * *

Jed couldn't sleep. It had been a long day, a productive one to a certain degree, and he had enjoyed a chat with Eloise on the phone as she had described the hotel and the beach she'd been to. She had also gone into some detail about a man who was a member of the coach party, a widower of five years, and with whom she shared a table in the restaurant for their meals.

'He's very nice,' she had enthused. 'Tomorrow, we're going on one of the trips included in the price, to Ryde.'

'Don't come home married,' Jed had warned her, laughing. 'I'm not convinced I need a new grandfather.'

'Too old for such shenanigans,' she had laughed in return. 'We'll just live together.'

He hoped she was joking, and changed the subject to the house. 'Would you have any strong objections if I moved into Mum's old room? Say if you would, and I'll never mention it again. I felt the need to go into it today, just for five minutes. Sitting in her chair, I realised the space is much bigger than mine, and a lot lighter with that lovely bay window. I can turn that part into my workspace, instead of the tiny little corner I'm currently using in my bedroom. I do have quite a lot of work to do from home.' He felt relieved at the confession to having been in her room.

There was only a momentary pause on Eloise's part. Then she spoke slowly, as if thinking it through. 'No, of course I don't mind. It's your house, Jed, not mine. All I ask is that you don't throw anything anyway. We can pack her stuff into boxes and store it in the attic with the tarantulas. Are you thinking of decorating the room? It was last done in that pretty blue about a year ago.'

'No, I'm just swapping furniture over really. It's a lovely space, and I know it was a bit of a haven for Mum. You're absolutely sure you don't mind?'

'It's not a question of minding...' He sensed honesty in her voice. 'It will just seem strange. But it makes sense, anyway; why should you be in the smallest room when there is that one free?

Kirsty wasn't about her surroundings, she was about her love of life, her attitude towards other people.'

'Then I'll make a start tomorrow.'

'Tomorrow?'

He froze. He'd forgotten she didn't know he was on annual leave. 'I've booked the rest of the week off, starting tomorrow, because we've closed our place for some construction work to start. I might as well; I'd only be sitting in my office twiddling my thumbs while the noise increases around me. I can deal with anything that crops up from home, and organise my bedroom as well.'

She seemed to accept it, and he breathed a sigh of relief. They finished the conversation with a promise to speak towards the end of the week, and he repeated his words of no marriages without consulting him.

But still he couldn't sleep. He had traced Nanette Lawton to the telephone number of a childcare group, one that bore the name: Lawton's Child Care Centre, so he guessed it was the same Nanette Lawton. He didn't want to ring her; he wanted to see her face when he started questioning her about his own paternity. He thought it would be difficult to lie about the subject, but he also appreciated the ties of friendship, and how long they could last. Would she still consider it important to keep promises made to Kirsty all those years ago? And how would she react when he told her Kirsty had died? He presumed she wouldn't know, as he couldn't recall any strangers at the funeral. Though would she really be a stranger? Her picture was on the website, and he believed he would have recognised her. His conclusion was that she wouldn't be aware of Kirsty's passing.

He felt quite alone. He had had several quite close friends while he was working in Bristol, mates he had shared a love of football, ten-pin bowling and real ales with, but they had now drifted away, replacing that camaraderie with the odd phone call. Since his arrival in Sheffield, he had been tied up with the death of his mother, taking on extra responsibility at work, and generally feeling out of sorts with life. Hence, no friends.

His quest for his father couldn't be shared with anyone, and he somehow felt if he could have done that, he wouldn't be tossing and turning, unable to close down his mind. At just after three, he went downstairs, hunted out Eloise's stash of camomile teabags and made himself a hot drink.

Within two minutes, he was fast asleep on the sofa, the tea gradually cooling as the night passed.

* * *

At just after nine, Jed was fishing the disgustingly bloated teabag out of the mug before he dropped it into the waste bin, switching on the kettle to make a drink that wasn't designed to send him to sleep, and opening a jar of instant coffee.

He sat out on the patio to drink it, nibbling on the toast he hadn't really wanted but thought he should have, letting his brain decide what the day held in store for him. In his head, decisions had already been made. He wouldn't approach John Staines first. That would be foolish, he realised, just in case he'd got the wrong end of a whole boatload of Jenga sticks. First he needed clarification, and that route led him towards Aunty Nette.

He would shower, put on one of the smart suits he normally wore for meetings with partners of his company, and head out towards the child care centre near Worksop. It would be a pleasant drive, no motorway, just easy roads. Nothing to distract him or wind him up. The day would begin well, and hopefully get better.

* * *

The car wouldn't start. He kicked all four tyres in frustration, but still the car wouldn't even cough, so he rang for roadside assistance. An hour and a half later, he was on his way, complete with a new car battery, his bank account a hundred pounds lighter.

With the sun streaming through the windscreen, he began to feel better, in a way that he hadn't been feeling earlier when he'd decided that the flat battery had jinxed his day.

He followed the A57, sticking to speed limits, enjoying driving with the window down. He was listening to Post Malone singing 'Congratulations', raucously singing along with it, trying to keep his thoughts away from what would happen in the next half hour when he hopefully would be meeting Nanette Lawton for the first time in several years. He trusted she would remember him, but he doubted it really. If she had remained in his life, he would surely have received birthday and Christmas cards?

His satnav directed him to leave the A57, and he turned off the music. He needed to be in a calm frame of mind, not buoyed up by listening to a rapper. He eased his foot off the accelerator just a little. He was in unfamiliar territory and needed to concentrate.

* * *

'Strange car just pulled into the car park,' Donna reported. 'Don't recognise the feller who's just got out of it. We expecting anybody?'

Nanette shook her head. 'Not as far as I know.' She stood and moved across to stand by her administrative assistant who was staring at the CCTV screen. Nanette leaned in and peered closely at the man as he walked across the car park towards the main doors. 'Well, he'll not get in without identifying himself, so be polite.'

Donna grinned. 'Aren't I always?'

'Occasionally,' Nanette said. 'Occasionally.'

The buzzer sounded, and both Donna and Nanette heard the man speak. 'I apologise for not having an appointment, but I'd like to speak with Ms Lawton, please. My name is Josiah Grantham.'

Nanette gave a quick shake of her long dark hair. 'Well, well, well. There's a name from the past. Josiah Grantham.'

'Smart-looking bloke. Looks to be in his twenties, though. Bit young for us, Nanette.'

'Twenty-three, I believe, next Christmas Day,' Nanette said. 'Let him in, Donna, and I'll go and meet him. I'll take him to our inter-view room, it'll be empty. Think you can rustle us up some coffee?'

'Certainly can, but your face tells me you might be better with brandy. This is a blast from the past?'

'Like you've never known, Donna, like you've never known. I kind of knew this day would come one day, but hoped it wouldn't.'

20

THURSDAY 15 SEPTEMBER 2022

Clare stood at the kitchen window staring out at the back garden. She sipped at her coffee, and wondered what the day would bring.

She had heard Vic get up twice in the night, but hadn't called out to her. She guessed her friend was dealing with Rob's death in her usual fashion – thinking everything through, even talking issues out loud to herself, never imagining for a moment that her night-time perambulations could be heard by her friend.

Footsteps came downstairs and then along the hallway, and a throaty 'morning' from somewhere deep inside Vic made Clare smile.

'Morning,' she replied. 'Sit down and I'll get you a drink.'

'Is it warm enough to sit on the patio?'

Clare shrugged. 'No idea, but we can make it warm enough. I'll make you a drink, you go and test it out. If it's too cool, put on the heater.'

Clare poured away what was left of her own drink, and made a pot of tea. Five minutes later she carried the tray outside.

Vic was snuggled inside the dressing gown Clare had lent her the previous night along with cosy pyjamas, but she had also fired up the patio heater.

'Summer's gone,' she said forlornly.

'Could be back again next week. It's still only mid-September. You ready to hear a suggestion?'

'Is it legal?'

Clare smiled. 'You ever known me do anything illegal? I was married to a solicitor, you know. No, I was going to suggest we go to your flat, collect anything you might need, and you stay here until you feel ready to be on your own again.'

Vic's eyes seemed to cloud over. 'I really don't want to be on my own, that's for sure. I was up and down all night, couldn't sleep. I must have dropped off around five, but I'm awake again now. I can't get the image of Rob with all that blood out of my head. Who would do that to him, Clare?'

Clare shook her head as she poured out the tea. 'I have no idea at this point, Vic. You think it's somebody random? And where's Rob's car? It doesn't make any sense. It was out on your drive with the engine running, for heaven's sake, as it has been every working day morning for all the time you two have lived there. If it was just for the car, they could have just taken it.'

'So the car wasn't the reason...' Vic said, her voice quietly thoughtful.

'No, I would say not, and I know this sounds a bit cops and robbers, but I think it was just a handy escape vehicle. If the killer had arrived on foot, then saw the car already primed to go, it would make sense to help him get away quickly.'

'Him?'

'Or her.' Clare shrugged. 'We'll not know until the killer is caught, but it could be either. And it seems they took the weapon, whatever it was they hit him with, because the police found nothing. He or she could hardly have caught a bus or legged it through the streets holding a hammer or whatever it was they used, dripping blood everywhere.'

'Do you have to be quite so graphic?' Vic said, brushing away a tear.

Clare reached across and touched Vic's hand. 'I'm so sorry. I haven't slept much either, been going over and over the scene in my head. Is it somebody Rob upset?'

Vic sighed. 'Somebody like me, you mean? I'm going to be top of the list of suspects, aren't I?' She took a sip of her tea. 'There's been enough photographs taken of what he did to me to fill an album, so they're obviously going to think I decided it was payback time.'

'But you didn't get here until after he was dead. No, there's no reason to blame you. In fact, there's no reason to link what he did to you with his death. It would have been more understandable if you'd stayed in the marital home and simply pushed him down the stairs. That could have been explained away as an accident. And you're pretty smart, Vic Dolan, smart enough to have worked that out.'

Vic shivered, and pulled the dressing gown tighter around her, seeking comfort. 'You're being quite brutal, Clare. And have you considered that the house is now wholly mine? That's another reason for me to have killed Rob. The police are going to work all of this out. I'm scared, Clare. I really didn't kill him, even though I wanted to.'

Clare smiled. 'Don't tell the police that, will you? Look, if they'd suspected it was you, they wouldn't have simply taken our statements and escorted us back to the outside world. They would have kept you there. But let's look at the facts as they see them. You had no blood on you, and neither did I. Whoever hit Rob would have had blood on them; it would have spattered, not dripped down gently. They've had the forensics team in your car, and there's no blood transferred to it...'

'How do you know?' Vic seemed lost.

'How do I know? Because you didn't kill him, did you? I don't need to see the report; I use logic. You didn't kill him, therefore there's no blood in your car.'

'Oh sorry, I'm being a bit thick, aren't I?'

Clare smiled. 'Yes, you are. And you're tired. You want more tea?'

Vic shook her head. 'No, let me take you out for breakfast. I'll go and have a quick shower, then we'll go to the pub, have a full English and go back to my place to pick up some clothes. I suppose eventually they'll release my house back to me, but heaven only knows what I'll do then. I'm never going to get that image out of my mind, am I? The blood...'

Clare spoke gently. 'It does fade. Don't forget that I also have the image of John dying in our lounge in my head. It took ages to make me unsee it, but I found that by getting rid of that bed and rearranging all of the furniture, it began to fade. Now I don't see it at all, and even the girls have stopped reacting when they walk through the lounge door. Time's a great healer, so they say, and it's true. Go and have your shower, and it will all look much better after our full English. And treat this home as your home for as long as you need, no asking if I mind you doing something, or treading gently around the place. It's your temporary new home.'

* * *

It was much later in the day when they caught up with the news – activities surrounding the Queen's lying-in-state, and the preparations for the funeral. Vic was now wrapped up in her own pyjamas and dressing gown, ostensibly with her eyes glued to the screen, but not taking in any of the details. She felt desperately sorry for the Royal family; they all had a lost look about them, and she knew she was feeling a little like they were feeling.

With the initial shock of knowing Rob was gone now beginning to be accepted by her brain, her mind insisted on drifting back to earlier times in their life when they had loved carelessly, wrapped up in each other, taking romantic weekend breaks and even longer romantic holidays – years when the love had been strong. She couldn't pinpoint the actual moment when things had begun to change, but change they had.

It had all culminated in that punch to her face, the pain that had shot through her eye following the blow, and the feeling as her legs had crumpled and she had dropped to the floor. The fear. There had been fear that he would continue to beat her, and she'd crawled away from him, desperate to be out of reach of his fists. She had felt the thud of a foot into her back, but with slippers on his feet instead of shoes it had caused minimal damage. She felt lucky she had already started to haul herself away from him; the damage to her spine could have been worse. And then he had stormed off into the kitchen, leaving her to climb slowly to her feet, and drag herself up to the bathroom where she could examine her face.

Already the bruise was forming down her cheek, and her eye was bloodshot, but her vision was clear. She breathed a sigh of relief.

This had to escalate matters.

Vic switched her mind back to the television and away from the memories of the past week, watching the Princess Royal, seeing the pain in the woman's face.

'Princess Anne is devastated,' Clare said quietly. 'She was so close to her mother.'

Vic nodded. 'They're no different to every other family in the land, really. They have their issues just the same as anybody else does, but they've lost the one person who held it all together.' She stood and walked to the window. 'They're still here.'

'The police? I know, but the forensics van has gone. I think it's just a couple of beat bobbies keeping watch overnight. I imagine by tomorrow they'll have finished, and you'll possibly be able to get back in, but whatever happens, Vic, you won't be going in alone. And we can organise a deep clean of the hallway, and anywhere else that may require it.'

'How come you know so much?' Vic was still staring across to her home.

'I know John didn't deal with criminal law, he found it singularly depressing and preferred what he called the "nicer side of the law", but he did have a criminal law department within the business, and had a controlling brief within it. He used to talk about stuff if he found it interesting, and I picked up lots about what the police do in the initial stages of an investigation. You do realise they may want to talk to you again?'

Vic turned away from the window to look at Clare. 'Why? What more can I tell them?'

'They'll have been through your home with a fine-tooth comb, believe me, and may have found stuff, stuff that may explain why Rob's been so different with you for the past two or three years. They'll want to talk about it with you, get your take on it, but if you didn't kill him, you don't need to panic. And, just for the record, I don't think you had anything at all to do with it.' Clare smiled, hoping Vic took it in the way she meant her to take it.

Vic walked back to the armchair, and curled her legs underneath her as she sat. 'What would I do without you, Clare? Who would ever have thought my home would be surrounded by crime scene tape, and my car removed on the back of a truck?'

Clare stood. 'I'll fetch the brandy bottle. Tomorrow is a new day, but we need to get through tonight with sleep. Brandy's a beginning.'

21

Looking across the road towards Vic's house had been Clare and Vic's occupation for ten minutes. They saw DS Franks and DC Waters glance over towards Clare's home and Vic shuddered.

'They know we're watching them, don't they?' Vic said. The tremor in her voice was evident. 'Oh my God, they're coming over here.'

Clare felt her friend stiffen, and she put her arm around Vic's shoulders. 'Hey, don't panic. They're not coming for anything other than to update you. That FLO said she couldn't tell you anything, but that Rosie Waters would possibly have something by the end of the day.'

'This is the beginning of the day.'

'I know, but you know what I mean.'

Clare moved away and opened the front door as the doorbell pealed. 'DS Franks, DC Waters, come in. Vic is in the lounge.'

Rosie Waters smiled. 'Nobody ever remembers our names. We're normally referred to as "those two coppers", so it's nice to hear you remember us.'

'It comes from years of living with my husband,' Clare

explained. 'He was a stickler for politeness, and said the first thing you had to do with anybody was remember their name. Common courtesy, he called it. Can I get you a drink?'

'No, we're good thanks,' Brendan Franks said. 'We only want a very brief word with Mrs Dolan.'

They followed Clare through to where Vic was still staring through the window.

'Mrs Dolan, I just need to tell you that you can go back inside your house from tomorrow. We've had our crime scene cleaners in, but you'll probably want to get your own in; we simply don't have the time, or the budget, to do a thorough clean.'

Vic stared at them. 'I thought you were coming to arrest me!'

Rosie Waters smiled. 'Why? What have you done?'

'Nothing, but you know he hit me. You know I walked unwillingly out of my home. Good reasons to kill anybody, I would have thought.'

'But your alibi is solid, Vic,' Rosie said. 'ANPR tracked you most of the way from your flat to here on that morning so unless you've a magic wand or something, you couldn't possibly have been the one to attack your husband. Mrs Staines confirmed your time of arrival, and we have no reason to doubt her. However, Mr Dolan has managed to upset one or two people according to the work files we found in his study and on his laptop, so that's where we're going to be concentrating our efforts.'

'He changed,' Vic said quietly. 'I've been doing a lot of thinking over the past month or so, because I could tell stuff was getting to him, even more so than usual. I reckon it started about three years ago. Until then, we were strong, there for each other through bad patches like finding out we wouldn't ever have children naturally, making the decision not to go down the adoption route. Just being there for each other,' she repeated. 'We were fine for quite a few years, but then, as I said, about three years ago he began to change. Frequent bouts of losing his temper, shouting at me, drinking too heavily. All this was out of character. And then of course it culminated in him hitting me. I knew then it couldn't carry on so I left. He never gave me any sort of clue as to what was wrong, just got progressively worse towards me. And yet he was an absolute tower of strength for Clare when she lost John, her husband; he was like a different person. But once the funeral was over, he reverted to how he'd been before John died.'

'You saw all this, Mrs Staines?'

Clare nodded. 'I did. And heard it even from across the road. When he shouted at Vic, he really shouted. We talked about it a lot, obviously, but neither of us could understand what had gone wrong. We've had to support each other many times during the last few years. Vic was my comfort through John's final few weeks, and now I'm here for her.'

'And neither of you can think of anybody Mr Dolan might have upset enough to cause his murder?'

The two women looked at each other.

'No.' Clare spoke first.

'Only me,' said Vic.

'Oh, Vic,' Clare said, and pulled her close. 'Stop it. Nobody believes for a minute that you're capable of this, and let's not forget that at under five feet you're hardly tall enough to whack a six-foot man around the head.'

'Hey.' Vic's voice was muffled against Clare's shoulder. 'Less of the under five feet, I *am* five feet.'

'And eight stone wet through,' Clare added. 'Vic, you simply aren't capable, neither mentally nor physically, but I'm sure if you talk to these nice police people, they'll lock you up for the night if that's what you want.'

Brendan and Rosie smiled as they left the house, promising to keep Vic informed of any developments. They left her with details of specialist deep cleaners, but when Clare and Vic were once more on their own, Vic began to sob.

'How can I organise somebody to come into my home to clean up my husband's blood? It's not right, it's not normal. I don't even want to go back there.'

'You don't have to do anything you don't want to right now. But the time will come when you can go in, when you'll remember it's your home, just as much as it was Rob's. We'll get through this, my tiny friend, we'll get through this.'

* * *

Grace and Megan were skirting around each other carefully as they tried to avoid touching one another with paintbrushes.

'I can't believe we're finished,' Megan said, waving a large brush with white paint on it. 'Done, completely. We can get these cleaned and put away for a thousand years, or until we want to change the colour scheme, whichever comes first.'

'Knowing you as I do,' Grace said, 'we'll need them again in about six months.' She handed Megan a brush with blue emulsion on. 'If you finish cleaning these, I'll go put the bedroom back to how it should look, so at least we can sleep in comfort when we collapse onto the bed later.'

'Think your mum will feed us tonight?'

'Probably. I'll check if she and Vic are going to be in.'

'I like Vic,' Megan said quietly. 'She doesn't deserve all of this upset in her life. It's good that your mum's taken her in; she shouldn't be on her own.'

Grace sent off a quick text with what seemed like fifty kisses, then the ping came to tell them they would be very welcome for a meal.

'Sorted,' Grace said. 'Eating at six, so we've bags of time to get finished here, put it all back to rights and have a shower.'

She left Megan to finish washing the brushes, and returned to the bedroom. She loved how it looked. Basically a blue room, but with accenting splashes of colour, it created an ambience that had been missing in their first home. She put on the new bedding, pulled out the new bedside lamps and set them on the bedside tables, then stood back and looked at the room as a whole.

'Wonderful,' she breathed softly. 'That Megan has a wonderful way with colour; I'd never have thought of all these shades coming together to create this.'

'You talking to me?' Megan called through from the kitchen.

'No, just to myself,' she called back. 'Wait until you see the new bedding and the room all set up. Be prepared to be astounded, Megs. I love it.'

She stooped and gathered all the bedding she had just removed and headed for the bathroom. She flicked open the lid of the laundry basket and leaned forward to drop everything in, then hesitated. The clothes Megan had worn for her run the day before were in the bottom, and had splashes of paint on them: red, green, orange and a light purple. These must have come from the colour splashes Megan had concocted in the bedroom.

Once again, she spoke to herself. 'It's only emulsion. It will come out in the wash. Stop being so particular.'

She dropped the whole lot of laundry in and put down the lid. They could think about the washing later when they'd recovered from all the decorating.

* * *

The two of them scrubbed up remarkably well and when they reached Clare's home, they immediately began showing the two women the pictures on their phones of the rooms, all now completed.

'Well done, you two,' Clare said. 'Oh, to be young again and have the energy the pair of you have. It hardly seems to have taken any time at all.'

'The walls were good,' Megan explained. 'We didn't have to do any filling, just paint. It's actually been a pleasure to do it. We only had two walls to wallpaper, so next week we're starting up as Staines and King, Painters and Decorators.'

'Not bloody likely,' Grace said. 'I'm knackered. How anybody can do it for a living I'll never know. Megan is so good at it though. Arty is the word. Everything she tries turns out to be a spectacular masterpiece. Except her clothes of course. Both of us have started a new fashion for paint-splattered outerwear. Wash day tomorrow, I reckon.'

Megan smiled. 'Day off tomorrow, I reckon.'

Clare looked serious for a moment. 'Vic can go into her house tomorrow – forensics have finished. I don't think they've found anything. Or at least nobody's said they've found anything, but you'll both be pleased to know that Vic has an airtight alibi thanks to them being able to track her car from leaving home to arriving here, and the timeline of that. She didn't have any time to go home and kill him.'

'Thank goodness for that,' Megan said. 'You're constantly on my mind, Vic. I can't stand it when men think it's okay to hit a woman, and he must have really walloped you to create that bruise on your face. I'm not saying he deserved to die, but he certainly deserved some sort of retribution.'

The other three women looked at Megan, surprise on all their faces. Quiet Megan, smiley Megan – it was the longest speech they had heard from her. And she rarely voiced her opinion.

'Thank you,' Vic whispered. 'I've felt quite alone inside for the last few days, but you've just made things better. And thank you for speaking aloud your thoughts. If ever they catch who did it, I shall take my lead from you and speak out in court. It's time to get it out there and let everyone see how bloody miserable life can be with an abusive partner.'

There was a brief moment of silence, and Clare clapped. 'Thank you, my special ladies,' she said. 'Now come through and let's eat, drink and be merry. Megan and Grace, I've made up the spare bed if you want to stay, but if you want to go back home to this lovely new bedroom, I'll understand. I'll pay for the taxi. I can put up with the little Aygo being outside all night. I'll even put a note of apology to the neighbours on it.'

'Mother,' Grace laughed, 'you're a car snob of the highest order. Leave our little car alone. All the neighbours love it!'

22

---

29 AUGUST 2022

Nanette smiled at the young man standing in front of her.

'Josiah, or is it still Jed? It must be around fifteen years ago that I last laid eyes on you.' She gave a gentle laugh. 'You've changed. How's your mother? And your grandmother? Both well I hope?'

In those few words, she had answered some of Jed's questions. 'It's always remained as Jed,' he said. 'I use Josiah when I'm meeting somebody through work, or in a more formal setting, but Jed is fine. And I remember you, I think, as Aunty Nette. Am I right?'

'You are. And I always felt like an aunty to you, because Kirsty didn't have siblings, so you never had a proper aunty. So why visit now? You're here to tell me something...'

'I am.' He gave a slight nod of his head as if to confirm the statement. 'Mum passed away in April. She had malignant melanoma initially, but the cancer had already spread to other parts of her body before they found it. They operated, but it was too late.'

There was a momentary silence, then Nanette reached across and touched his arm. 'Jed, I'm so sorry. Beautiful Kirsty, gone. It doesn't seem right. We were the same age, and now she's not here.'

She paused for a moment to let the information sink in. 'We were so close, but things changed in our lives, and we lost touch. I was given the opportunity to buy this place as a going concern, but she didn't want the journey twice a day from Sheffield, so she took another job. I believe it was with a haulage company but I'm not sure. I gave her a fantastic reference not because we were friends, but because she deserved it. We drifted apart after that but I suspect that was my fault. Building up the clientele took all of my working hours at the start. We kept in touch for six months or so, but then I assumed she'd found other friends to take my place.'

'She didn't,' Jed said. 'She rarely went out, kept herself to herself, although there were lots of people at the funeral. I'm guessing she touched many people's lives but kept them at arm's length. A very private person.'

The door opened and Donna entered, carrying a tray of drinks and biscuits; she placed it on the coffee table.

'There's tea and coffee,' she said with a smile. 'Just ask if you want more. Nette, I've rung little Carly's mum and asked her to collect her. She's been quite sick, much to the disgust of most of the children. Hannah is with her at the moment until Carly's mum can get here. Everything's taken care of, so you're not needed anywhere.'

'Thank you. Come and get me if there are any problems.'

Donna left the room, and Nanette leaned forward to pour out two drinks. 'Your mum always drank coffee,' she said. 'Was never bothered about tea back in the day, rarely touched alcohol, but loved a good coffee. I have so many lovely memories of both of you until you reached about four or five, then as I mentioned before, we simply drifted apart.'

Jed picked up his drink and sipped at it. 'She almost died

when I was six. We were on the motorway heading towards Meadowhall for the cinema, and we were in an accident. She died by the side of the road but the paramedics wouldn't let her go. They worked on her and got her back but she didn't come home for about a month. She survived all of that, and cancer took her.'

'And your gran?'

'Eloise is fine. I've sent her off to Sandown on the Isle of Wight for a few days' holiday, where she appears to have latched onto a feller. She's awesome, just as she's always been. But I bought her the holiday for a reason. I've decided I want to know who my father is, and I won't be fobbed off any longer. I've done a bit of research, and I reckon Granny genuinely knows nothing. Not for definite anyway. I think she has thought about it a lot over the years, but I don't believe my mum ever told her the truth. I don't think she could, because I think my father was a married man who couldn't acknowledge me. Am I right?'

Nanette placed her cup on the coffee table, stood and walked over to the window. She said nothing. Jed waited.

When she turned to face him, her face was stony.

'Have you ever considered there might be a good reason why your mother didn't want you or your granny to know? Am I to understand that, from this visit, you believe I know who he is?'

'Somebody must.' His words were plain, simple.

'I agree,' she said, 'but I can tell you now, Jed, that never once in all our years of friendship before and after your birth did Kirsty say a name. I never saw her behave in a loving way towards any male except you. She adored you. She may have adored your father, and I wouldn't be surprised at that because she was a... loyal... type of person. I think that's the right word to describe Kirsty. Loyal, deeply loving. She never married?'

'She never had so much as a boyfriend as far as I'm aware. I think she loved him, my father. I need to know who he is. I can be careful. I won't approach his family, just him.'

'I'm sorry, I can't help you, Jed, and even if I did know I wouldn't give you any information. Kirsty was like a sister to me back then, until life moved us into separate circles, and there's a degree of loyalty there even now. If Kirsty had wanted you to know, then that is what would have happened.' She paused. 'Be careful what you're stirring up, Jed; it may not be what you want when you dig deep enough. I really am truly sorry that Kirsty is no longer with us but I don't believe she would have confided in anyone. And that's for the simple reason that if she had, it would have been me she trusted with the information.'

Jed knew when he was beaten. He felt the same as when he had asked Eloise for help.

He put down his empty cup and stood. Walking towards Nanette, he held out his hand. 'I'm sorry to have disturbed your day. I won't trouble you again, but if you think of anything, or you simply want to get in touch, this is my card.'

He handed it to her, and she looked at it and smiled. 'I always knew you would do well. Even at three and four you were a bright child, inquisitive, in a rush to learn. You've done well, Jed.'

He gave a slight nod in response. 'Thank you. And thank you for listening to me. It genuinely was nice to meet you again. You seem to have done well, like me, and I think Mum would have been pleased to know that.'

He moved towards the door, and Nanette felt a little lost. She had told him all she knew, which was negligible at best, but she hadn't told him what she guessed. Those years were behind her, and what was more important was her loyalty to Kirsty. No, she had to let this smart young man go, and hope he would never track down his father. If her guess was right, it wouldn't do anybody any good for it to come out.

* * *

Jed headed back towards Sheffield, deep in thought. He couldn't make up his mind whether he believed Nanette but deep down he knew it was irrelevant – she wasn't going to tell him anything. Despite his earlier car troubles, he had felt full of hope when he had left home that morning, but now it was more a feeling of deflation. He acknowledged that he had been lucky in tracking down Nanette and he doubted he would have the same sort of luck with Jenny Pointer.

One thing was clear though: he was inexorably being drawn towards John Staines – the man either being his actual father, or someone who may know who the man was who had fathered him with such a complete lack of responsibility.

He called at the Tesco Express to pick up some milk and other bits of food he thought he might enjoy at some point during the week, and returned home, parking on the drive. He sat for a moment, enjoying the heat of the sun and listening to his music, before switching everything off. He would take the rest of the day to plan things, to work out where to go next. Tonight, he would have a walk down to the local pub, have a meal there, and possibly a pint of bitter or two, take his iPad with him.

Maybe he could spend some time trying to track down Jenny Pointer, but deep in his heart he felt she hadn't been a friend, not someone with the same closeness as Nanette Lawton. If he couldn't trace her, he knew it would be no great loss in his search for answers.

There was only one person who could give him the resolution he needed. His father.

23

SATURDAY 17 SEPTEMBER 2022

Jed's life moved on at a pace, albeit under the watchful eye of his grandmother. Eloise had returned from her holiday feeling much happier, more settled than she had felt before she went.

She was a little unnerved by the change in her grandson. He had become reserved, not in a shy sort of way, but a quiet one, as if he had something on his mind that wouldn't leave him alone. She hoped it had nothing to do with the obvious interest in finding out who his father was.

The worst part of the whole debacle was that Kirsty had been aware that one day this would happen. They had talked about it, and all Kirsty had done was shrug, and change the subject. Several times.

It was only when Eloise received a letter from Nanette Lawton that she knew for definite just how serious he was about finding the mystery man in Kirsty's life. The letter was really one of condolence, with Nanette saying how sorry she had been to hear of Kirsty's passing, and how proud she must feel of Jed, who had proved to be everything he had promised in his early years.

Eloise had been shocked by the letter. Jed had said nothing of tracking down Nanette, and although 'Aunty Nette's' letter said nothing of Jed trying to find his father, Eloise knew exactly what had been on Jed's mind. He hadn't trailed Nanette all that way to tell her of his mother's death; he'd gone for another reason, made sure he was there personally, to watch out for any clues in her words or facial expressions.

She wrote a short letter in reply, and hoped that would be the end of that little episode.

Time moved on, and on that Saturday morning in September she could almost believe Jed had given up on the search. Nothing had arrived in the post for him of any significance. Yes, she knew about the DNA test results from several weeks earlier, having watched as Jed briefly scanned the letter and put it in the side-board drawer, making a comment about waste of time and waste of money.

She had the television on watching the news surrounding the Queen's funeral, and wondered what plans Jed had for Monday. He had already mentioned they wouldn't be opening up the branch, because of the bank holiday, so she presumed he would be home with her.

Eloise picked up her mug of tea, sipped at it and replaced it on the side table. Cold tea wasn't a favoured drink.

'You mashing?' She spoke to the quiet Jed, and he glanced up at her.

'You've got one.'

'Gone cold.'

He sighed and put down his iPad. 'Okay. Mop up your tears, and remember to drink this one.'

'I'm not crying.'

'You are.' He placed the iPad on the side table, and walked out of the room. She quickly picked up the tablet, and looked at what was on the screen. It was Google, and it said 'Staines Sheffield' in the search box.

He hadn't given up his search. And like her, he had reached the conclusion that the father was a member of staff at Staines Solicitors, someone Kirsty had met when she had worked there. Eloise knew Kirsty would have been horrified by this turn of events, but Jed was old enough to understand all possibilities in the workplace environment, and nothing she could say or do would help matters. The lad wanted to find his father, and that was an end to it.

Over the years she had drawn her own conclusions, and believed that the absentee father wasn't quite so absentee in another family. She had always thought he must be a married man who hadn't been able to resist Kirsty. He had clearly wanted to eat both slices of cake for as long as he could get away with it, and had never had any intentions of leaving his wife, and possibly a family.

She heard the click as the kettle switched off, so hurriedly put down the iPad, and returned her gaze to the television screen.

Jed carried two mugs of tea through and placed one on her side table. 'Here you are, old lady. You want any biscuits to go with it?'

'No, I'm good, thanks,' she said, smiling as she saw David Beckham on the screen. Such a delicious man. Was that how Kirsty had viewed Jed's father? A delicious man.

Jed picked up the tablet once more, and returned to what he was doing.

'Thought it was your Saturday off?'

'It is,' he responded. 'This isn't work. Listen, Gran, think about this carefully. Did Mum ever say I looked like my father?'

Eloise felt an ice-cold tremor wash through her body. Should she lie? She stared at him, knowing that if he pursued this quest, everything would change. And not just in their house – another household would become drawn into the maelstrom of deceit that had gone on for so long. Could she bluff her way out of it? Or had he already seen the truth written in her face?

She thought back to the day the envelope had dropped through the letterbox. InstantPrints it had said on it. The pictures were of the fourth birthday tea they had done for Jed, the new bike she had bought him, the dinosaur that walked across the room, controlled remotely. It had been a really good birthday.

She had handed the envelope to Kirsty when she came home that evening, and Kirsty had laughed. 'Well, I've had a rubbish day, let's hope these pictures have turned out well.'

She spread them out on the kitchen table, and they peered at them, inspecting each one. Kirsty had eventually picked up one where Jed was about to blow out the four candles on his cake. His eyes were flashing up to his mother as if asking for permission to blow. It was a stunning snapshot of a moment in time, and Kirsty had whispered, 'He's the double of his daddy.'

That was the moment Eloise realised that the affair had never finished. It had carried on long enough for it not to be father, but *daddy*. But then it had stopped, because it was too dangerous if Jed were to remember things. She was surprised he'd never said he could remember snippets, but he hadn't.

Through Eloise's scrambled thoughts, she realised she'd only ever seen that picture one day. Where was it now?

'Gran?' Jed could see the myriad of thoughts and feelings flashing through her brain and across her face, and knew that maybe he should have asked the question long before this time.

She nodded. 'She said it once. A picture of you on your fourth birthday, about to blow out the candles on your cake. It was a cake in the shape of a four...'

'I remember it,' Jed said slowly. 'It was on the kitchen table. A blue four.'

Again, Eloise shivered. 'I've never heard you say you remembered anything of those times. I always assumed the car accident affected your memory, but it seems it didn't.'

'I can't remember much,' Jed said, a wistful note in his voice. 'But the cake I can remember. And didn't I have a big green plastic dinosaur that walked everywhere?'

'You did, and a bike with stabilisers, although it wasn't long before we had to take them off. You wanted to be a big boy and ride it properly.'

'Do you have that photograph?'

'No, I'm sorry, I don't. I suppose it's quite possible it was sent to your father, but don't forget she never mentioned him; I knew nothing. Do you ever remember seeing him, meeting him?'

Jed stared into space. 'Sometimes I think I can. It's like a memory that floats off into outer space, and even though I reach out for it, I can't get it. It's quite frustrating, believe me. Please help, Gran. Even if I only meet him once, it will be enough.'

'Sweetheart, if I could, I would. I never thought of Kirsty as secretive until the baby was conceived, and from the point of confirmation of the pregnancy, she withdrew into herself, wouldn't talk about any of it in detail, just snippets of how the pregnancy was going, that sort of thing. Oh, Jed, I wouldn't lie to you. If I knew for definite who your father was, I would tell you. She paid cash for this house, you know, and I believe he bought it for her. She never said anything about it, it was just an impression I got.'

'I'm sorry,' he said. 'I know I'm becoming obsessed with this, and I'm pushing you. Just hit me on the head with a frying pan or something, if I get on your nerves too much. That will shut me up.'

Her eyes twinkled as she looked at her grandson, this man she would willingly give her life for. 'I'll remember that.'

'And I'll shut up now. You get back to watching your funeral preps, and I'll just continue scrolling a little longer. There are some bits and bobs I want to check out before giving up for the moment.'

Jed returned to tapping away on his iPad and Eloise swivelled her head back towards the television, the cameras now focused on the coffin on the catafalque. Again, tears were in her eyes, and she had no idea how she would get through the ceremony on Monday without being a blubbering wreck.

She wished from the bottom of her heart that Jed would drop the search. She felt concerned – and reasonably certain – it would all end in disaster. Suppose he found his father and his father said piss off? It would destroy him. And not just for a day or a week – for the rest of his life. If his father had wanted to know him, he would have stepped up to the plate, especially if he had been aware of Kirsty's death.

She could hear the tap tap tap of Jed's fingers on the iPad, strangely soothing as she watched the television, and then suddenly they stopped. He reached down and picked up his notebook which had fallen from the arm of the chair onto the floor, and he removed the pencil from behind his ear.

Eloise felt mild panic. What had he come across that required a transfer to a notebook? And what was with the notebook anyway? She couldn't remember him ever writing in one before. He was much more likely to tap memos into his notes on his iPhone than do any physical writing.

He was scrolling, then writing, scrolling, then writing, and she knew he had found something he considered significant. She eyed the notebook, paying particular attention to the cover. She needed to see what he was doing, remember which notebook this was; she didn't want to purloin the wrong book later.

'Anything you particularly fancy for our meal tonight?'

Jed looked up at her. 'Chips.'

'Just chips?'

'No, chips and something, but I've been fancying chips all day. With vinegar and tomato sauce on them. And salt.'

'Well, I can provide all that, but we actually need something to go with the chips.'

'Bread?'

'You mean chip butties?'

'I do. That's a good idea. I'm glad you suggested it.'

She stared at him. 'I didn't. You suggested it. I was thinking about a chicken pasta bake. Now it seems we're having chip butties.'

'On bread cakes?'

She stood slowly, aware that at her age she shouldn't cabbage around watching television for hours on end. She groaned as she moved, and he grinned at her. 'Getting old, are we?'

'You're not, but it seems I am. I'll go and get some bread cakes out the freezer.'

He laughed. 'I'll go and find some. A pack of four?'

'Yes. In fact, if you can find the Marks & Spencer's ones, it's a pack of six. I can't believe all I have to do is chip butties; we haven't had them for years.'

He put down his tablet and notebook, and walked to the lounge door. 'I'll only be a minute. You need anything else?'

'No, just the bread. I'm quite looking forward to this, you know what I'm like with vinegar. I'll make a start on peeling the potatoes; can't stand frozen chips.'

Jed walked out of the room, and as soon as she heard the kitchen door squeak, as it always did, she picked up his notebook.

She stared at the assorted notes, swiftly scanning the last ones he had written. It was a name and address, a name she recognised, an address she didn't. She closed the book, returned it to the same place, and left the lounge, heading for the kitchen. The potatoes wouldn't peel themselves, and such culinary delights as chip butties required care to cut them perfectly. Chip butties... what was the lad thinking of?

She pulled out the bag of potatoes, ferreted in the drawer for her little sharp knife, and began the preparation, a smile plastered across her face. She thought of the name in the notebook, and wondered if John Staines ever had chip butties for his Saturday evening meal. She thought not. But she did think that maybe her grandson had hit on the right person.

24

SUNDAY 18 SEPTEMBER 2022

Jed was out of the house before Eloise had even stirred, and it was the sound of his car engine that woke her. By the time she'd reached her bedroom window, his car had got to the end of the road, and was indicating left.

She knew where he was going, and felt helpless that she couldn't stop him. She was almost tempted to throw some clothes on, run a brush through her hair and follow him in her own car, but she knew it would cause friction between them. She had to let him do this, whatever it was he was planning, on his own. And be there waiting to comfort him when it all went pear-shaped.

She dragged on her dressing gown and headed downstairs, smelling the coffee as she descended. She smiled. He had left the coffee ready for her, knowing she'd be woken by the sound of his engine.

She poured out her first cup of the day, and sat down to enjoy it at the kitchen table. It didn't stop her worrying about Jed, but it was excellent coffee. The second cup tasted even better, and she took it through to the lounge where she switched on the television, all too aware that her normal life, without the death of the monarch, would hardly ever see the television in use. She watched as the queues still filed past the catafalque, and thought back to her earliest memories of this woman, which were of the death of her father, followed a year later by the Coronation. She smiled at the thought of the little purple tin she had received at school on the day of the school party for the Coronation, a little rectangular tin filled with small bars of Cadbury's chocolates, the Queen's crest imprinted on the front. She didn't have to think too much about it, she could lay her hands on it with only a moment's notice. It now contained her calligraphy pens, and was in the top drawer of her desk, along with her inks.

She remained on the sofa for an hour, watching the various items on the screen before standing up to head back upstairs for a shower. Because of this, she didn't hear Jed return. She did smell the bacon though, and shouted down to tell him she might be able to find room in her stomach for a bacon buttie. It was waiting for her when she reached the kitchen, her grandson sitting at the table eating his own.

'You've been out,' she said, picking up her third coffee of the day and sipping at it.

'I have. Just drove to an address I thought my father might live at, though I just sat in my car. I opened my book of maps and had it on the steering wheel so that it looked as if I was looking for a place. I didn't want anybody getting worried about me being there, thinking I was casing the joint or something. You know, Gran, sometimes you just feel that when you know, you know.'

'What?' She looked puzzled.

'I know it's him. I just know it. I know it's the right person, I know he's my biological father. But I made no move to contact him. I just sat there and watched. There was nobody about, probably all watching the TV just like you've been doing, no doubt, but there were two cars there. One was pulled up onto the front of the house, a big one, and a little runabout thing, was on the road outside. A woman came out and walked across the road to another house, pulled a few weeds up in the garden then went in that house. I assumed she was a neighbour, so I added her into my little book, with her address as well, but that was the sum total of activity. I guess Sunday isn't a suitable day for surveillance. I'm going to pick a normal midweek day, book it off work, and do it all again.'

He noticed Eloise's face crumple, and he reached across to her. 'I only need to know, Gran. This won't change anything really; I'm not claiming son's rights or demanding that he spends time with me, I just need to know. It's all I ever wanted, and Mum could have given me this, but she chose not to. So now I have to find out for myself.' He stared at her for a moment. 'And I will. I accept finally that you know nothing, but I don't accept that you didn't put your thinking cap on all those years ago, and didn't come up with any answers. You're a smart cookie, Gran, and I think you made a guess twenty-odd years ago, which is probably the answer I've come up with too.'

Eloise carefully put her bacon sandwich back on the plate, and lifted her head. 'And I think you're pretty much right in all these assumptions, my lovely boy, but don't ask me to say names out loud because that would be some sort of admittance that your mother's secrets aren't secrets any more. And that's not good. She kept silent for a reason, and it was to protect your father. She didn't need to protect you – she was there for you always, as was I – but you could be stirring up a real hornet's nest if you approach this man. I can't tell you to drop the whole thing, but I can explain that actions have consequences. I love you so much, Jed, but I can't support you in this, because I think that whatever happens, there's a strong possibility you will be hurt.'

'If I'm hurt, I can take it, Gran. I'm a big boy now,' he said, and smiled at her. 'I have to do this.'

'And how did I know you'd say that? Because you're your mother's son. She didn't understand the whole actions and consequences bit. I'm not being brutal here, Jed, but she made the action and you're the consequence.'

'Ouch. Say it like it is, Gran.'

'It's true, and there will be some consequences that won't even affect you, but possibly somebody in this man's family. In another twenty years, you wouldn't even be thinking about doing what you're planning to do, because you would have more experience of the world, would know about consequences, but at the moment you haven't come across anything like that. Think carefully, Jed, about the problems you are likely to be creating.'

'I have.'

'Then all I can say is you haven't thought carefully enough, because a whole avalanche will probably descend on your head the minute you approach this man. Also, think what his job is...'

'Haha! So you do know who I'm talking about.' There was almost a note of triumph in his voice.

'Only guesswork, Jed, only guesswork.'

* * *

Vic staggered across the road carrying a huge flowerpot, which she deposited with a thud outside Clare's front door. She went inside, gasping for breath.

'That's blood heavy. Who'd have thought something as sweet and pretty as an anemone could need a crane to lift and carry it from mine to yours.'

Clare laughed. 'Well, thank you for doing it. I'll get Greg to transport it through to the back garden. Want a drink?'

'Coffee, please. It might reboot the energy levels. I've been transplanting and potting up bulbs all morning.'

'Did you see that car?'

'Car?'

'Yep. Don't ask me the make because I wouldn't know a Mini from a Rolls Royce, but I know colour and it was a silver one. Parked almost opposite here.'

Vic frowned. She seemed to feel permanently on the alert these days, worried about the slightest thing, and here was her best friend causing her grief by talking about strange cars on this little backwater of a road. 'No, I didn't see it, but I've been pottering around the back of my place all morning. It felt strange, as you said it would, but I've coped. I stayed mainly outside, so I don't suppose it counts as being back inside. So, this car. You didn't know the driver?'

Clare shook her head. 'No, but he seemed youngish. Had a map spread out across his steering wheel and was studying it pretty damn carefully. I almost went across to ask him if he was lost, but then thought twice about it in view of what happened to Rob. It seems strange the police haven't come up with anything at all beyond telling us yesterday they'd found his car and it was with forensics being tested.' There was a moment of hesitation. 'When this funeral is over and done with and everywhere is open again, can we go chase up the mysterious child on that photograph?'

Vic stared at her, her eyes open wide. 'You think that was him?'

'God, I don't know, Vic. I see him everywhere. Every young man in his early twenties I'm ogling, to see if I can see any resemblance to John. It feels as though I'm living on a knife edge, and I can't talk to the girls about it. There's only the two of us that know, and at the moment that's the way it has to stay, but supposing the young man knows...'

'Look, if he'd known, he would have been round here before

now.' Vic spoke firmly, aware that Clare sounded at breaking point. 'John's death was in the papers, a beautiful obituary for a man who was a large part of the professional group in this area, so I think young Jed probably has no idea who is father is. But on Tuesday morning I'll get on the phone, find out if we have to book a slot for the microfiche thing if it's still in existence, and get the ball rolling for us. You making that coffee or what?'

'Sorry, I was lost in my thoughts. I'll do it now. You want to go outside or stay in here?'

Vic looked at her. 'Let's stay in here. We can see any comings and goings on the road, any strange silver cars that could possibly be a Rolls Royce – yes, let's have it in here. And we can spot if anybody tries to steal the plant pot.'

She was gratified to hear a laugh from Clare, and hoped her mind had moved on from her worries about the man in the car – which was probably nothing whatsoever to do with anything in their lives, just a random bloke who was a bit lost.

Clare didn't take long to make the coffee, and when she came back, she brought with her several small squares of fabric.

'I've been playing for half an hour while you've been doing your bulb planting,' she announced. 'I started out with six assorted fat quarters that I chopped up, and ended up with all these pretty blocks in shades of cream. I'm going to put them all together to make a cot quilt for the new baby, but I'll wait until we know the gender and make extra blocks in either pink or blue that I can mingle in. I think it'll look lovely. All those classes I took many years ago are now filtering back into my brain, and if this turns out okay, I've decided to make a king size one for Grace and Megan for Christmas, in colours to match their new bedroom. Think they'll like it?'

'They very easily might love it, you dork. When I move back into my home I will be changing everything. I have to. And that means my bedroom will be decorated soon. I could quite fancy a quilt for that. Happy to pay for it, but can I say I had no idea you were this talented? Light under a bushel and all that? Now I understand why you've done what you've done with John's study. Smart lady, Clare Staines.'

Clare sipped at her coffee. 'Not that smart that I can easily dismiss that silver car though. What if it's him, Vic? What if it's John's son?'

25

MONDAY 19 SEPTEMBER 2022

Jed and Eloise were both downstairs early, each of them deciding they wanted nothing other than a slice of toast and copious amounts of coffee to start their day. Jed stared out of the kitchen window, mug of coffee already half drunk.

'Let's hope the weather's like this in London,' he said, and put his arm around his gran's shoulder as she joined him at the large window.

'Fingers crossed it doesn't rain later. There'll be thousands and thousands of people there for the full day. Should we have gone?'

He smiled. 'I didn't even suggest it, because I knew you'd say yes. I'm not as daft as I look.'

She punched his arm. 'That's what you think. Some of us know the truth.'

She left him to continue his vigil of the back garden, and went through to the lounge. She intended spending the whole day in here, although she doubted she would be joined by her grandson for much of it. He seemed to be ambivalent about the Royal family, but in her eyes they were such an integral part of the UK, and losing the Queen without any sort of general warning to prepare her subjects had been hard to bear.

Eloise placed a packet of ginger biscuits and one of digestives – dark not milk chocolate – on the coffee table, and sat in her chair, still holding on to her mug. She switched on the television and saw the crowds.

Jed joined her, slumped into the second armchair, and said nothing. He stared at the screen, but Eloise knew he wasn't really seeing anything, his thoughts elsewhere. She suspected they were at the Staines' house but fervently hoped he wouldn't do anything stupid like going round there. She guessed Staines and his wife would probably be home as it was a bank holiday, and watching television too.

She pushed the biscuits across to him and smiled. He picked up the ginger ones, opened the sealed end, and removed three. He thoughtfully began to dunk them in his coffee, his unseeing eyes still fixed on the screen.

Eloise could stand it no longer. 'Jed, talk to me.'

He jumped, startled by her voice. 'Sorry, Gran, I was miles away.'

'Where?'

'Doesn't really matter. But, looking at all those people, I'm glad you didn't mention us going. You know I would have taken you, don't you?'

'I know.' She smiled. 'But I wouldn't have asked. You're changing the subject. What's going through your mind that's putting that bleak look on your face?'

He hesitated for a moment, but knew she could see straight through him. 'John Staines. I know it's him. I just know it. And all I want from him is confirmation before it's too late. So many people who are looking for birth mothers and fathers find out who they are, but they've already died. I don't want that to be me; I want to see him face to face, even if he disappears after that. For all I know, he's possibly never even seen me. My memory isn't clear at all. That accident took a lot away from me.'

'Jed, whoever your father is, he does know about you. As I said, I'm almost 100 per cent sure he paid for this house, even though your mother never said how she'd been able to finance it. He definitely knew of your existence, but they could never be together as a couple. That was the top and bottom of it, but that doesn't mean John Staines is your father.'

'Gran...' There was almost a warning note in the way he spoke. 'It is him. I've seen a picture, and I look like him.'

'You've seen a picture? On the Staines company website?'

Jed felt his face go hot. Confession time? 'No, it's quite indistinct on that, but I saw one in the attic.'

The air suddenly felt claustrophobic, and Jed could see Eloise's face change as she digested that piece of information.

'So that's why you sent me to the Isle of Wight? So you had free rein to investigate? If you'd asked me, I would have helped you look. You didn't have to do it behind my back.'

'Yes, I did. You've never wanted me to know who he was, and don't tell me you've never guessed. I've brought up the subject lots and lots of times, so in the end I had to search for myself. Don't worry, I put everything back...'

'It's not about that, Jed. It all belongs to you anyway. I just wish you felt you could trust me enough to tell me. I found out you'd been to see Nanette because she wrote to me, not because you said anything. It hurts. I've given you my life from the day you were born, and now I can see you on the edge of that chair itching to be somewhere else in this crazy quest to find a father who has never wanted to know you. If he had, he would have come looking.'

'And to add insult to injury, I'm eating your ginger biscuits...'

'Exactly,' she said, then allowed the tears to roll down her cheeks. 'And now you're bloody making me laugh.'

* * *

Two hours later, just as the state funeral service was starting, Jed stood, bent over Eloise, planted a kiss on her head and said, 'See you in a bit.'

She reached up and squeezed his hand, knowing in her head, and her heart, where he was going. A deep sigh and an acknowledgement that she could do nothing to prevent what was to follow, caused her to wave him goodbye, raising her hand and wiggling her fingers. He recognised it as a take care sign from her, and smiled as he left the room. They were friends again.

* * *

There were Union Jacks everywhere. They fluttered in the gentle breeze, and were quite mesmerising. Jed drove along in the sunshine that held little warmth, aware of how few cars were on the road, how silent everywhere seemed. He imagined the real person inside of King Charles III's public persona would be feeling exactly as he had felt back in April when he had followed the hearse carrying his own much-loved mother.

For a moment he felt engulfed by the memories of that day, by the anger he had still been feeling and displaying towards his grandmother, and he felt ashamed. Eloise had been acting on Kirsty's instructions, and Jed knew that what his mother said, his mother meant. What Jed realised now was that Eloise had been the one with the weight of everything on her shoulders, restricted from telling him the truth until the final couple of weeks, carrying the pain of Kirsty's cancer everywhere with her. And she had been forced into that situation because he wasn't even in Sheffield.

He shook his head slightly, trying to clear his mind, and turned left onto the road that held John and Clare Staines' home. He drove slowly past the house, then turned in the turning circle at the end of the long cul-de-sac.

He parked in the turning area for a moment, his engine still running, as he debated what to do next. He figured the funeral service would be almost over, and people would start to move, to maybe make some lunch before re-joining their viewing at St George's Chapel in Windsor.

Jed switched on his music, listened to a couple of Post Malone tracks, then turned off the engine, killing the music at the same time. Music certainly wasn't soothing his soul today in quite the same way it normally did, and he sat quietly, watching in case anyone headed towards him wanting to know why he was there. Neighbourhood Watch had a lot to answer for, he thought, grinning at the thought of the membership card for his own area of Sheffield that resided in his wallet.

He waited a further fifteen minutes, then decided it had to be over now; he started his engine.

Pulling up outside the Staines house, he saw the large Toyota was hiding the smaller Aygo on the paved area in front of the garage. It seemed people were inside the house. Staines' family.

If he was right, his own half-siblings, Jed thought, but squashed the brief flare of temper that shot through him. Today wasn't about anger, it was about answers, and he was determined to get them.

His phone pealed out and he glanced at the screen. Gran. He considered ignoring it, but then had a mental image of her lying on the floor, injured. 'Gran?'

'You're okay, Jed?'

'I'm fine. Did you want something?'

'Yes, I want you to come home. This feels so wrong...'

'It's not wrong, Gran. What is wrong is that nobody has told me anything for all of my life. So it's kind of payback time now.'

'Oh, Jed,' she sighed. 'Just be careful.'

He laughed. 'I will. And polite. I've thought it through, and I want him to realise what he's missed all these years by not acknowledging me. Stop worrying, I'll be home soon.'

They disconnected, and he slipped the phone into his jacket pocket. Time to go door-knocking. He froze as the front door opened, and the woman he had seen on his previous stake-out ran across the road to what he assumed was her own home. A friend of Clare Staines, he assumed. He waited until there was no more activity, and pressed down on the car handle, before stopping once more.

* * *

Vic returned to Clare's house after a quick trip to her own home, carrying a bag containing two bottles of Prosecco and a box of teabags to replenish Clare's supplies that had been used in the many drinks consumed by all six of them. It had felt good to be all together for such a momentous occasion, and now there was a brief lull in proceedings as the cortège proceeded to Windsor.

She glanced back as she went through Clare's front door. Silver car. Young man.

'Clare, look out the window. Is that the same silver car?'

The driver door opened, and Clare froze. Whether it was the same car or not was irrelevant, she knew what was about to happen. It was almost as if a younger version of John was walking up her driveway, and if she was right, her whole world was quite possibly going to implode.

She walked slowly to the front door as she heard the doorbell peal out, and opened it.

'Mrs Staines?' The young man sounded so polite. 'My name is Josiah Grantham. I wonder if I might have a word with your husband, please. I won't keep him long.'

Vic was standing quietly at the doorway to the lounge, ready to help Clare if she needed it. She didn't know what was going on, but she could see Clare was white. Scared.

'I'm sorry, that won't be possible,' Clare said. 'Can I ask what this is about? Maybe I can help.'

Jed had been so sure the man would be in his home today that he felt quite overwhelmed by Clare's words, and for a moment wasn't sure how to respond. Then he turned slightly, as if in thought. 'Will he be in later?'

Clare shook her head. 'No, I'm sorry, he won't.'

'Then can I have a word with you?' Jed knew there was a touch of desperation in his voice. He hadn't planned on this; he thought he would be able to see John, and just know.

Clare didn't move. 'You're Jed, aren't you? As in Jed Bartlet?'

For the first time, Jed allowed a smile to appear. 'I am. Although as I said, my name is Jed Grantham. How do you know me?'

26

MONDAY 19 SEPTEMBER 2022

'I think you'd better come in,' Clare said quietly. She stepped aside and Jed entered her home.

'Thank you.' Jed followed Clare through to the kitchen, aware of Vic's eyes on her all the way.

* * *

'Vic? Who was that?' Grace asked.

'I'm not sure. But your mum seems to know him, so I'm sure she'll tell you when he's gone.'

'Hang on a minute.' There was a touch of anxiety in Greg's words as he stood. 'He's a stranger and she's invited him in? I'm sure I don't need to remind all of us we've had a murder in our midst, and nothing seems to be progressing with that. Who is this person?'

Vic hesitated. Even she was only guessing, but she had seen his face and she was sure that her guess was pretty accurate; it was the four-year-old Jed in the birthday photograph, all grown up now. And this could only mean trouble was heading the way of this family that she considered to be her own.

'It's not for me to say because I don't know. Your mum is only in the kitchen. I'm sure she'll be fine, but we'll leave the lounge door open just in case.'

'Just in case what?' Megan said. 'Just in case he's an axe murderer? I'm not happy about this, I don't know about anybody else. It can't be a workman, or a double-glazing salesman or anything like that; it's a sodding bank holiday, for heaven's sake. Shouldn't somebody be with her?'

'He's not an axe murderer,' Vic said quietly. 'Trust your mum. She knows what she's doing, although she probably doesn't want to do it, not today anyway. Let's get back to what we were doing, and I'm sure your mum will fill you in when that young man goes.'

Vic looked at the faces of Sara, Greg, Grace and Megan and knew they didn't believe a word of what was coming from her mouth. She left the lounge door open and returned to her seat.

* * *

'So,' Clare began, 'you're Jed... Grantham?' The name Bartlet was stuck firmly in Clare's mind.

'I am,' he acknowledged, and took a business card from its small leather case. 'This is me.'

She looked at the card, then placed it carefully on the table. 'You wanted to see my husband?'

Jed gave a slight nod. 'He does live here?'

'He did. Look, I think we're slightly at odds here, Jed. Would you like to tell me why you want to speak to my husband?'

Jed could feel a lump in his throat, and he swallowed. 'There's something I need to discuss with him. Something personal.'

She looked at his hands as they lay on the table; his thumbs were circling each other. This was a nervous young man, and she knew she wasn't helping. But she also knew the second the truth started to come out, her whole life, and his, would change. And that second was imminent.

Clare sighed. 'You believe you're John's son?'

The twiddling thumbs circled faster.

'You know?' he asked.

'I don't *know* anything, nothing more than you do. But I do know something that you clearly don't know, and that is that John died in January.'

The thumbs stopped circling, and he held his hand to his mouth. Shock was etched onto his face. She stood and moved towards the sink. She took an empty glass, filled it with cold water and carried it back to him.

'Sip this,' she said, 'and we can talk.'

He muttered a thank you, and allowed the cold water to trickle down his throat. Of all the outcomes, this was the one he definitely didn't want.

And he had only missed seeing his father in the flesh by a mere nine months or so.

He placed the glass on the table carefully and looked across at Clare. 'I'm so very sorry, Mrs Staines. This is unforgivable; I should have done deeper research. Obviously I haven't seen any mention of his death anywhere, but I have only been seriously looking for a month or so. My mother died in April, and since then it has nagged at me, the fact that only she knew the identity of my father. My gran and my mother brought me up, but nobody, not even Mum's friends, knew who my father was. I think Gran could hazard a guess, but it was only ever a guess. Never confirmed.'

'What makes you think my husband is the man?'

'My name. She called me Josiah, shortening it to Jed, and you were right when you mentioned Jed Bartlet; she and my gran were massive fans of *The West Wing*. My gran is currently rewatching it.' He stared at his hands. They had stopped trembling now, and he picked up the glass to take another sip of water. 'Mum gave me John as a second name, and then I found a picture, hidden away in the attic with all my baby things. It was some sort of fairly formal event, and the names are on the back – your husband's was simply on there as J, whereas all the others had full first and second names. Seeing him was like looking at my own face. Even at that point I didn't immediately think "this is it, I've found him". That came later when I started to give everything even more thought. I'd always thought it was strange that I had such an unusual first name, followed by such a commonplace and simple second name. It was like a flash of lightning. And the thought led onto the picture with J written on the back. Three months after that picture was taken she was pregnant with me.'

Jed reached into his inside pocket, and took out a folded piece of paper.

'This is a photocopy of the picture.'

Clare spoke slowly. 'I remember it well. It was an office party to celebrate moving into new premises. It had been hard work and all the staff had really pulled their weight, so John and I hosted the evening.' She flattened it in front of her, and looked at it. 'Which one is your mother?'

He pointed to Kirsty. 'This one. She left the company before I was born, so you possibly didn't know her beyond this evening. I was born Christmas Day, 1999.'

'I know when you were born,' Clare said. 'Give me a minute.'

She left him sitting at the table, and headed into the lounge. Everyone looked towards her, and Vic said, 'Okay?'

She nodded. 'I'm fine. Just need my handbag. I promise I'll talk to all of you in a bit, but for now I just have something to do. And don't worry about me, everything's fine.'

She picked up her bag and took it through to the kitchen. Jed was staring at the picture of his mother, his finger touching her face.

'She was very beautiful,' he said.

'She was. It still doesn't mean that it was okay to fuck her.'

There was a sense of shock at her words from both her and Jed.

'I'm sorry,' she said. 'I don't normally use language like that, never use it to be perfectly honest, but I didn't expect a visit from my husband's potential offspring today. There may be stronger words used before the end of this particular Monday. I now have to tell my family who you are and why you're here.' Clare reached into her handbag and took out a plain white envelope. 'This is why I know your date of birth.'

She pushed the envelope across to him. He opened the flap and slid out the picture.

He gasped in amazement. 'Gran and I were talking about this picture the other day. She remembered it, this one exactly. I remember this day, the cake, the blue four. It's really the only memory I have of my early years, because when I was six Mum and I were in a serious road accident. How...?'

'How did I get it? John saved it. I found it not long ago. John had an antique desk in his home office, and I decided to move it, then give it a thorough clean out, so I could use it. During that clean out I disturbed a lever which released a hidden drawer. Inside it was this picture and a Father's Day card. Your mother wrote the card for you, but you signed it, Jed. The card and the original envelope are still in the drawer, but I wanted to carry this around with me, a sort of "just in case" item in my bag.'

He touched the photo, his finger stroking the four cake. 'Gran said Mum took this photo. I'd had a large walking dinosaur and a new bike for my birthday. I don't know what happened to the dinosaur but the bike is up in my attic now.'

He raised his eyes to Clare. 'I wish I had met him. And I'm so sorry to have caused you any distress, Mrs Staines. I know you're going to have to tell your family now, but I'll leave you to work out how best to do that. My gran will be going out of her mind worrying about me, so I'll head back home. Just tell me – was he a nice man?'

Clare gave a brief smile. Her muddledness hadn't recovered in any way, but this young man didn't need to know that. 'He was a lovely, caring man, Jed. And I'm sure that if the circumstances had been different he would have been truly proud of his son. You've clearly done well for yourself.' She tapped the business card he'd given her. 'May I keep this?'

'Of course. I've already written my personal phone number on the back. I'll let you go back to your family, and I am truly sorry for disturbing you. I could have written and sort of pre-warned my father, or who I think is my father, but I was concerned he would fob me off. It honestly never occurred to me that he could have died, although in view of the fact that Mum has died, that was a pretty stupid assumption to make, wasn't it? I'll always think of John Staines as my father, but I won't trouble you again, Mrs Staines.'

Clare walked with him to the front door, passing by the open lounge door. He didn't look inside. He turned and shook her hand.

'Thank you for listening to me, and if ever you feel you can do it, I would appreciate a copy of that photograph. You can send it to my office address.'

'Of course I will, Jed. But there's something we should do, I think. How would you feel about a DNA test to confirm, or deny, your beliefs once and for all?'

27

Clare returned to the lounge, sitting down with a thud. Everyone looked at her, the silence unbroken until Sara said, 'Well?'

Clare coughed to clear her throat. When Jed had confirmed he would happily take a DNA test, she had felt a choking feeling in her throat, and she was struggling to clear it despite drinking a full glass of water. She looked around at them all. The worry was etched on Vic's face, but her family members simply looked puzzled.

'First of all,' Clare said, then coughed again, 'it was nothing to do with Rob's death. I know this has taken over our lives of late with it being so close to us, but this was something else that has happened, with regard to your father.'

Vic stood and moved to sit on the arm of Clare's armchair. She reached out to take her hand.

'The young man you saw me take into the kitchen is someone I have been half expecting to see. I promise you I did not know he would be coming here today, and I would not have wanted you to see him before I had processed everything in my own mind first anyway. It will completely take you by surprise. Vic knows as much as I do, or did up to the point the man rang our doorbell.'

Grace reached across for the remote control and switched off the television. 'Okay,' she said, 'we're listening.'

Clare gave a quick glance upwards to Vic, who gently nodded and squeezed Clare's hand.

'His name is Josiah Grantham. He was born on Christmas Day, 1999, so I believe that makes him twenty-three in December.'

'Our Daniel would have been twenty-three in December,' Sara said quietly.

Clare nodded. 'He would, and what I'm about to tell you is not about Daniel at all; he will always be our much-loved son, and your beautiful brother. This young man who has been here today was born six days after Daniel's birth. Four days after his death.'

Again, Vic squeezed Clare's hand.

'His mother was called Kirsty Grantham, and she died this year. Kirsty Grantham used to work for your father until she had her baby, and then she moved on. The young man was brought up by both Kirsty and his grandmother, a lady I believe to be called Eloise Grantham, though I'm not sure I'm remembering her first name correctly.'

'No father then?' Sara asked.

'Not an active father who had any part of the boy's development, no. He did have a father, of course, but purely genetically. I believe your dad is also Josiah's dad. I've spoken briefly with Jed, as he prefers to be called, and he has willingly agreed to a DNA test, but only if the whole family agree with it.'

Grace frowned. 'Whoa. This is all a bit sudden, isn't it? And how come you and Vic had an inkling this was likely to happen? What's going on, Mum?'

Clare reached into her bag, and took out the white envelope. 'I found this in a secret drawer in Dad's desk. It came with a Father's

Day card, and this, along with the original envelope, is still in the drawer. Jed remembers the cake quite clearly and confirmed he had a large walking dinosaur and a new bike for this birthday. He doesn't remember his father.'

'You believe him?' Greg asked, taking the photograph from Clare's hand. 'He's not conning you?'

'For what? I genuinely think he's someone who wanted to meet his father. He's gutted that he left it too late. He jumped at the chance of a DNA test to prove it one way or the other, so, no, I don't think he's conning me.'

It was Sara's turn to speak; to question. 'Is he like Dad?'

'Very much so. He has your dad's face, and when you meet him, *if* you meet him, I think you'll be a little unnerved by it. He also does that slight nod of the head your dad used to do when he was about to say something important. But it seems his mother would never admit to who had fathered her baby, although Jed thinks his gran had accurately guessed.'

'Where is he now?'

'He's gone home to his gran, who he knows will be worrying about him. We've left it that I will organise a DNA test, then contact him. Luckily, I have one of your dad's hairbrushes, plus a couple of toothbrushes in the kit he used to keep packed for away trips. I agree I've had some knowledge of this for the last week or so, but I'm not finding it any easier than you are. I have discovered my husband had an affair, and it seems the young woman fell very hard for him. Jed told me she never had a boyfriend, and though Jed can't remember ever seeing your dad, he did admit he has memory issues due to a severe car accident he had as a child.'

'So his actual name is Josiah?' Greg asked.

'It is,' Clare confirmed. 'Josiah John Grantham.'

'She gave him Dad's name,' Sara mused. 'Just as I will use Greg's name for our baby's second name if it's a little boy.'

Megan joined in. 'There's a lot to think about with this. Grace, come in the kitchen with me and we'll make a pot of tea. I think we all need to settle down, and if we think of anything else to ask, we can do so in a quiet way with a cuppa.'

Clare smiled. 'Thank you, Megan. That would be lovely. And while you're doing that I'll go and get the Father's Day card and the envelope from the desk, so you can all see. Then you'll know as much as I do. Funnily enough, Vic and I were going to start trying to track him down next week, after everything opened up again following the funeral. Now we don't need to.'

Jed drove as far as the end of the cul-de-sac, and turned left. He stopped the car, and clasped his shaking hands together. He felt sick, and suddenly immensely tired. He leaned his head back on the headrest and closed his eyes, allowing his thoughts to roam wherever they wanted. And they were roaming, that was for sure.

When he'd left Eloise watching the funeral that morning, he hadn't had any preconceptions about what the day would bring. Would John Staines deny all knowledge of him? Would his wife throw a proper wobbly, or had she lived with the information that her husband liked to play away from home for all her life? And did he have a family? Would he discover he had a whole heap of half-siblings?

The reality had proved to be beyond anything he could have imagined. He had noticed a picture of John in the hallway, atop a small antique hall table, and even at that point it hadn't occurred to him that the man might be dead. It was only Clare's words that had made him realise his true status was orphan. No mother, no father.

Throughout the ensuing conversation with the calm and lady-like Clare, he had come to realise that he would never know the truth of the situation, that his mother had taken the details to her own grave with her, and he recognised the moment when he knew it was time to leave this woman who knew so much, yet so little.

She hadn't spoken of her family, yet there seemed to be quite a few people in the lounge as he'd passed the open door – open, presumably, so that the occupants of the room could ensure their mother's safety.

He opened his eyes as his thoughts drifted to Clare Staines' words on the doorstep. The offer was to find out once and for all if he was John's son, and to take a DNA test. She had his personal phone number and she had promised she would only ring on that, not his work phone. She would find out how they could do it in view of the fact that her husband was deceased, but he had no doubt she was a very capable woman, and if she wanted to arrange something, it would be arranged.

She had closed the door before he had clicked shut the garden gate; enough was enough, she had obviously decided.

He sat for a few minutes longer, then started up his car once again.

Driving home was a sedate sort of journey. He wasn't convinced he could react swiftly in an emergency. He pulled onto their driveway, and within seconds, his grandmother was at the front door, waiting for him.

'I've poured us a brandy,' she said.

'You think we need one?'

'Your face says you do. Come on, let's go in. We can either talk or not talk, it doesn't matter to me, but you look shell-shocked and that does matter.'

On the front doorstep, he reached out and pulled Eloise towards him. She relaxed into his warmth, and let him hold her.

Inside, the lounge was dark; Eloise had drawn the curtains as the sun had reached the point where it was shining directly onto the television screen. On the coffee table stood two brandy glasses, both filled with a fair amount.

'I poured these when I heard your car engine,' she said, and handed one to him. He sipped at the amber liquid, and allowed it to trickle down his throat. 'That's good,' he said, and followed it with another sip.

'You needed it?'

'Well, I didn't realise I needed it, but now I think that's the case. It's been a strange sort of day, and nothing's resolved yet. I've lots to tell you, Gran, but give me a few minutes. I need to digest it all, make sure I don't get it muddled up, and then we'll talk.'

She smiled at this maturity that was suddenly evolving. 'Whenever you're ready, Jed, whenever you're ready. You've missed most of the funeral, but I don't suppose you'll fret about that. She's had a good send-off, with all her family there, including that young whippersnapper, Harry. He's trouble, that boy, you mark my words.'

He laughed. 'Hardly a boy, Gran. They need you there, at the palace; you'd sort all of them out, I'm sure.'

'Just give me the chance. Now, is there anything special you fancy tonight, or shall we go out, my treat?'

He shook his head. 'No, I think I need to stay in, and just think. And when I tell you all I've discovered today, we'll probably have a lot to discuss. Let's just have something on toast, and a big dish of ice cream for afters. That okay with you?'

She looked at him. Ice cream. His go-to food when he was out of sorts. So it hadn't gone smoothly for her boy. Ice cream it would be then.

28

DS Franks stared out of the window knowing he had missed something, yet not having a clue what it was.

'Come on, Bren,' he said to himself, 'go back to the beginning. We may not know much, but they've now found his car. Surely that should tell us something.'

He walked back to his desk and sat down, flipping open his laptop. He pulled up the forensic report of the car found in the multistorey known as the cheese grater because of the outward appearance of it, and read through the words once again.

It had arrived in the city centre car park within half an hour of the attack, confirming the timings given to him by Clare Staines, and whoever was driving it hadn't been visible on the camera. They had no idea of the gender of the driver, nothing at all. No fingerprints that shouldn't have been in it, only Robert Dolan's own prints and a couple that belonged to his wife, so Brendan could only assume that the killer was definitely a savvy customer, knew about wearing gloves, wiping down if accidentally touching something, that sort of thing. It was frustrating. ANPR had picked up the car going through the centre of Sheffield, but had only revealed the car, not the driver.

He had sat with Rosie the previous evening, talking about the case in general and the feeling that now the funeral was over, they could get back to full strength on their team and maybe start to advance the case, but neither had felt optimistic. Five days, and precious little progress.

He looked up to see that Rosie had just walked through the door, and he waved her over. She mimed getting a coffee, and two minutes later was sitting opposite him.

'You not slept either?' she asked.

'Not really. I think we need to re-interview, find out if we still get the same stories. I was kind of optimistic we would get something from his work files and laptop, but there really is nothing that's standing out. I checked out two that troubled me, but they proved to have been settled amicably. He seems to have been good at his job, conscientious, probably overworked which I suspect is the reason he took his nastiness home, but on the surface there seems to be nothing that would make us sit up and take notice. Do you agree?'

'I do.' Rosie gave a slight nod. 'I thought that from the very beginning. He's worked for that company for years, climbed the ladder, has specific customers who trust him with their finances. I felt it didn't lead in that direction right from the start, but it had to be checked. This feels personal, but having got to know the people who were close to him, well...'

'I know what you mean. They don't fit any sort of pattern, do they? And yet he's dead by unnatural causes.'

Rosie took out her notebook. 'After we'd chatted in the pub last night, I went home and listed the people that we would consider to be close to him. But more importantly, close to Vicki Dolan. We only have the wife's word for it that he's only just started hitting her, and maybe that's true, but somebody decided it was time to stop him, didn't they? Would you agree?'

'Wholeheartedly. Probably somebody in the Staines family, but they all have pretty strong alibis. And according to Mrs Dolan, she has no family. No kids, parents long gone for her. More recently for him, but also no siblings for either of them.' He stared across the room for a moment. 'Must be awful to have nobody at all, wouldn't you think?'

'Soul-destroying. I know I moan about my kids, but I wouldn't want to be without them.' She pulled her notebook towards her and made a note of the 'no family' fact against Vic Dolan's name, then closed it again. 'Somebody believes they are her family because one of them has done this, I'll lay money on it. So, it's alibi breaking time. Fine-tooth comb and all that. We bringing them in individually to re-interview?'

'I'm considering going out to their homes. Keep it informal, but make damn sure they're aware it's official. And we'll start with Mrs Dolan. Whether she wielded the weapon or not, she's bang at the heart of it all.' He checked his watch. 'Okay, let's leave here at nine, and go to the crime scene. I know she can now return there, but he's only been gone six days so it will probably be a little early to move back in. She may still be at her mate's house over the road. Either way, we'll catch her somewhere. And we'll have a talk with Clare Staines afterwards.'

'And then?'

He looked at his screen. 'And then we tackle Greg Carter, Sara Carter, Grace Staines and Megan King. Individually. Without prompting and corrections from partners who are pretending to be upset by the death of a man they didn't like, a man who had hit his wife, maybe not for the first time. I wonder if Mrs Dolan will admit to us there were earlier beatings? It just seems odd that he smacks her for the first time, and somebody whacks him over the head with a blunt instrument that we haven't been able to find. In fact, we've found bugger all to point us in any direction, so let's hope by the end of today something seems clearer. A way forward for this investigation to follow.'

Vic was walking across the road from Clare's home when she saw the police car turn the corner at the end of the cul-de-sac. She hesitated, unsure whether to go back to Clare's or continue to her own home where specialist cleaners were currently working to get rid of the smell and the sight of her husband's blood. They had promised that by lunchtime everything would be back to its normal state, and she wanted desperately to believe them.

She had almost decided to go back to Clare's when the two police officers pulled up.

'Glad you're here, Mrs Dolan,' Rosie Waters said as she climbed out of the passenger seat. 'We need to continue our chat with you, make sure we have all the facts. Can we go inside?'

'The cleaners...' Vic tried to explain, and pointed to the van parked on her drive.

'That's okay. They should only be doing the areas where the body was found – the kitchen and hallway – so we should be fine to go in the lounge, right? We'll not interfere with anything they're doing.'

Vic felt as though she wasn't being given a choice.

The three of them walked past the van and in through the door leading directly into the hall. Two men were working at getting rid of all stains, and Vic led the two police officers into the first room on the left. Brendan closed the door to separate them from the cleaners, and they all sat.

'I can't really offer you a drink...' Vic began, but Rosie held up her hand.

'That's fine, Vic. Do you prefer to be called Vic, or Vicki?'

'Vic, please. I was only called Vicki when I was in trouble.'

Rosie smiled. 'That's just like me. I'm always known as Rosie, but my full name is Rosanna. So, we're here to go through your statement in more depth. We're making a little progress in the case, as you know. At least we've found your husband's car, but it's given us nothing. Whoever took it knew to drive in gloves, and probably wore a hoodie with the hood up. There's absolutely nothing of any help. Just your husband's prints, and some of yours on the passenger side.'

'It's a fact they wouldn't be on the driver's side,' she said. 'I've never been allowed to drive it—'

'It's actually your relationship with Robert we wanted to look at a bit more closely. We know he hit you a couple of days before his death.' Rosie lifted her head and looked closely at Vic's face. 'The bruising is still there, but only just. Was that the first time, as you intimated in your statement?'

There was hesitation on Vic's part. 'It was the first time on my face. That was why I knew I had to leave. I couldn't hide a purple cheekbone. Purple shoulders, ribs and legs can be covered, but other than wearing a mask, you can't hide the face.'

Both officers remained silent, hoping she would give more detail, but Vic simply shrugged as if to say water under the bridge, and Rosie wrote in her notebook while Brendan took over.

'So he beat you regularly?'

'I wouldn't say it was regularly, but one or two people noticed if I limped, or favoured my arm. You know, up to a couple of years ago he was the perfect husband. Then he got a massive promotion at work, more high-profile clients, that sort of thing. He worked longer hours. We seemed to lose any social life we had, it was all about work, and he became moody, then violent.'

'Did Mrs Staines know about this?'

'I think she guessed, but I didn't tell her everything. She had her own problems, because John had been diagnosed with terminal cancer. But she's not stupid.'

Rosie continued to make notes, then looked up. 'Did all of them know or guess?'

'All of them?'

'Clare and her family. Sara, Greg, Grace and Megan. Did they all know?'

Vic looked uncomfortable. Her mind had instantly flashed back to a couple of months earlier when Grace and Megan had arrived at her door to tell her their news of finding their perfect flat to buy, overlooking the Don in the centre of Sheffield. 'Possibly,' she muttered.

'Enlighten us,' Bren said quietly.

'They're almost like my own children, Grace and Sara; I've been such a large part of their lives, so whenever the girls had something really important happen, they – and I now include Megan in this – naturally came to tell me. Not to tell *us* – Megan was wary of Rob – but she hadn't known him when he was lovely Rob; she only knew him when he was bully Rob. Anyway, one time they had walked straight in, as they normally do, because it was a warm evening and we'd left the door open. He had punched me in the stomach after I'd asked him to pour us a glass of wine so we could sit outside on the patio for an hour before bedtime. I asked twice, which was my big mistake. He swung round just as they walked through the door, too late to pull back on the punch. I dropped to the floor, and then he glared at them before stomping off upstairs.'

'And the girls?'

'They wanted to kill him. Just words of course. They're both martial arts people, that's how they met, and I genuinely think they wanted to hurt him, but he'd gone upstairs and I needed help. I told them he was simply in a bad mood and I'd aggravated it. I'm assuming they told Clare, but she never said anything. The bruise on my stomach was pretty spectacular, but he must have known it would be hidden.'

'You didn't leave then?'

'No, I tried to stop irritating him. I loved him, but the love died. That was why I left. Megan and Grace never spoke to him again after that. I don't think they'll be sorry he's gone; they'll probably want to congratulate the random thief who decided to kill him as well as take his car.'

Rosie glanced at Brendan. 'You might need to reconsider those words, Vic. We're not looking for a random thief. The car was technically stolen, but it was only driven into the city centre and then abandoned. It was used purely to get the killer away from this house. This was no random act; this was premeditated murder.'

29

TUESDAY 20 SEPTEMBER 2022

'That came as a bit of a shock to the grieving widow,' Brendan said as they walked across the road to seek out Clare Staines.

'She must be very naïve to think this was a randomer who saw a car with the engine running, but decided to kill the owner first before taking the car. How do you read what happened?'

They stopped to talk just outside Clare's front gate, not wanting Clare to hear their words. 'I think whoever has killed him knows his routine. They have to. I believe they must have been in the back garden, watched him taking the car out of the garage, and then slipped inside the house, knowing his routine was to get out the car, collect anything he needed from the house then head off to work.' Bren's face was thoughtful as he chose his words carefully, seeing what he was saying almost as a film in his mind. 'They also knew his wife wouldn't be in the house at that point.'

Rosie smiled. 'I totally agree. I can't see yet who it is, but somebody slipped into his house, waited until his back was towards them, and then hit him with whatever the blunt instrument is. I suspect they quickly changed their clothes, dumped them and the weapon into a bag, and legged it out of the house and into the car. This is a small cul-de-sac, not many people about, and the car would have been very close to the back door. It's a pity there's so little ANPR round here, but we got nothing really, not until the car got closer to the city centre. Everything was well-planned and executed, but it was definitely somebody who knew Vic Dolan wouldn't be here. I know they're still checking the CCTV of the cheese grater car park, but I'm not convinced the murderer's car was there for them to conveniently swap over to it. There are four people in this equation who could have walked to their home from that car park.'

Brendan nodded. 'Sara and Greg Carter at Norfolk Park, and Grace Staines and Megan King bang in the centre. I haven't ruled out our two older ladies, but time frames don't really give them the opportunity to kill him, drive into Sheffield and then get back to the Dolan house.'

Rosie pushed open the garden gate. 'Let's go and talk to Clare again. Let her see we know a bit more about how her best mate was being treated by her bully of a husband.'

'Allegedly,' Brendan qualified.

* * *

Clare was on the phone with Jed, confirming she had organised a DNA test, and would need him to complete it as soon as the parcel arrived. She was just telling him that the company had confirmed that hairbrushes and toothbrushes were valuable sources of DNA although they couldn't guarantee results, when the doorbell pealed.

'I have to go, Jed, I think the police are here. I'll ring you when everything arrives.'

She disconnected and opened her door, unsurprised to see the two police officers. She had watched them escort Vic into her own home half an hour earlier.

'Come in.' She didn't bother smiling.

'Thank you, Mrs Staines,' Brendan said, his face just as serious as Clare's.

'We just need to build on your original statement,' Rosie said, surprised at the seeming frigidity oozing from both her boss and Clare Staines. 'We won't keep you long.'

'You've been with Vic?'

'We have. Again, just a couple of things to clarify.'

'I'd rather you didn't speak to her on her own, that's all. She's quite fragile at the moment, as you've probably realised.'

'Well, unless you're a solicitor in your own right, Mrs Staines, I'm afraid that's the way it has to be. Mrs Dolan is free to appoint a solicitor at any time, if she deems it to be necessary, but I don't think anything we've discussed today can possibly lead her along that path.'

She led them into the kitchen, and waved her hand towards the kitchen chairs. 'Would you like a drink?' Ever the hostess.

'No thank you,' Brendan said. 'We've a full day in front of us, and need to crack on.'

Rosie took out her book and opened it.

'I just want to double check your movements on the morning of the murder,' Brendan said. 'You went to pick up a shower screen for your daughter and her partner. Is that right?'

'You know it is.' Clare stood and walked to the kitchen drawer. She brought two receipts back to the table and pushed them towards Brendan. 'The first one is the receipt for the shower screen, the second is the receipt from the McDonald's drive-through where I went immediately after leaving B&Q. Both are timed. I found these in the bottom of my handbag last night, so I hope this proves that what I told you was accurate.'

'We don't doubt your version of events, Mrs Staines,' Brendan said quietly. 'But thank you for these, they will corroborate your statement.' He picked them up and dropped them into an evidence bag.

'I've photocopied them,' Clare said, completely apropos of nothing. She just felt she should make the point.

'Good,' Rosie said, trying to lighten the atmosphere. 'You might need the B&Q one if the screen falls apart.'

Neither Brendon nor Clare even smiled, let alone laughed.

Brendon coughed. 'Mrs Staines, we're not disputing any part of your statement. Before Mrs Dolan arrived did you notice any sort of activity on the road outside? And I mean from the moment you got out of bed to Mrs Dolan finding her husband's body.'

'I've already told you I saw Rob get his car out of the garage, but prior to that I don't recall seeing anything. It's a very quiet cul-de-sac, mainly retired people, and when I heard Rob's car screech away it was his normal time of nine o'clock. Most of the people who live on this road wouldn't even be up at that time. I was up because of the trip to get the shower screen but I can't remember seeing anybody other than Rob.'

'Describe his actions.'

For a moment Clare closed her eyes, recalling what she could of that early morning. 'He came out of the door, left it open and went to the garage. I heard the car start up, then he drove it out of the garage and put it facing the front gate ready for heading off to work. He left it running – he always does – and walked back through the door he'd left open. I came away from the window, and then I heard his car pull away and roar off down the road, just like normal. Now that you're forcing me to rethink it, there was one thing that was different – he didn't close the garage door. He has a bit of a routine where he pulls the car down to the sliding front gates as he's ready for driving off to work, uses his remote to operate them, then goes back while they're opening, to close the house door and the garage door. Now we know it wasn't him driving the car, that kind of makes a bit more sense. Whoever killed him wouldn't be bothered about open garage doors, would they?'

'No, they wouldn't, you're right. Mrs Staines, we believe there is the possibility that the killer knew you and Mrs Dolan would be arriving imminently, which is why they got away as fast as they could.'

'But who would know that?' Clare looked bewildered.

'If I read you a list of names, will you confirm if that person knew of your plans with Mrs Dolan for that morning?'

'Of course.'

Brendan gave a brief nod, and opened his own notebook. 'Gregory Carter, Sara Carter, Grace Staines, Megan King.'

A look of horror flashed across Clare's face. 'They're my family!'

'Did all of them know of your plans to clear out the craft stuff from Mrs Dolan's home that morning?'

'Yes, but—'

'I just needed confirmation, Mrs Staines,' Brendan said. 'We're going to re-interview them all at some point, but, like you, we also don't believe they could have done it. Do they all have cars?'

The question was abrupt, and Clare visibly flinched. 'Sara and Greg share one, because Sara doesn't need one for work, and Grace and Megan share an Aygo because they can't afford one each. They've just bought a new flat.'

'Thank you,' Brendan said, and stood. Rosie took the hint and got to her feet as well; they moved down the hallway to the front door.

'Lock your door, Mrs Staines. We haven't caught the killer yet, and we don't want them coming after you. We'll add everything we've discussed today into your statement and get somebody to bring it back out here for you to sign, unless we need to ask further questions. Thank you for your time this morning, have a good day.' He stared at the baseball bat which was almost blending into the doorjamb. He looked at Rosie, and she pulled out a large evidence bag. 'We'll have to take this in for testing, Mrs Staines.' He placed the bat in the bag and sealed the opening before heading down the front garden path.

Clare slammed the door behind them, and felt a seething anger exploding out of her. Where the hell was John when she needed him?

She watched from the small side window in the hall and waited until the police car had turned out of the road before ringing Vic to check she was okay.

'For fuck's sake, Clare, put the kettle on. They didn't say much, but I feel as if I've been put through a spin cycle in the washer. I'll be over in one minute.'

Clare switched on the kettle, took down the large teapot and popped in three teabags. This was a serious tea-drinking session. She couldn't ring any of her family because they were all back at work, but she could text them. Sara was the one causing her the most concern; it was bad enough that she felt sick all the time without having the police harass her about the death of a man she had nothing to do with.

The front door opened, and she heard a couple of swear words preceding her friend's entrance into the kitchen. She smiled. Vic could always make her smile.

'I'm in the kitchen,' she called, and Vic came through.

'Well, I think I'm in the doghouse with the way those two spoke to me,' she said. 'I might not have killed Rob, but I think they're ready to charge me.'

'No, they're not. They're ready to charge somebody from my family.'

'What? And they're my family as well, not just yours. What do you mean?'

Clare poured the water into the teapot, and shrugged. 'I'm not sure what I mean, but it seems that anybody who knew Rob's routine is fair game for DS Franks and DC Waters. I think we're actually in the clear because of the timings. They managed to track your journey because of CCTV in shops. You were pretty smart without realising you were being pretty smart, and drove past businesses with working CCTV. So they know exactly what you were doing at the time Rob was killed. I've got proof because I've got timed receipts from B&Q and McDonald's for my purchases, but now they've moved on to the kids. I know we talked about it being some random scrote who stole Rob's car, but they're not thinking that it seems.'

'They said that to me very clearly. So what do we do now?'

'We drink a full potful of tea, eat biscuits, and after the cleaners have finished, we go over to yours and make plans for you for a life without Rob.'

30

Jed watched as the forklift truck backed slowly away from the trailer being loaded, then gradually moved forward as the driver pointed it in the direction of the next part of the load that was required.

Jed's attention wasn't on his work; he had been surprised to hear the ringtone of his personal phone, and had instantly felt a degree of panic, assuming it was his grandmother needing him in some way. It had been a shock to see Clare Staines' name on his screen.

It had been a welcome surprise to hear why she had rung him; she had organised the DNA test.

The previous evening had been filled with talking about the man who still had to be proved to be his father, but he knew that Clare Staines believed it. She had had a little more time than he had to get her head around it, and she had reached the somewhat obvious conclusion that the child was the mirror image of the father.

Eloise, of course, had been full of questions, questions he couldn't answer. They had talked late into the night, and now this morning he felt a little spaced out with tiredness. Having seen the loading of the trailer progressing smoothly, and with the right goods, he headed back into the office to make himself a black coffee. He needed to wake up, and fast.

His mind went back to the hurried phone call – he was sure she had said *the police are here.* He hoped it wasn't about anything bad; she had seemed such a nice woman, in control of things, and quite straightforward.

He spooned the instant coffee into a mug while the kettle was boiling, and sat at his desk, staring at the memo from head office congratulating him on the turnover increase over the last month. He had sensed he had done well, but seeing the figures in front of him made him think that most of the local population must be doing some form of DIY instead of going abroad for their holidays. He smiled. It was all looking good for his annual bonus payment in March.

His thoughts returned to the man who he was now thinking of as definitely his genetic father, and he typed his name into Google. When he'd started his quest, he had looked at his business's website; it basically only told him what they did as solicitors. He hadn't taken the search any further than that; the man was a solicitor and clearly the head of the business.

But now things had moved on, and his foray into the real John Staines, the person, revealed his death. He sat back, picked up the boiling coffee and carefully sipped at it. He wondered if his trip the previous day would have gone ahead if he had seen this. If he had known Staines was dead, would he have pursued it? He thought not.

Eloise had done her best to ground him. She had said a couple of times that until the DNA test revealed the absolute truth, he mustn't close his mind to the possibility that he had got it wrong, and he had nodded his head in agreement. But he wasn't wrong.

He had seen Clare Staines' face when she had seen his. And he knew that one day his grandmother would meet Clare...

His thoughts veered away from Clare slightly, and towards the others who had been in the lounge, presumably other relatives of his. It would be a good day when they could all meet as equals, because in his heart he knew what the DNA test would reveal.

He finished the coffee, responded to the head office email, and went back outside. The corpulent forklift driver was chatting to the equally corpulent artic driver as he fastened his sides on the trailer, and both men held up a thumb towards him, indicating it was all done. He returned the thumb, and walked around the side of the building, taking extra time out to get his thoughts in order.

His day passed slowly, and locking the gates was his last action before heading home. He rarely finished on time, but today had definitely been a five o'clock finish day.

* * *

In contrast, Brendan Franks and Rosie Waters felt as if their day was starting at five. They had been to the homes of the people they wanted to talk to, but everybody had been at work. It suddenly felt as if the whole country had forgotten the Queen and the previous day's activities, and had gone about their normal business.

Rosie did the amendments, few as they were, to both Vic's and Clare's statements, wrote up the report on their visits to the two women, and then read up on the statements of the four remaining members of Clare's family.

Bren had been in conference with the DI, going over the case and explaining the limitations because of the mourning period that Rob Dolan's death had been a part of. The DI had nodded in full agreement of Bren's words, but he'd made it very clear he expected significant results within a couple of days.

'A couple of days?' Rosie exclaimed in disbelief. 'He does know Dolan was killed on the fourteenth, doesn't he? And it's only the twentieth today, six days later, with a whole country in mourning, and half our team helping out down in London?'

Bren grinned at her. 'He does know, but it's over now, and everybody's back in tomorrow. We'll get these interviews finished today, and spend tomorrow checking everything. I know we didn't get much on the car park CCTV, but that car was parked up at a peak time, so we might be able to get dashcam footage from other cars parking up at the same time. We need to get out an appeal on Facebook for it.'

'I'll do it this afternoon; fingers crossed we get some sort of response. Then at least the DI will know we turned up for work.' The sarcasm in her voice was obvious, and Bren laughed.

'He's just doing his job, Rosie. He'll have got the DCI breathing down his neck, don't forget. They know the score, we're working against the odds on this one, but it'll get easier.'

'So we'll interview all four of them tonight?'

'We will. I'd like to get them on their own, so if we make a point of taking one each in separate rooms at the addresses, it'll stop them protecting each other. If they object, we'll bring them in here. That'll shut them up with their objections.'

She grinned at Brendan. 'So we go in prepared to terrify them? I love that sort of interview.'

'Perhaps terrify is too strong a word, Rosie, but we can lay it on thickly if they do start trying to wriggle out of talking to us. And I'm pretty sure they know the law around police interviews; they are John Staines' kids when all's said and done.'

'You came across him?'

'Not a lot, because although he was really good at it, he didn't like working the criminal side of the business. He preferred what he called grown-up work – wills, probate, that sort of stuff. We didn't know he was ill of course, which I suspect was another reason he dropped out of the criminal. He must have felt unwell before his terminal diagnosis, because nothing happens quickly with cancer. You feel out of sorts, then a bit worse, then you risk going to the doctor in case they want you to attend a hospital, then there's all the tests, and then the "sorry it's too late" bit. I think Staines backed away from court appearances when he first started to feel ill.'

'Horrible way to die,' Rosie murmured. 'And he really wasn't very old, was he?'

'Early fifties, lovely family, everything to live for. And he's only been dead nine months or so. We might have to watch our words carefully when we interview tonight. Tell me your thoughts on Vic Dolan.'

Rosie pursed her lips. 'Not sure, but I like her and I think she's pretty genuine. She was absolutely grey and covered in vomit the first time I saw her, and she seemed completely in shock. Nothing would have got her back into that house; she was proper freaked out by it. She's very close to Clare, but that's been a close friendship for years and years, so I understand.'

Bren nodded. 'Exactly my thoughts. I know they always say look at the spouse first, but she's only a slip of a thing, and if he had seen her in that hallway, she would have been in a lot of danger. She didn't need to kill him, she'd already moved out, and the two ladies were taking the rest of her stuff that day. She already had a new home... no, it doesn't point to her having done it. Now Clare Staines is a different breed. I think she would protect anybody she felt was being bullied, and her friend Vic was definitely that.'

'You think we'll get anything from that baseball bat?'

He shook his head. 'Not a thing. It didn't even smell of bleach, and there were no stains on it. It just unsettled her a bit, and that's always good. She's smart enough not to have used that anyway. It's obviously a permanent fixture in her hall, so if she's the killer she would have thought of a different weapon to that. I'm hoping somebody comes up with an answer to what the blunt instrument could be, but so far they're still testing, it seems.'

'Well they'll certainly test that baseball bat against the indentation in the head, but there was no blood on the bat. In fact it looked as though it has been polished on a regular basis. Every home should have one.' Rosie laughed. 'I wouldn't dare, my kids would wreck the house with it.'

'Anybody would think your kids were proper hooligans the way you talk about them.'

'You've met them...'

'I know. Little darlings, they are.'

Rosie stared at him. 'It must have been somebody else's kids you met. Little darlings does not describe my three. Come on, let's go and snag a squad car, and we can sit and wait outside the Carter house, get all the neighbours talking. It'll be good to get there before they do, wrong-foot them from the start, because I bet they think that first interview was it, and it's all over for them now.'

'We could dangle handcuffs from the car aerial, really scare the shit out of them. And switch on the lights and sirens as they turn onto the road...'

They were laughing at further lurid suggestions as they left the office and headed downstairs to the car pool. The pressure was on, and the need to get these four interviews done and out of the way was uppermost in both their minds.

31

TUESDAY 20 SEPTEMBER 2022

Sara saw the squad car before Greg did, and drew in a breath. 'Why are they here?' she asked quietly.

Greg grimaced. 'I have no idea, but let's find out and get rid of them. You need to rest.'

She nodded. 'Tell me about it. I'm on intimate vomiting terms with the ladies' toilets at work. It's okay saying don't tell anybody yet, but they're not daft. And most of them have got kids, so they know what being pregnant is like.'

Greg pulled on the hand brake, and slipped his arm around his wife. 'Come on, I'll do the talking, and you just sit back.'

* * *

Rosie took Sara into the kitchen, and Bren led Greg into the lounge.

Sara felt uncomfortable without her husband by her side, and Rosie waited until she was ensconced at the kitchen table before opening her notebook.

'This is a follow-up visit to see if there's anything you've remembered that we can add to your original statement,' she said. 'I need to record it so that I don't miss anything of what you say. It's to protect you as well as help me. Are you okay?'

Sara waved a hand in front of her face. 'I'll apologise now if I vomit all over you and/or your recording machine,' she said. 'It's been one of those days...'

'Vomit? You're pregnant?'

'I am, but it's not sitting very well with me. It's not public knowledge yet, only a handful of people know, and we'd like to keep it that way for the time being.'

Rosie smiled. 'I understand exactly what you mean, but anyone who's gone through it will recognise instantly why your face looks ghostly white. Let's crack on with this, and then you can relax. So, according to your statement, you walked to work on the day in question. You didn't go in the car with your husband?'

'No, he said he needed to put air in the tyres, so I said I might as well walk. It's not far, and I set off before he did. I work in the casino – I think I've already said this. Three days a week, in the accounts. I haven't a clue about the gambling side of it, but figures float my boat. Greg encouraged me to go part time when I was looking for a new job, and this one is perfect. Ten minutes' walking distance, and numbers. Couldn't be better. It's not so good walking back home because it's quite a steep hill, is Park Grange Road, so I tend to hang around at work until Greg can get me, but the walk to work is lovely.'

'So you went nowhere near your mother's house that morning?'

'No, but I came out of work as soon as she rang with the news. I contacted Greg, he left work and picked me up. We went to Mum's, but I can't remember much about it, it's all a bit blurry. Vic was kind of spaced out, couldn't take anything much in, but she was the one who found Rob so I understand why she was like that.

Mum was trying to be brave, but they both really fell apart when you took them to the station to make their statements. We stayed there until Grace and Megan brought Mum and Vic back home from the police station, and I think we had a takeaway instead of cooking a meal. We were all shocked, as you can imagine. Rob was such a huge part of our family and he hadn't always been like that with Vic. They were brilliant together for years. Greg and I were talking about it, about how he'd changed...'

Sara let herself trail off. It was almost as if she suddenly realised her words were exploding out of her mouth, and she had no idea what she was saying, or how it would affect anything.

'So the change in Rob was noticeable to all of you?' Rosie spoke gently, leading Sara back into the conversation.

Sara nodded. 'It was. We actually wondered if he'd found somebody else, but if he had it was well hidden. I think they just fell out of love – or he did, I'm not saying Vic did. I think she left him because there was nothing else she could do.'

'And I'm sure you're right, Sara. So, just to clarify what you've told me: you left for work, walking rather than travelling with Greg in the car; you were working until your mother rang to tell you of what had happened to Mr Dolan; and then Greg picked you up in the car to take you both to your mother's home. What time did you leave your house to go to work?'

'It would have been around quarter past eight, I guess. I start at nine, but I'm always there early.'

'So from quarter past eight until the time your mother called to tell you of Rob's death, you didn't see or hear from your husband?'

There was a vast chasm of silence. The small recorder kept running, and eventually Rosie said, 'Sara?'

Sara shook her head as if to wake herself. 'Sorry, I hadn't thought about it like that. No, I didn't hear from Greg, but that doesn't mean he took himself off to Vic's house, to kill Rob, if that's what you're inferring. I never see him after I go to work until we come home at night.'

'I wasn't inferring anything, Sara. I was merely checking I had the facts correct. We have to look at your version of events against what Greg is saying to my colleague, and we have to be accurate. Shall we have a cup of tea?'

Sara gave a half smile. 'I'll have a drink of anything as long as it's not coffee. I'll make it.' She stood and walked towards the cupboard where she took down two mugs. She switched on the kettle and turned to Rosie.

'I'm not out of my mind with grief that he's dead, but that doesn't make any of us the killer. I will, at some point, begin to remember the good times with him, and then I'll miss him. Surely it's the person who stole his car who killed him?'

'We believe so, yes. We just don't know who took it. Have you given it any thought?'

Rosie saw the colour disappear from Sara's face, just before she began to run to the bathroom. Rosie moved across to the work surface, and continued to make the two mugs of tea. Sara eventually returned, looking definitely washed out.

'I'm sorry,' she whispered. 'A week this has been happening, and I can't do anything about it.'

'It will pass,' Rosie said. 'Sit down and enjoy this.' She handed Sara the mug, adding that she hadn't put any sugar in it.

'I don't take it,' Sara responded, and sipped at the hot drink. 'It seemed such a good idea, having a baby. Now I'm not so sure.'

'As I said, it will pass. Just about everybody has to work through this phase, but it kind of slips away almost without you realising you're no longer feeling sick. I was the worst with my third one. But it went by the second trimester.'

Rosie switched off her recorder, and the two women sat and

chatted, mainly about having babies that ultimately turned into children; as Rosie explained, that was a whole different ball game.

They were laughing when they were joined by Brendan and Greg. Greg wasn't smiling, and as Bren entered, Rosie stood. 'I hope everything goes well with the rest of the pregnancy, you two,' Rosie said, and moved to Bren's side. 'Are we done?'

He nodded. 'For the moment,' he said. 'If we need to speak with either of you again, we'll have you brought into the station. It will be more formal then, because we'll probably have to read you your rights.'

There was an audible gasp from Sara, and Greg moved to place his arm around her shoulders.

Rosie and Bren walked outside and headed back to the squad car. He handed Rosie the car keys, and climbed into the passenger side.

She didn't start the engine straight away, merely sat and stared through the windscreen.

'That didn't go too well, then?'

He growled in answer.

'That good?' Her tone was conversational, knowing she had to snap him out of this bad mood. What the hell had Greg Carter said to upset her boss so much?

Bren gave a huge sigh in response. 'Sorry, Rosie. Look, I'll drive if you want.'

'Not bloody likely. I want to get back to the station in one piece.' She glanced at her watch. 'Shall we leave Grace and Megan until tomorrow morning? It looks as though you need to calm down before we interview them.'

'Yes, we'll go early. That always unnerves people. Seven o'clock good for you?'

'It is, but I need to know what the hell Greg Carter's said to make you like this. Did you expect him to confess to the murder and he didn't? Because it could easily have been him. He didn't take Sara to work that morning; she walked. He was putting air into his tyres, so she said she'd walk down the hill.'

'Oh, I know what he told her. I also know it wasn't the truth, and he's now wondering if it's going to come out. He told me he was going to put air in his tyres, but when I delved a bit deeper and asked for the exact time and location of this activity, he backed off. I pushed him a bit more to find out why there was a change of plan, and he said he just carried on driving and went to work. He panicked when I asked for his route, said we always thoroughly check alibis, and he would continue to be a person of interest until his alibi was proven.'

Rosie laughed. 'So what was he doing that he couldn't tell us first time around, when his wife was there?'

'I knew you'd click on.' Bren turned to his partner and grinned.

'He's got a bit on the side?'

'Did have. He met up with her that morning to tell her about the pregnancy, and that they would have to split up, he was going to make it work with Sara, et cetera, et cetera. He was pacing up and down, couldn't sit, his hands were shaking. All he could say was he didn't want Sara to know. I asked for the name of his floosy, and he said she's not a floosy, she works in the Town Hall. I'm not sure why that makes her not a floosy, but he seemed to think it did. Anyway, her name is Helen Bowler. We'll go and interview her at work tomorrow, I think. I don't doubt she'll confirm it all happened exactly as he described it, but she's now a lady scorned. She was pretty unhappy it was all coming to an end apparently. Let's see if she can tell us anything else about our lothario.'

Rosie started the engine, and pulled away from the kerb. 'This has really pissed you off, hasn't it?'

'Certainly has. Sara seems a nice lady, although going through it a bit at the moment from the sound of her vomiting. I stopped him going to her, didn't want any conferring between them for our report, but she did sound pretty bad.'

'I made her a cup of tea. It's first trimester sickness, she'll get over it, but it's horrible while it's happening. If she finds out about his activities though, I don't see her dealing with it very well.'

'Well, he'll always wonder whether we're going to drop him in it, won't he? He's getting no assurances from me, and in fact, I might have to drop hints that there's a possibility it will come out in court when we catch whoever killed Rob Dolan.'

Rosie laughed. 'Brendan Franks, you're bloody evil.'

32

WEDNESDAY 21 SEPTEMBER 2022

Grace had just wrapped her towel around her following her shower when she heard the loud rat-a-tat-tat on the door. She wandered down the hallway, frantically trying to anchor the towel more firmly, almost with a feeling of dread about who could be knocking so early – and so loudly.

She peered through the spyhole, instantly recognising the man standing on the other side. She removed the chain and unlocked the door, then stood blocking his entry. Their entry. DC Rosie Waters was standing behind him.

'It's only seven o'clock,' she said. 'Is something wrong?'

'We need a chat,' Brendan Franks said, 'with both of you. Megan is here, I take it?'

'She is, but we've got work you know.'

'I know. It's why we're here so early. We need to speak with you today, and if we hadn't caught you both at home, we would have had to take you out of work to talk to you.' He let the inference of taking them in formally, to an interview room, hang in the air.

'You'd best come in then.' There was a hint of a grumble in Grace's voice. 'Is it okay if I get dressed?'

'Of course,' Brendan said. 'And can you ask Megan to join us as well, please.'

Megan appeared in the bedroom doorway, fully clothed. 'I'm here. Some noisy bastard woke me by hammering on the front door. Grace, go and get dressed, I'll put the kettle on.' She looked pointedly at the two police officers. 'For the two of us. We have to have some breakfast and a drink before we go to work. We don't get to choose our hours like some people do.'

Ouch, Rosie thought, *this was one unhappy lady, and would be difficult to interview, difficult to ferret out any truth or lie underneath all the anger.*

Grace disappeared into the bedroom, and reappeared dressed in jeans and a sweatshirt as Megan finished making their drinks.

It was obvious Grace was uncomfortable, and she turned to Rosie. 'I'm sorry, would you two like a drink?'

Rosie smiled. 'No thanks, we had one at Costa before we came here. And just for the record, we were both in work by half past five this morning. Now, bring your drink please, and we'll go into the lounge. Grace, DS Franks will speak to you in here.'

Somehow Rosie knew that Bren would get nothing out of Megan; he would be better with the gentler Grace.

Megan slumped down onto the sofa, curling her legs underneath her. 'Not a good start to my day,' she began.

'No, and carry on like this and it will get much worse,' was Rosie's short, sharp answer. 'I can have you taken in for formal interview if it should please me to do that, so I suggest you give yourself a shake, stop blaming us for disturbing your sleep, and start answering my questions. Answer them truthfully and we can be gone from here in fifteen minutes, leaving you to do whatever it is you do that is so bloody important. I'm going to switch on my recorder now that we've had that little conversation, so get your head ready to sound like a half-decent human being.'

Megan uncurled her legs and sat in a better position, watching as Rosie placed the recorder on the coffee table, and logged both of them in.

With the interview started, Megan became less aggressive, and Rosie breathed a sigh of relief. She asked her about her movements on the day that Robert Dolan was killed, confirming that she got up early to go for a run along the riverside, then headed up into Sheffield's legal quarter around Paradise Square and the area's hilly terrain. The added workout sounded tortuous as she described it but Rosie made no comment. Megan thought carefully before confirming she continued past the Cathedral, down through the very heart of the city centre, eventually arriving back home just before Clare Staines pulled up to deliver their new shower screen.

'So you went nowhere near the Dolan residence?'

'Of course not. I didn't have the car; I was out running. The car was in our car park, as I'm sure somebody can confirm.'

'I'm sure your route would have taken forty-five minutes, and according to Mrs Staines' statement she arrived here between nine and nine-fifteen to drop off the screen, so that means you left here to start your run around eight thirty-ish. Would that be right?'

'If you say so, but I can't honestly remember.'

'So what time did you get up? You said it was early? You see, Megan, I'm thinking maybe you had a taxi out to Mr Dolan's house because you were up so early. And maybe the route you've described to me is a route taken on another day, not that day.'

Megan looked horrified. 'You think I killed Rob? Why? Why would I want to do that? Vic had already taken the first steps towards getting away from the toxic atmosphere of her home, so none of us had any reason to bump him off.' She stood. 'And look at me! I'm not even five feet two with my shoes on! If I wanted to kill anybody, trust me I'd have to do it with poison because I'm sure as hell not big enough to do it any other way.'

'So, tell me the name of someone other than Clare Staines and Grace Staines who can confirm they saw you out running on that day at the times you have stated. Just for the record, do you have a tracker on your phone to show exactly where your route took you, and how far you ran?'

Megan shook her head. 'No, I've never bothered. It started out as a fun thing to do, and as I've increased my distance it never occurred to me to track them. Sorry.'

* * *

Grace cradled her drink and said nothing, waiting for Brendan to open his notebook and set up the recorder. She did briefly wonder if she could object to the recorder, but then quickly realised he could exercise his right to take her in for questioning, and that was the last thing she wanted.

'Can we begin by you stating what you were doing on the morning of Mr Dolan's murder?'

'I was here. We've only just moved in, and we've had lots of decorating to do. Nobody can confirm it because Megan went out for her morning run, but Mum came around nine-ish with a new shower screen for us.'

Brendan stared at her. 'Did you like Robert Dolan?'

'I used to. He was like my uncle. Rob and Vic couldn't have children of their own, so they always treated us as if we were their kids. We even went on holiday with them a few times, me more than Sara really, because she began seeing Greg and started work when she was sixteen, and didn't like leaving him while she swanned off with the neighbours.'

'What made you stop liking him?'

'Nothing to do with you.'

'It is, I'm afraid.'

Brendan could see the search for a lie flash across Grace's face. 'I could see how he was with Vic.'

Brendan didn't believe a word of what she'd just said. There was something else.

'According to what everybody's said, Vic and Rob's relationship changed about three years ago.' He checked his notebook. 'You were born 1997, so that makes you coming up to... twenty-five,' he said thoughtfully. 'When was the last time you went on holiday with Vic and Rob?'

'When I was fourteen, almost fifteen. They took me to Greece, to Rhodes. Sara didn't want to go, made some excuse about having to work – she was doing a part-time job to earn a bit of money ready for her starting uni. Dad encouraged this, said it was character building. It got her out of that damned holiday, whatever it was.'

'You didn't enjoy it?'

'I didn't go on any more holidays with them.'

'So, this was ten years ago. Do you think things have been going wrong between them for longer than three years then?'

'You want an honest answer?'

'Of course.'

'I think things have always been strange between them. I also think the three years keeps getting mentioned because he became more violent then. It wasn't violence initially, it was things like sarcasm, always denigrating her, knocking her confidence. She had to do everything in that house, he never helped at all – but don't get me wrong, he could be a good laugh. We had some cracking barbecues round at their house, and he was very generous. When they took us on holiday they always paid; they didn't ask Mum and Dad for anything.'

'Are you and Sara close?'

The question seemed to throw Grace off balance. 'We are.' She thought about her answer for a bit longer. 'We were closer before she married Greg, and I know that's an odd thing to say, but being married made her a lot more serious. We always had fun together, but not now. However, having said that, they hadn't been married long when we found out Dad had terminal cancer. None of us have handled that well at all; Dad was only fifty-three when he died.'

'And you and Megan?'

She looked at him, unflinching. 'Strong,' she said.

He closed his notebook. 'Thank you, Grace. I think we'll probably have to talk further because I sense there's something you're not saying. But next time we'll have you in at Moss Way.'

'Not saying?' He sensed a note of panic in her voice.

'I came here today to find out about things that I feel have been glossed over – such as the situation with Robert Dolan and his wife. And then I find out there was some bad blood between you and Rob as well, yet you've deliberately squashed it. Answer it now, or answer it in court, it's all the same to me. But we will sort out who is lying and who is covering for somebody else, I promise you.' He deliberately softened his tone. 'Grace, you have to tell me about Rob Dolan, about the favourite uncle who suddenly wasn't. Does your mum know anything? Or Vic Dolan?' Bren knew instinctively he was getting somewhere and he wasn't leaving the interview to be controlled by Grace.

She gave a huge shiver and tears appeared in her eyes. She was silent, and he didn't push. He was so close to finding what was troubling her. 'It was that holiday,' she whispered eventually, and

Brendan felt relieved that he hadn't switched off the recorder. The closing of his book had been enough of a trigger warning to get her talking honestly.

Bren said nothing, simply waited.

Grace wiped her eyes, and sniffed. 'We'd been there for almost the full week. It was the Friday, and we were flying home on the Saturday. We'd been down by the pool all morning but it had been a real scorcher, so we went and had some lunch, then Vic said she was going for an hour's nap, or she wouldn't have the energy to go out at night. Rob went with her, so I went and got a Coke and took it to my room. My skin was burning, so I decided to have a shower.'

Bren hated himself. He could see what he was putting Grace through, and he hated himself. She was clearly remembering every second of that day, and he knew the actions and any consequences would never leave her memory. Truth was emerging.

'I was nearly fifteen. Yes, I had my own room, but because I was younger than sixteen the hotel gave a key card to them for my room, as well as one to me. If I had thought to actually lock my door as I did at night, nothing of what happened would have been possible, but I didn't. I just let it close. It was locked of course, but could be easily unlocked with the key card from the outside.'

Still Bren said nothing.

'I went in the shower, and suddenly he was there. He slid back the shower screen and he touched me. Everywhere. Never in my life, before or since, have I been so afraid as I was that day. And then he went. I crumpled to the floor, and I don't know how long I stayed there for, but the next thing was Vic knocking on my door to tell me they were going for a walk to the shops and did I want to go. She didn't come in, didn't see the state I was in. We flew home the next day, with me pretending I had period pains to explain how unresponsive I was. I only spoke to Rob after that if I had to.'

Finally Bren spoke. 'I'm so sorry I've forced you to go through this, Grace, but solving this murder is going to be as much about the character of the victim as it is about the murderer. I just have one more question, then you can re-join Megan. Grace, did Robert Dolan rape you?'

33

Helen Bowler glanced at her watch as the telephone rang, and she considered ignoring it. It was one minute to nine, and while she was thinking along the lines of *I don't start till nine*, the digital numbers clicked over to the hour. She reluctantly lifted the receiver, said, 'Planning Office,' and waited.

'Helen? It's Sandy on reception. I have two police officers wanting to speak to you. DS Franks and DC Waters.'

'Okay, thanks, Sandy. Put them through.' Helen briefly wondered what damage had been done to one of their sites, then it registered what Sandy was saying.

'No, they're not on the phone. They're actually here in reception, and they've asked that you come down to talk to them as they need privacy with you.'

'Oh... okay. I'll be down in a minute.'

She replaced the receiver and began the long trek to the opposite end of the building. She loved working in the beautiful Victorian Town Hall, but considered it a drawback that it was always a journey to get anywhere else in the building. She dodged around cleaners busy hoovering the carpets, and headed down the curving stairs towards the magnificent entrance.

The two officers stood as she approached.

Brendan spoke first. 'Ms Bowler? Is there a spare room where we can speak to you for a few minutes?'

'Can't we just sit on the seats you just vacated?'

'Not really. I don't think you'll want everybody hearing our questions.'

'Questions? You're not here to report vandalism then?'

'No.'

Helen stared at them for a moment then walked towards Sandy. She said a few words, and Sandy handed her a key. Bren and Rosie followed her down a corridor, and she unlocked a door.

'I hope this won't take long,' she said. 'I am at work, you know.'

'We could have you check out, and take you back to the station. Would that be better?' Bren spoke very politely, no trace of a threat in his tone, but there was in the words he used. He opened his notebook and placed the recorder on the desk.

Helen stared at the small silver object almost in disbelief at what was happening. 'What? What the hell is going on? I can't think of anything that I could possibly have done wrong.'

'You know someone by the name of Greg Carter?'

She bit her lip. 'I did.'

'Then presumably you still know him, even if you're no longer seeing him?' Rosie could see this wasn't going to be easy.

'Yes, I can tell you know I know him, so what of it?'

'We understand your relationship with this man ended. Can you tell us when?'

'I bloody can,' she grumbled, glaring at both officers. 'Although I can't see what it's to do with you. What we did wasn't criminal. A bit immoral perhaps, but surely an affair isn't illegal?'

'We didn't suggest that in any way, Ms Bowler,' Rosie said,

pleased to see the woman was starting to panic. 'If you can just answer our questions, we can leave you to return to your office.'

'Well, I can tell you when he dumped me. It was my birthday, of all days to choose. He gave me a bunch of garage flowers, a kiss on the cheek and said it was all over. His stuck-up wife is apparently pregnant, and he's staying with her. Well good luck to them. And his bloody flowers only lasted three days.'

With a degree of patience, Bren spoke once more. 'And what date is your birthday?'

'Fourteenth. A week ago.'

'For clarification for the recorder, that is the fourteenth of September, is it?'

'It is.'

'And at what time did he meet you?'

'Around eight thirty. I thought he'd be dropping me at work, but he dumped me and ran. I had to catch a bus into work, and it made me late. Sandy on reception will confirm that. I told her I wasn't well, which was why I wasn't on time, and why my eyes were a bit red. Nothing came of it.'

'And you've had no contact with him since?'

'None. Let his bloody wife have him. He was crap in bed anyway.'

They ignored her final barbed comment, and Bren asked her for her home address. She was reluctant at first to give it, but he explained they would obviously have to contact her if they had any more questions. He thought it would be better in her home rather than her workplace where people were quick to gossip. She pondered for a few seconds and told him her address and mobile number.

They thanked her and left her still sitting in the unused office, her face a picture of misery. She had no idea what ratbag Greg had done, but she hoped they sent him down for a long time.

* * *

Brendan and Rosie headed back to the station via Starbucks and picked up a couple of coffees and two croissants at the drive-through before returning to Bren's office.

Bren needed to listen to the interview between Rosie and Megan, and Rosie needed to catch up on the interview between her boss and Grace. Neither gave each other any clues as to what was on the tapes, believing that listening to it for the first time kept their minds alert, so they finished their late breakfasts and then plugged in earphones to hear the conversations, before uploading all seven of them to their computers – Vicki Dolan, Clare Staines, Sara Carter, Greg Carter, Grace Staines, Megan King and Helen Bowler, all immortalised forever in police files.

With everybody now back at work after the temporary post-ings down to London for the funeral, Bren wanted to have a briefing to bring all his team up to scratch, sending a link to the conversations that had been held over the past couple of days.

And then he wanted feedback. He needed officers out on the streets around the crime scene, something that they physically hadn't been able to do with a murder just five days before the most important funeral of the last century. He wanted them knocking on doors, finding CCTV that they hadn't already discovered – and partly, Bren suspected, because it wasn't only the police that were down in London. Half the population seemed to have been there as well. It was difficult finding anybody at home.

He dipped the last bit of his croissant into his coffee, swallowed and emptied his cup. 'I needed that.' He tipped all the detritus into his waste basket, and dusted all the crumbs off his keyboard by the simple action of turning his laptop upside down and shaking it.

'That'll have done it some good,' Rosie said with a laugh.

'Yeah, smart how we had breakfast in here and not at your desk, isn't it. How did I fall for that?'

'You're a man and not quick enough to catch when a con is in play.'

He thought for a moment. 'Maybe you're right,' he finally conceded. 'Right, I'm going to listen to you and Megan. Anything you want to forewarn me about before I start?'

Rosie shook her head. 'No, don't think so. I'd rather you hear it fresh as we usually do. I'll listen to yours with interest though; Grace looked... wrong... when she came into the room to be with Megan.'

'I'll not say anything, but make sure you listen to the end. I actually thought I'd done all I could, and was getting close to switching off the recorder, but then it took a turn for the better, or worse, whichever way you want to look at it. I don't think it gets us any nearer to discovering who killed Dolan, but it does lead us to other avenues.'

Bren leaned back in his chair, inserted his earphones and switched on the recorder used by his partner that morning. He listened to the aggravation evident in Megan's voice, her dislike of cooperation, and the way she was expertly turned by Rosie. When he got to the end he rewound it and listened again, searching for any nuances in view of what he knew about Grace, but got no sense that Megan knew of fifteen-year-old Grace's troubles on that Greek island of Rhodes.

He could see Rosie was still listening to the longer interview, the one he had imagined would be short and sweet because Grace was definitely the quieter one of the two women. It had proved to be twice as long, because of his instincts kicking in and telling him there was something Grace wasn't saying.

Bren saw Rosie brush away a tear and knew she was almost at the end. When Grace had answered his final question, he had wanted to pull the young woman into his arms and hold her, let her see that not all men were of the calibre of Robert Dolan. She had pulled tissue after tissue out of the box on the side, and he had let her cry it out; all the emotion flowed around the room, and he suspected it was the first time it had been mentioned since the arrival home from that hated holiday.

Rosie lifted eyes shimmering with tears to Bren. 'I couldn't have done this, got this information from her. That was awe-inspiring, the way you let her talk, let her get it all out there with somebody else finally knowing about it after all these years.'

'Did you believe what she said at the end, that she didn't know if he had raped her? She says she passed out, crumpled to the floor, so he could have done anything to her. She didn't know how long she was unconscious for; she woke to hear Vic knocking on her door. And she was cold. She had to quickly put clothes on to get warm – in Greece! I didn't want to ask too much about pain, bleeding and soreness, because let's face it, there's no comeback on this for him, is there? I thought she did amazingly telling me as much as she did. When I asked her about Vic, and if she thought she suspected what Rob had done, Grace said no. Vic didn't change at all towards her, and she thought she would have done if she'd suspected Rob of any wrongdoing. And you heard her at the end pleading with me not to tell Vic.'

Rosie nodded. 'And unless we ever have to, we mustn't. Grace and Megan have a good relationship with Vic, a very close one, and what Robert Dolan did to Grace is something that Vic never needs to know about. I need a drink of water. Listening to that has left me with a nasty taste. We starting the briefing at noon?'

'We are. I want as many of the team as we can get in, and it's time to start allocating who's doing what jobs. It's been damned hard work with the just the two of us doing basically everything. You have any thoughts on Helen Bowler from this morning?'

'I know I could have opened my mouth and ripped her a new arsehole several times, but my gut feeling says she's not involved in anything. I don't think she's that bright, to be truthful. She thought she saw a good future with Greg, but what she didn't reckon was that Greg actually loves his wife, and the baby has put the icing on Greg's cake. I don't think we'll be interviewing her again, despite our assorted threats to her.'

Bren smiled. 'Exactly my thoughts, but let's not reveal our thoughts to Greg, eh?'

34

Jed saw the text from Clare just after lunch. The package from the DNA company had just arrived, and she said it was up to him when to do the test. She had already bagged up the items required to hopefully get John's DNA.

He immediately responded saying he would be there by around half past five, complete his side of the requirements and they could sit back and wait for the results to arrive.

She sent a thumbs up in response, and he smiled. Then it occurred to him that if this test showed he had no connection to John Staines, he would probably never see her again. He would have to politely thank her for not instantly throwing him out, and apologise for troubling her and her family. But what if it showed a positive match?

Would she allow him to meet her family? Was it enough for him that he would know who his father was, even though he would never meet him?

He slipped his phone into his pocket and left the office to take a quick walk around the yard, pausing to watch as the smaller forklift truck didn't seem to want to start. Suddenly it spluttered into life, and he made a note to get it serviced as soon as he could. It was used more often than the larger one, and could get into tighter places. They couldn't manage without it. He did a thumbs up towards the driver, who mimicked wiping sweat from his forehead, and Jed laughed. He had a good gang of workers, and he could rely on all of them.

He returned to the office, opened up his emails, and began to respond to any that needed answers.

* * *

Clare felt a little lost. She didn't know why, but knew once again that she was muddled. The police visit the day before had unsettled both her and Vic, and yet she hadn't felt inclined to talk about it with her. She actually wanted to bury her head in the sands of muddlement, not lifting it out again until the police had arrested whoever had killed Rob.

That thought, of course, led her onto the baseball bat that had been taken in for testing – nobody had got back to her, and it amused her to think that she had come pretty close to whacking Rob with it when he had come around in such a threatening manner, trying to find Vic. They would definitely have found blood on it then, and she might, at this present moment in time, have been getting used to new accommodation in a cell.

She hung the tea towel on its hook, and left the kitchen to head upstairs. She needed the peace of her office. Indeed, it was starting to feel like her office, no longer in her head as John's.

The sun was beginning to sink lower, and the room felt warm. She went towards her cutting out table, where she touched the fabrics she had chosen to make a quilt for her own bed. Her bedroom, complying with John's wishes of two years earlier, was a classical grey, very smart, extremely sophisticated, and utterly boring. She didn't want to lose all the grey, but wanted to change the wall by the bedhead to a wallpapered one, a patterned wallpaper. Watching Megan and Grace do up their flat had inspired her, and she had found a perfect wallpaper. She had bought three rolls of it, and then went searching through her stash of fabric. John had never approved of her sewing activities, saying everywhere felt such a mess when she was using her machine, so this stash had almost been viewed by her as forbidden, and as a result, she had let it all slide. Now the fabric was back in the light, folded carefully and placed on her shelves, and she had matched up the ones she wanted to use to tone in with the wallpaper.

She stood for a while just looking and stroking the fabric, then moved across to the desk. This was where she felt John the most. She had moved his leather chair back to its original place at the desk, freeing up the other chair to be used at her sewing machine, and she sat down, enjoying the feeling of the leather as it wrapped her in its warmth. She opened the hidden drawer and took out the Father's Day card. She wanted Jed to see it, to see if he remembered writing in it. Although she had been the one to suggest the DNA test, she knew what the result would be. She had known from seeing the little four-year-old boy on the photograph that he was John's son. It was simply something else to add to the complete muddled phase of her life.

She left the room taking the card with her, and went back downstairs, surprised to see Vic sat in the lounge, her legs curled under her.

'Hi, there. I didn't hear you come in. You okay?'

Vic shook her head. 'No, it's like living in limbo. Nothing seems to be happening. I felt quite rattled after they came to re-interview us yesterday, and I can't get my thoughts away from it. It felt as if they suspected me, and yet of everybody I've probably got the clearest alibi because they've tracked my car's whereabouts. Tell me honestly, Clare, who do you think could have done this? And so brutally? Whoever killed Rob wasn't a stranger to him, it was somebody who had a reason to hate him. And let's face it, that all points directly to me. The only issue I have with that is that I know I didn't do it, and that scares me. Because somebody did. Do you understand me? I know it all sounds a bit garbled, but right at this moment there is only one person in this entire universe who can say with complete certainty that I didn't bash my husband with a hammer or whatever was used, and that one person is me. That's not good odds.'

Clare laughed. She couldn't help it. The woebegone expression on her friend's face was a sight to behold, and although all the facts were perfectly true, the real truth of the matter was that she did have a spot-on alibi, and there was no denying that.

'Let's get drunk.'

Vic stood. 'Good idea. Why haven't we thought of that before?'

'Just don't let me be falling down drunk before Jed Grantham gets here.'

'He's coming here?'

'Yes, the DNA kit arrived at lunchtime, so he'll be here by half past five. I'd like you to meet him; you're usually spot on with your judgements. I think he's a nice young man, but maybe he's putting it on, I don't know.'

Jed arrived on time, and brought with him a bunch of flowers. He handed them to Clare as he crossed her doorstep.

'These are to say sorry for disturbing you on Monday when you were clearly watching the funeral. It was thoughtless of me; I acted on the spur of the moment, coming here, and I should have thought it through. I believed Mr Staines would be here, but even if he had been, it wasn't the right time or the right way to go about things. I'm an idiot, so the flowers are to say sorry.'

'Thank you, Jed.' Clare smiled. 'Come through to the kitchen. I've left everything on the kitchen table so we can do whatever has to be done in comfort.'

His face didn't show surprise when he saw Vic already in the kitchen.

'Jed, this is my closest friend, Vicki Dolan, usually known as Vic. She's staying for a few days. Vic, this is Jed.'

Vic held out her hand and shook Jed's.

'Good to meet you, Vic. I think I saw you before, crossing the road?'

Vic smiled. 'You probably have. I live almost directly opposite. But there's been a bit of trouble so I've been here for a few days.'

Clare stepped in to steer the talk away from Vic's *bit of trouble* understatement, and the three of them sat down around the table. 'Okay, Jed, this is the stick you have to run around inside your mouth. Read through the leaflet and you'll see what needs doing. We'll get this out of the way, then I have something to show you.'

Jed quietly read the piece of paper, picked up the stick and stared at it for a moment, before putting it in his mouth. He followed the instructions as closely as he could, then placed the stick inside the container provided by the company.

'Is that it?'

'It is. This little bundle here is a hairbrush and two tooth-brushes that belonged to John, and they seemed to think there wouldn't be a problem. I'll wrap it all up tonight, and take it to the post office tomorrow. Letters will be sent to both of us with the results.' She took a deep breath before continuing. 'Jed, I know you look very much like John, but try to keep an open mind until we know for definite. If this proves that you are John's son, then I will introduce you to your half-sisters. They do know about you. Mixed feelings obviously, but prepared for a result either way.'

'Half-sisters? How many?'

'Two – Sara who is twenty-nine, and Grace who will be twenty-five the day before your own birthday.'

'Then more than ever I want this test to return a positive result. I never had any siblings, and it's a lonely life without one.'

Clare reached across the table to pull her bag towards her. 'I want to show you this. It was in the envelope it's still in, along with the photograph you've already seen.'

She handed the envelope to Jed, and he looked at the front before opening the flap. He carefully eased out the card, and inspected it without speaking. Clare waited, letting him savour the moment.

He looked at the front, at the sports car drawing, at the Happy Father's Day wording, then he opened it. He read what it said, and still didn't speak. He reached into his pocket and pulled out a tissue, which he used to mop his eyes.

When he did speak, his voice was guttural. 'I'm sorry, I don't know what to say. I don't remember writing my name on this, but I do remember the cake on the photograph. I didn't know your husband, or at least I don't think I knew him, but was he the sort of man who would have welcomed this card?'

'He would, Jed. He'd kept it hidden away, and I suspect he must have realised I would find it one day and attempt to track you down. He was definitely a family man, and it's my guess that the decision to not acknowledge you as his son was decided by both he and your mother. We already had two girls, and he wouldn't have hurt them for the world. Believe me, if I had known about his affair and its consequences, he would have lost not only me, but Sara and Grace as well.'

She took a second, pristine envelope out of her bag and passed it to him. 'This is for you and your grandmother. It is a copy of the card, a copy of the envelope it arrived in, and a copy of the photograph. I know you said your Gran remembered the picture – well, now she can enjoy it again.'

'Thank you, Mrs Staines. I'll leave you in peace now, and hopefully next time we meet we'll have some good news we can both share. Bye, Mrs Dolan.' He picked up the envelope, and Clare walked with him to the door.

'Jed, thank you for coming. And please, it's Clare from now on. Mrs Staines is a little formal. I'll go and sort out my flowers, but they really weren't necessary. You behaved impeccably on Monday, you're a credit to your mum and gran.'

35

Brendan and Rosie were in Bren's office sifting through reports that had arrived from members of their team, and Rosie felt a draught on the back of her neck as the door opened.

Bren looked up. 'Boss? Everything okay?'

DI Philip Vickery closed the door behind him. 'Everything's fine. Just checking you have enough of a team to get cracking with this now. We've had a meeting upstairs and I assured everybody you were well on top of it, but then thought I'd better check just where you are.' He smiled at Rosie. 'Morning, Rosie. You enjoying working in Major Crimes?'

'It's different to traffic duties and late-night shifts in the town centre, so thank you for thinking of me. It took me a while to get used to the different way of working, and the fact that people listened to me when I had anything to contribute, but I reckon I've found my little corner in this job.'

'Good. That's all I wanted to check. And indications as to a possible arrest?'

Bren shuffled uncomfortably in his chair. 'We've certainly

narrowed it down to a possible three suspects, but one of them will break before much longer, I'm sure of it.'

'Three suspects? And pretty solid?'

Bren grinned. 'Pretty solid, boss. Remember these names, ready for when you see the arrest go through – Greg Carter, Grace Staines and Megan King. I'll bet Rosie's job on it that it's one of those three.'

'Oy,' Rosie said. 'Bet your own job on it; you leave mine alone.'

Vickery turned, opening the door. 'Let me know when you know. And just for the record, Rosie, he can only bet his own job. Yours is safe, from what I can see.' He winked at her and left the office.

'I like him,' she said.

'He's okay. I like that he leaves us to get on with things, just needs an occasional update. He's not pestered us for results on this one, because he knows we've only had the two of us to do all the running around a team would normally do. I suggest when we find out the date of the new King's Coronation, we book our annual leave. It's been damned hard work and longer hours than usual having this murder dropped on us.'

He turned the report round that he had just skimmed through. 'Check this and we can file it. It's the forensic report on the baseball bat we removed from Clare Staines' home. It's showing lots of spray polish, no bleach at all, ever, no blood, no brain matter – in short, nobody used this baseball bat to bash Dolan over the head. I don't doubt we'll be talking to them again in the near future, so we'll return it to her. She obviously leaves it standing by the front door for protection.'

'So what was it? What did he or she use to kill him? And did they take it with them?'

'Nothing's definite on the forensic report but it does say they tested the baseball bat in Dolan's head wound that had caused his death. They are 95 per cent certain that it was a baseball bat that was used, but it's definite it's not this one. As they say, it may be another baseball bat, but until we know who actually killed him I doubt we're going to get much joy pursuing the weapon. I believe whoever it was proved smart enough to take it with them in Dolan's car. And I also feel that car was a bonus for getting away from the house. Dolan certainly helped our killer flee the scene by leaving the engine running, the front gates open and the car pointing out to the road. He couldn't have been more considerate if he'd tried. According to Clare Staines the car was noisy as it was driven away, which leads me to think it was driven at excessive speed by someone not used to driving it, not a more cautious build up to the twenty miles an hour limit for that road.'

'Suddenly we seem to be in the mindset of this character – and it seems to have followed on from yesterday's interviews.' Rosie frowned. 'Did I miss something?'

'No, you didn't miss anything, it was more a case of you didn't see the state Grace Staines was in after she'd given that additional statement. That's kind of opened my eyes. She's never forgotten the horror of it, and I imagine not knowing whether he raped her or not has always eaten away at her.' He banged his fist onto the desk in a gesture of frustration. 'Why the hell can't women just report it if they've been sexually attacked, because even if he didn't force his penis into her, it was still a sexual attack.'

Rosie spoke quietly. 'She was fourteen, Bren. She was a child, and the man who attacked her was a friend of her parents. And the husband of the woman she considered almost like a second mother. Of course she wouldn't tell anybody.'

Bren squeezed his hands together, as if he needed to warm them. 'I hardly slept last night; this was constantly on my mind. I made a hot chocolate around two this morning, an act of desperation. I did end up having a couple of hours' sleep, but that was all.

I went over and over it in my head, wondering if I'd missed something, if I could have been more helpful towards Grace Staines, but I'm sure I handled it correctly.'

'You did. That's why sometimes this is such a shit job, being in the police. Yesterday was a bad day, but we have to have the belief that today will be better. I've listened twice to that recording, and I don't think you did anything wrong at any point. She was totally open with you, probably for the first time ever in her life, and you responded in exactly the right way. I'm not sure I could have handled it as well as you did; I'd probably have gone all soppy on her, given her a hug, told her everything would be all right, when you know it can never be mended, ever. Come on, show your masterful skills and let's go get this briefing underway.'

* * *

Bren listened to the various reports brought in by his team, aware that there was still nothing much to go on. Someone had spoken to a neighbour closer to the end of the cul-de-sac, who had been aware of the fast departure of Dolan's car, and had tutted to herself about it. *He'll kill a child one day* had formed the basis of her thoughts, but then she had changed her thoughts because she realised it hadn't been Rob Dolan driving his car, it had been what she thought was a woman, but she couldn't be certain about that. She could only say with a degree of certainty that it wasn't Rob Dolan; she'd known him for a number of years. The person driving it had pulled a hood over their hair, but the hoodie was a feminine colour, a pale colour, lemon or cream.

That report proved to be the only one that held any new information, and Bren thanked them all for their hard work. He went on to discuss the recorded interviews with the seven potential suspects. He stopped and tapped all the names listed on the white-board behind him.

'There are degrees of suspicion about all of these people, but I feel absolutely convinced that one of them will be arrested. I have never felt this was a random attack to steal the victim's car, that never felt credible. So, yesterday, DC Waters and I went to re-inter-view them. All the interviews were recorded, and I include this woman in this.' He tapped on Helen Bowler's name. 'You'll find out from listening that she is the mistress of him' – he tapped on Greg Carter's name – 'but it's more ex-mistress than mistress. He dumped her on the morning of the death of Robert Dolan. However, bear that in mind. You know what they say about a woman scorned...'

'You're seriously considering her though?' someone called out from the back of the room.

'No, not really, but she is Greg Carter's alibi. Bear that in mind as well.'

He stood and moved towards the whiteboard. 'I am aware it is only a small circle of suspects, and in all honesty my own mind would rule out four of them, but I don't want you to have precon-ceptions so I'm saying nothing more. Listen to everything, jot down anything that springs into your mind while you're listening, and we'll meet up in the morning at nine to discuss further thoughts and make decisions about what comes next. Any questions?'

Everybody stood as one, and Rosie said quietly, 'I guess no questions then. Bet there are when they've listened to the recordings.'

The team members drifted back towards their desks, and to open up their laptops. Headphones went on, and silence fell as they listened to what Rosie and Bren had already heard. He hoped they wouldn't have the sleepless hours that he had experienced, but he guessed being with the victim as she told her story had been the main thing that had stopped his sleep.

Grace Staines had been almost unable to breathe while telling her story; he deserved a sleepless night for forcing it from her. He hoped her future would be better for bringing the actions of ten years earlier out into the open finally.

* * *

Clare picked up the parcel and walked out to the car. She had asked Vic if she wanted to go with her to the post office, but Vic had said she would prefer to stay in, maybe make a couple of cards for upcoming birthdays.

Clare got in the car, switched on the engine and pulled away. The journey didn't take long, and she paid the postage fee of almost four pounds with a grimace.

The postmistress laughed at her. 'Sorry, I don't set the charges.'

Clare sighed. 'I know, it just seems that whatever you do these days costs a fortune. I would make the usual inane comment that I could have taken it there myself and delivered it for cheaper, but that's blatantly untrue, with petrol at God knows what astronomical prices now. Thank you, anyway; it's an important package.'

She left the post office, crossed the road to the bakery and bought two huge vanilla slices. She had to do something to bring a bit of light into Vic's life, because she had the troublesome feeling that whatever had already happened was nothing in comparison to anything that was still to happen.

The police had treated them with respect, had definitely been good with Vic, but there had been an underlying feeling that something wasn't right with the investigation; there was something they weren't in a position to pass comment on, not yet.

She added a Coburg loaf to her order, and then saw a huge

fresh cream cake. By the time she came out, the bill made the post office payment look like peanuts. She carefully deposited the squashy items on to the passenger seat, then drove home hoping nothing had happened to upset anybody while she had been unavailable to calm troubled waters. Or indeed a troubled Rosie Waters. She smiled to herself at the pun, parked her car and entered her house to find Vic cutting and pasting tiny pieces of paper to an A4 piece of card, her fingers stained dark brown with the Distress Oxide.

'You need a bun?' Clare asked, looking on with some amusement at her friend's hands.

'A big bun?'

'A very large vanilla slice.'

Her smile lit up the room. 'I'll go wash my hands then, best friend in the whole wide world.'

36

The afternoon was full of rain. It made the day feel as though winter was well on its way, missing out the beautiful bit that was autumn. Bren stared out of his office window wondering why he'd laughed at his wife that morning when she'd said it was going to rain later. He'd left the house in a lightweight zip-up jacket. What sort of detective couldn't detect it might rain later?

He heard a tap on his door and turned to see Rosie enter, clutching some pieces of paper.

'One or two thoughts from the team, Bren,' she said, and placed them on his desk. 'I've had a quick look through them, and there're a few valid points that have been made.'

'They've listened to all of the recordings?'

'Most of them have listened to all of them twice. I don't have to tell you that the one from Grace has numbed them.'

'I knew it would, but I didn't want to pre-warn them, I wanted them to hear the rawness in her voice. Are most of the comments about Grace?'

'Not really. There are thoughts about skips near to the cheese grater. If the killer took the weapon, it could be dumped in a skip now, but we're nine days on from the murder, so will the skips that could have been there, still be there?'

'Who's mentioned the skips?'

'Layla and Matt. Shall I send them down to have a scout around?'

He nodded. 'And make it now. We don't want to miss this by being a day too late.'

Rosie left his office, then watched as the two officers disappeared to commandeer a car to head down to the city centre. She returned to tell Bren they'd gone. He was now sitting at his desk going through the many comments and suggestions.

'Listen to this smart piece of work.' He pulled a piece of paper towards him that he had put to one side.

When was the holiday? If she was fourteen, wouldn't that make it 2012? When in 2012? Sorry, boss, just my thoughts. Shaz.

'Think I was too dumbstruck by what she was telling me to ask the obvious question?'

'I think we perhaps should have had Shaz with us.' Rosie grinned. 'I didn't think about getting specific dates. What's occurred to Shaz that hasn't occurred to us?' She paused for a moment. 'Oh my God. Is it an anniversary?'

'I'd reached that conclusion as well. So now I have a quandary. I definitely don't want to warn anybody that a lot could be riding on the answer, but I need to know what the holiday date was. How do I find that out without asking anybody?'

'Well, me being a mother to three little darlings, I can tell you the answer to that. School. If they're going on holiday outside of school holidays, you have to jump through hoops and come up with a damn good reason to take them out. Unless she just went back to school a week later and said she'd been ill. Her mother could have rung school to say she was poorly, but either way, there will be a week's absence that shouldn't be there during the school year. And if this murder is an anniversary date, it means they went on holiday halfway through September. If it's not an anniversary date, then the holiday could have been at any time in that year, and we'll have to ask either Vic Dolan or Grace.'

'So now we need to know where she went to school.'

'Westfield. She hated it.'

'You seem to know a lot.'

'I ask a lot.'

'Okay, smart arse, see if you can get anything from Westfield, before we have to give hints to our suspects that they are suspects.'

She held up a thumb, flashed a quick smile at him, and left his office, grabbing her coat and umbrella as she went.

* * *

One and a half hours later, Rosie was collecting two coffees from the Costa drive-through before returning to the office. It had been a battle to get the information from the school, who did eventually deliver when they realised it was homicide and not just a simple bit of vandalism that was in question. It would have been so easy to ring Vic Dolan and ask, *When did you go to Rhodes in 2012?* But supposing the chatty and friendly Mrs Dolan proved to be not quite so chatty and friendly with her bastard of a husband, more murderous? Yes, she had an alibi, but not one of the cameras verified it was her, just her car. Just supposing this was all a set-up...

Rosie placed the coffees in her car cup holders and drove back to the station, laughing at herself for allowing her imagination to run riot just because she'd had to wait in the Costa queue. Vic Dolan had the strongest alibi of all of them.

She headed straight for Bren's office, and handed him a coffee. He thanked her, sat back and said, 'Well?'

'Very well,' she responded, taking a sip of her drink. 'I need this. I had a bit of a battle to get the information we needed, and they ummed and aahed about it being ten years ago, but they eventually came up trumps. Yes, it was September, and the week was booked off as it should be. She booked the break from 9th to 14th September, which was the Monday to Friday. This ties in with Grace's statement saying that he molested her on the Friday and came home the next day. She was back at school the following Monday.'

'And there we have it.' Bren sipped at his own drink. 'This is bloody hot.'

'Sorry, I'll blow on it before I give it to you next time. But you're right, there we have it. Dolan was killed on 14th September, the ten year anniversary exactly to the day of when he attacked Grace.'

'And we're still no nearer solving who killed him because we didn't ask the question we should have asked when we were taking Grace's statement.'

Rosie sighed. She hated it when he was being all enigmatic and know-it-all. She thought they'd be going out, picking up Grace, and bringing her in for further questioning with a probable arrest at the end of it.

It seemed not. It seemed he'd actually been doing some thinking in the peace and quiet of his own office, while working through the notes and thoughts of his team.

He reached forward and pulled a piece of paper towards him. He looked at it, then pushed it across to where Rosie was sitting with her coffee, facing him across the desk.

Just had a thought boss. Did the young lass say she'd ever told anybody else about what happened?

Rosie stared, then lifted her head to look at Bren.

'Did she?'

'I don't know. That's the second question we didn't ask. Let's just think this through before we go tearing off with our handcuffs at the ready. Who would she have told?'

'Not her mum, definitely not her dad, and I guess not Vic. I suspect at such a young age she wouldn't have wanted to talk about it with any of those three. Sara? Maybe. Although they don't strike me as being that close. I think they're a little too different to confide in each other, and I'm pretty sure she wouldn't have told Greg. So really that only leaves Megan. Would she tell her? I understand they're planning on getting married, so it's not just a bit of a romance; they are life partners and they've just bought that apartment together.' Rosie paused. 'I can't believe we're actually saying all of this, but is it the fact that it's the tenth anniversary of the attack that's triggered all this? Has Grace simply had enough, and seeing Vic Dolan's face escalated it? Do we think she couldn't take any more?'

'We need to talk to Grace again, don't we? And maybe have a bit of a shufty around and see if we can spot a baseball bat. Daddy might have provided Sara and Grace with one, but they're all so bloody tight-lipped nobody will ever mention something like that.' He looked at his watch. 'We'll not approach her at work, we'll wait outside their flat until she arrives home. It always puts people off when we're waiting for them.'

'I'm so sick of getting into stinky squad cars. I'll be glad when this one is over and done with,' Rosie laughed. 'I think every copper at this station lives on chips, because that's the over-whelming fragrance inside every car. I swear after this when we're using squad cars to scare people into being grovelling wrecks, I'm going to spring clean them and buy twenty air fresheners.'

'Stop whingeing, woman. Tonight is breakthrough night. I

don't believe we're looking at Grace for this, but I do believe she told somebody about Rob Dolan and his attack on Grace, and whoever she told has used the anniversary of his actions to take him out. It just seems odd that it's a ten-year anniversary – does this mean that they've only been told recently? And is that the third question we should have asked? Crap at this game, aren't we?'

Rosie finished her coffee and sat back. 'We definitely are *not* crap. By the end of this evening I think without any doubt we'll have a suspect in custody, forcing us to work tomorrow to question him or her. And I'd promised the kids a trip to the cinema...'

'Then do that. If you need to take tomorrow off, then do it. We've put enough hours in over the last couple of weeks, and I can bring Shaz in for the interview; she's pretty good at them, but needs to do more. Well done with her mentoring, by the way. I keep thinking to say something to you, and then some other issue crops up and I forget, but she's really coming on.'

'She makes me laugh. It's always good to work with someone who makes you laugh.'

'Do I make you laugh?' His brow creased as he asked the question.

'Bren, I laugh at you, not with you, and that can be even better.'

He digested her words, and then said, 'Sarky cow.'

* * *

They left work just after half past four and drove down to the block of flats by the riverside. Rosie pulled her hood up and tightened the drawstring slightly, put on her gloves and opened her umbrella as she got out of the car. Bren shivered in his lightweight jacket and followed her as she walked across to where they could watch the river.

The Don is the largest of Sheffield's five rivers, and ultimately all of them flow into it before it heads out to the east coast and into the North Sea. It almost always looks dark and forbidding, and today, in the heavy rain, it looked exactly that.

'I could live here,' she said, 'by the waterside. I know it's a bit bleak at the moment, but during the summer months I bet it's wonderful. I also bet it was sunny on the day they came to view it, because who wouldn't want this view from their balcony?'

'Could that be where our baseball bat is?' he said quietly, as if ruminating on the possibility.

'Either there or the bin depository.'

'Then shall we get out of the rain and go and have a look in the bins?'

'Thought you'd never ask, Bren. You take me to the nicest places.'

It was a large room, built as the lower ground floor of the flats. Each flat had their own numbered bin, but they had to check every one – it would be just too convenient for any of their suspects to have thrown it into their own bin. When they walked back outside to even heavier rain, they saw the little Aygo had arrived home.

FRIDAY 23 SEPTEMBER 2022

Rosie took her umbrella back to the car, figuring it would be a hindrance once they were inside the flat, and they headed towards the stairs; Bren was aware of the unease always obvious in Rosie when they had to take a lift, and if the level they were heading for was four or below, he would always suggest the stairs.

Bren sent a text to Shaz while Rosie knocked on the flat door. Megan opened it. There was no welcoming smile.

'You need us again?'

Rosie smiled in an effort to lighten the atmosphere. 'I'm sorry, but we do. We've a couple of further questions for Grace, and we didn't want to trouble her at work. Is she home?'

'She is. She's the main user of the car, so if that's here, Grace tends to be as well. I try to run everywhere; she thinks I'm crazy, but I'm fit. Come in.'

Megan led them through to the kitchen where Grace was stirring a huge pot of food.

'I'm actually still working,' Megan said. 'I've a Zoom call in about five minutes, so do you need me?'

'Possibly. Can you postpone it for an hour?'

'No. I'm not leading it, my client is.'

Rosie looked at Bren for guidance.

'Okay, Megan,' he said. 'Join your Zoom call, but if we need you for anything while we're chatting, I will come and get you.'

'Hang on a minute,' Grace joined in. 'You can't do that. This is Megan's work.'

'I can do that, I'm afraid. We're here with further questions, and we will get our answers. If we need Megan, then she either leaves her Zoom call and joins us in here, or both of you will be taken to Moss Way and interrogated there. And if that happens, don't forget to turn off the stew.'

Rosie desperately wanted to laugh at the final sentence.

The atmosphere inside the flat was palpable. Megan removed her mobile from her pocket and sent off a quick text. She waited until her phone pinged a reply, and she said, 'It's done.'

'Good,' Bren said. 'Now let's cut out all the threats and start talking common sense and the truth.'

Megan and Grace looked at each other and Megan spoke. 'I thought we had told you the truth last night. Do we need a solicitor?'

'If you feel you do, then by all means contact one. Tell him or her to meet you at Moss Way.'

'Thought you said no more threats.' Megan almost growled the words.

'That's definitely not a threat. It's a fact of life that if you ask for a solicitor, for your protection and ours, it has to be at a station, in an interview room. I'm sorry if it sounded like a threat, but it really wasn't meant to be one.'

Liar, Rosie thought.

Both the girls stared at Bren. Grace switched off the heat under the stew and moved away from the cooker. 'Shall we sit in here?'

With the four of them around the table, the kitchen felt full to overflowing, and there was no offer of a cup of tea. Bren switched on the recorder, said the usual registration of who was there, and the date, then turned to Grace.

'Grace, it seems that the indentation in the head of Robert Dolan was very similar to a head wound caused by being hit by a baseball bat. We are aware your mother has a bat that stands by her front door on the instructions of your father, who felt she needed some sort of protection when he was away with his job. However, that bat has been forensically tested, and it has never been in any contact with blood or anything else except furniture polish. My first question is, did he provide baseball bats for you and Sara too?'

'He gave one to Sara as soon as they moved into their house, but for me, only did so reluctantly. You see, when Megan and I moved in together he didn't approve. Therefore, no baseball bat. I mentioned it one day as a joke, but I think Mum picked up that he'd hurt me by not getting me one, and so she had a bit of a go at him. A week later one was waiting at Mum's for me.'

'And where is it now?'

'Gone.' Megan was straight to the point.

'Gone?'

'It is,' she continued. 'We fell over it all the time, and when we left the little house to move in here we realised a third-floor flat was so much safer than a house anyway, so we decided to get rid of it, along with all the other useless bits and bobs we'd acquired. The skip went before we moved in here, so it's long gone now. And, I might add, it was long gone before Rob Dolan met his untimely but welcome end.'

'Welcome?' Rosie said.

'Very welcome. Just look at how it's changed Vic. She smiles again now. We haven't seen many from her for a long time. That smack into her face wasn't the first, you know.'

Bren wrote in his notebook as if it was an important point. He didn't need to, it was all on the recorder, but he wanted them to think what she'd said was significant.

'So' – he lifted his head and looked at them – 'it's either in that skip, in the bins downstairs, or in the river.'

'No, we have to stop doubting ourselves. It's not in the bins,' Rosie said, her eyes on Bren, 'we've looked through every one, black, blue, green and brown. I'll book the divers for tomorrow.'

He nodded.

'But I've told you what we did with it, and it wasn't used for anything, ever.' There was a hint of desperation in Grace's voice.

'We check everything, Grace,' Rosie said, deliberately keeping her voice gentle. 'But we do need to move on to a couple more questions. We are returning to the attack on you in September 2012 on Rhodes.'

Bren's eyes were locked onto Megan's face, a face that had instantly turned to Grace with compassion. It told him everything. She knew all about what Rob Dolan had done that day.

Grace's face drained of all colour. 'I've told you everything.'

'Not quite, Grace, and actually Megan's silence gives us the answer to one of the questions.' Bren paused for a moment to let his words sink in. 'Have you ever told anyone else about what he did to you in that hotel room that day? Fourteenth September 2012, it was. Exactly ten years prior to the date he was murdered.'

Megan stood. 'She told me. She bloody told me!' Her voice was getting louder.

Rosie stood and moved towards Megan. 'Sit down, please. And allow Grace to answer for herself.'

'I told Megan,' Grace replied. 'Nobody else knew. But I could feel it building up inside me and then when I realised it had been almost ten years and it still filled me with horror, I couldn't control the tears and I told her everything.'

The two officers could clearly hear and see the panic in Grace, but neither spoke, waiting for Grace to continue.

'Over the days that followed she didn't leave me alone, but I was planning. I thought I could get away with it – a solicitor's daughter planning a murder? It just wouldn't happen, would it? But that man has ruined my life because I can't get him out of my head. Even if I didn't see him every day, I saw his wife, or that bloody ridiculous car with the noisy exhaust. So I killed him.' Grace spoke with belligerence, anger aimed at Rob Dolan and all he had done to her, and Rosie sensed she had finally told the truth almost with relief at getting it out in the open.

Rosie sat with a thud. Of everything she had thought would happen today, this hadn't figured at all.

'And how did you do it, Grace?' Bren's voice was gentle.

'Knew his routine, didn't I? He always took his car out of the garage, left it ready, and that day I knew Vic wasn't there. I waited till he left to get the car out, slipped in through the door and hid round the base of the stairs till he came back in to pick up his briefcase. As he turned his back, I hit him. I was so incensed that I was standing so close to him, it only took one whack with the bat. I'd taken a backpack with me with fresh clothes in, got changed very quickly then ran outside and into his car.'

Bren sensed a lie.

'You drove after killing him?'

'I did.'

'How did you get there?'

'Tram to the Hackenthorpe stop, then I walked to Vic's home.'

'I think we have a lot more questions to ask. Don't say anything else now, Grace. Stand up, please.'

Grace was trembling as she pushed back her chair.

'Grace Staines, I am arresting you on suspicion of the murder of Robert Dolan on 14 September 2022. You do not have to say anything, but it may harm your defence if you do not mention, when questioned, something which you later rely on in court.'

Megan wailed. Rosie could find no other word to convey the sound that came out of Megan King. 'Noooo!'

She pushed Rosie to one side to get to Grace, and for a moment there was chaos in the kitchen. Megan reached for Grace who had collapsed onto the floor, and whispered something to her. Then she helped her to her feet and sat her on the chair that Bren had moved back to its upright position.

'Grace,' he said, 'do you understand what I have just said? That you are under arrest for murder?'

Grace gave a very small nod, but said nothing. Megan was distraught, staring around the kitchen with a wild expression on her face.

Bren changed his stance and faced Megan. 'Megan King, I am arresting you on suspicion of the murder of Robert Dolan on 14 September 2022. You do not have to say anything, but it may harm your defence if you do not mention, when questioned, something which you later rely on in court.'

It was Grace's turn to scream.

'No!' she shouted. 'Megan did nothing.'

And Rosie knew exactly where Bren was leading. 'I believe you both went on the tram that day, in disguise probably. You didn't want to be recognised. You made your way to the Dolan house and then it all happened exactly the way Grace has phrased in her confession. But then I think she's omitted to tell us that you drove the getaway car, Rob Dolan's car, knowing Grace wouldn't be able to drive anywhere after killing a man in cold blood. You were already in that driving seat, possibly lying low, until Grace had done the deed, then you were instantly ready to drive away fast.

Megan, you were complicit in this murder. You knew it was to happen, how it would happen, and that a car would need driving. You will be charged jointly with this offence. Stand up both of you, please.'

* * *

Within ten minutes, the two women were in handcuffs and being helped into the back of the two police cars Bren had summoned from outside the flat, before they went in. Bren and Rosie watched as they were driven away, and then Rosie allowed herself to sag. She leant against Bren, who held her for a moment.

'You okay?' he said.

'Kind of. How the hell did you know to order two cars to be waiting? I thought we'd come to arrest Megan. When you arrested Grace first that completely threw me. I decided I was a rubbish detective at that point, but then you arrested Megan so I decided I wasn't that rubbish.'

'Don't be daft. Everything you've said, or just thought aloud, during this investigation has led us to this point. You're definitely a smart cookie, Rosie Waters, and I know this may stop you taking the kids to the cinema tomorrow because I think with two to question you'll have to be there, but take them next week, and I'll pay.'

'You're all heart, Bren Franks. Does that include popcorn and drinks?'

* * *

Telling Clare Staines and Vic Dolan together an hour later was even more difficult than arresting Grace and Megan. Vic Dolan had taken the news without flinching, but had said very little.

Clare had been drained of all colour, and had wanted to know if she could see Grace.

Once Bren and Rosie had left, Vic returned to her own home for the first time since Rob's death, and slept on the sofa for the night.

Clare didn't sleep at all.

EPILOGUE

There was a feeling of relief throughout the Moss Way station that the forensics had come up trumps with the baseball bat found embedded in the mud of the River Don. It was the final seal on the case, and nobody had expected that they would find the bat anywhere, but Bren requested twice that divers be sent down, just to rule it out. His request was initially refused on the grounds that it was unlikely in such a fast-flowing river that it would be anywhere near the flats occupied by Grace Staines and Megan King, but he persisted and requested again. His superiors gave in and said yes, for one day only. With the recordings and the subsequent confessions from both girls, they didn't need this final piece of evidence. Bren wanted it.

He had been there all day on his one-day allocation, and it was found. It went immediately to forensics, who mournfully said don't expect much, it's been in the water a long time, but his hope never died. And there was blood. Rob Dolan's blood.

He celebrated quietly with Rosie, who was as surprised as he was that they could still get some forensics from it, but she enjoyed the coffee and doughnuts they munched their way through as they toasted the persistence they had demonstrated with regard to the baseball bat.

'They took it exactly as I expected them to take it, the Staines family.' Rosie gorged happily on the doughnut but her thoughts had drifted back to the day when they had gone to see Clare Staines, after the arrest of her daughter.

Bren nodded. 'Ever the lady, isn't she?'

'She is, and I like her. And the awful thing about all of this is I can empathise with Grace. She was a child, Bren, a child. But murder is murder, and she wasn't a child when she decided taking that action was one way of wiping it from her memory. She wouldn't have to see him again.'

'You think all of this will be classed as mitigating circumstances when they get to being sentenced?'

'The judge will know about it, but to take a man's life... no, I think they'll both get a hefty number of years. Of course, by pleading guilty and not going to court it's not going to come out about the affair Greg Carter was having. That's a blessing, because there's a baby involved, and I would hate to see them split up because of a stupid little affair that was never going to last the course.' Rosie picked up a second doughnut. 'This was very nice of you to treat us to coffee and doughnuts.'

'I am nice.'

She spluttered with laughter. 'Yeah, right.' She was quiet for a moment. 'That family has been decimated by this. The shock on Vic Dolan's face was almost too much to see. She not only had the shock of it being Grace who'd actually struck the killing blow, but she had to be told why Grace had done it. It's been an awful year for all of them; let's hope 2023 sees them pulling together. I know Clare's seen Grace a couple of times, and she'll get into the routine of doing that, but it's not going to be easy from now on.'

'You're too soft, Rosie Waters. Grace killed him, and she should have thought of all actions having consequences.'

Rosie shrugged. 'I know. If I pick up another doughnut will there be consequences?'

'Too bloody right there will,' he said, and closed the lid of the box. 'Besides, it was only last week you said you were dieting.'

'Look, smart arse, I wanted three, and I've only had two. That is dieting, isn't it?'

He sighed and reopened the box.

* * *

Christmas Eve 2022

The air in the Staines house wasn't a festive one. Clare knew that if she was to impress Jed and Eloise, she would have to introduce at least a smile into the evening. She looked at the small Christmas tree, hoping it wasn't too small. She simply hadn't wanted to take on her usual role of Mrs Christmas to all and sundry this year, and everything was very much muted.

She couldn't imagine how Grace and Megan would be feeling, and she was finding that to retain her own sanity she was having to continually push the two girls to the back of her mind, particularly her daughter.

She would never stop her two letters a week, written at her desk in her office – one to Grace, one to Megan – but if she was to exist for any length of time without going mad, she would have to place the whole situation onto a different plateau to the rest of her life.

Already there was a massive rift between her and Vic. When

Vic had told her she had put the house on the market, she had been shocked, but not unhappy. Seeing Vic every day just reminded her of what had happened on that final holiday and it made the friendship between the two fraught, to say the least.

She thought back to the day of the arrest, the arrival of DS Franks and DC Waters to tell them the girls had been arrested, and the exact truth of why. Vic's panic attack had been spectacular, and had taken some time to bring under control. Tears had flowed from both women, and as soon as the two police officers had left to prepare their interviews for the Saturday morning, Clare had summoned Sara and Greg to her house. At least that was how Sara referred to it. A summons.

Knowing it would be in the papers the following day, Clare considered it imperative that she told her elder daughter immediately. It turned into something like a funeral wake, and Clare hoped that intense feeling of grief they'd been feeling since it happened would disperse with the meal she and Vic would be sharing with her newfound relatives, aided by Sara and Greg.

Initially she had decided Vic wouldn't be a part of it, but ever-sensible Sara had persuaded her otherwise.

'Vic is grieving over this as well, you know, Mum,' had been her words, so the following day she had asked Vic if she would like to be there.

And so tonight Clare would be hosting a Christmas meal, feeding Vic, Sara and her growing bump, Greg, Jed and Eloise. She knew they would all skirt around the subject of Grace and Megan and that of their sentencing court date of late January, but she had felt a certain warmth following the unexpected phone call from Jed as soon as the news broke in the newspapers. He had offered immediate support – if she needed it, of course, he had said hesitantly – and they had chatted for some time, mainly about John, but she felt she knew him just a little bit more by the end of the call.

The DNA results had come as no surprise; he was John's son without any doubt.

And tonight would be the sealing of some sort of commitment. Clare knew the young man would be a part of her life from now on, perhaps not as much as her own two daughters, but definitely a part of her life.

By seven o'clock, everyone had arrived, and Clare led Jed and Eloise into the lounge, where Vic was handing out drinks.

'Okay, everybody, can I introduce all of you to John's son, Jed, and his lovely gran, Eloise. Eloise is Kirsty's mum, and the late Kirsty is Jed's mum. Please welcome them into my home, and our family. Having spoken to Jed several times over the past few months I happen to know he is delighted to have siblings, even if they are sisters. I think he's a bit aggrieved I didn't have a son.' She ended with a laugh. She was determined there would be some jollity on this first Christmas without Grace.

Sara put down her orange juice and walked across to Jed. She wrapped her arms around him, and hugged him. 'Welcome to our family, Jed. We're a bit depleted now, but I know Mum has kept you informed, and one day you'll get to meet Grace.' She stepped away, and hugged Eloise. 'And I hope this influx into our family makes you my gran too, Eloise. But I do have to warn you that if you take on that role, you'll soon be a great-grandmother.' She patted her stomach. 'Due the end of March,' she added.

Eloise smiled at her. 'I'll be delighted to be a great-grandmother. And a grandmother, to both you and Grace.' She pulled herself a little straighter. 'Jed has kept me informed of all the happenings of the past few months, and believe me, I know of unexpected things that can happen in families. I almost lost my daughter and grandson in a car accident several years ago, and waiting to hear if they would survive was the hardest thing I've ever gone through. One day Grace will come back to you, and Jed and I will welcome her just as warmly as we want to officially welcome you tonight. Thank you for inviting us to share your Christmas Eve.'

Clare clapped her hands and led everyone through to the dining room, where Christmas carols played softly in the background and the little tree glowed brightly on the stand in the corner of the room.

Place names had been set, and Jed found himself with Sara to his left and Vic to his right. He took a deep breath. He felt he somehow belonged around this table, just as much as he belonged at the kitchen table in the home he shared with Eloise.

Greg did the honours with the wine, and they all pulled crackers in order to have a Christmas tissue paper hat. There was laughter at the corny jokes, and they worked their way through the totally delicious meal, chatting and getting to know each other. Vic was a little quieter, but she clearly enjoyed the meal, and Clare asked for her help when she went into the kitchen to get the desserts.

'We need to talk,' Clare said. 'I hate this estrangement, and I shouldn't blame you for the actions of your thug of a husband. Please don't go home to your empty house tonight, stay here. Your room is still made up for you. Sara and Greg are staying over – I think really it's because Sara would still like Santa Claus to be real, and he always was here.'

Vic gave a strangled sob and walked into Clare's open arms. 'You know I worshipped your girls as if they were my own. I would never knowingly have put them anywhere near a paedophile, because that's what he'll always be known as now. Grace did this world a favour, doing what she did.'

'So you'll stay?'

'Thank you, I will. Now let's take these desserts through and we can relax.'

* * *

With everything cleared away, they were in the lounge by just after nine, talking about Christmases of the past, and the fact that the younger members in the group couldn't ever remember a white Christmas.

The Echo Dot was now regaling them with Christmas songs rather than Christmas carols, and a sing-song appeared to be on the cards.

The knock on the door startled them all. Knocks on the door over the past few months had tended to indicate a police presence, and Clare hoped desperately they wouldn't do that on Christmas Eve.

She peered through the spyhole and saw red. Literally. She cautiously opened the door and the fat man standing on the other side said, 'Ho ho ho.'

She couldn't speak. Why was Santa Claus standing on her doorstep? He leaned forward and handed her a sack.

'Merry Christmas, Mrs Staines.' Then he turned and walked down the path, then continued to walk down the road, waving at anyone he saw.

Clare took the sack into the lounge and turned to Sara. 'I apologise, my love, for telling you once that Santa Claus isn't real. He's just delivered this to our front door. I didn't see Rudolph, so don't go tearing off down the road after him...'

She opened the sack, and there were several gifts inside all addressed to people in the room. Only Jed knew the identity of the man in red; his forklift driver had been only too willing to earn an extra £100 to turn up with a sack on his back. As he watched the delight on the faces of everyone, including his own as he opened the gift he had addressed to himself, a wallet from the Sheffield Wednesday shop, he knew it was the best £100 he had ever spent.

They finished opening their gifts, and Sara asked that they excuse her. Her back was aching, and baby was jumping around all over the place, so she felt bed was calling. Greg went with her, and shortly after, as Jed helped Eloise out of the comfortable armchair that he was sure she could happily sleep in all night, he thanked Clare for a wonderful night.

'Happy Christmas, everyone,' he called as he reached the front door, and he held out his arm for his grandmother to take. He helped her into the car and went round to the driver's side, checking she was safely strapped in. He'd seen the number of sherries she had imbibed.

'They're nice,' she said, sounding sleepy, and he hoped she wouldn't nod off before they arrived home.

'They're lovely,' he agreed. 'Do you think my new stepmother will put me in her will if I hang around, as Dad didn't bother to put me in his?'

* * *

The woman walked up to Greg and Sara's home, glancing carefully around her. She didn't want to bump into her ex-lover, but he would surely pay for dumping her. She had chosen the card with care, the front declaring it was for *The One I love*.

I miss you, Greg, she had written, adding *with all my love, Helen* just to make it very clear.

She took the Christmas card from her bag, and slipped it quietly through the letter box before turning and walking away, a smile on her face. 'Happy Christmas, Greg and Sara,' she said.

ACKNOWLEDGMENTS

My truly grateful thanks go to the amazing team at Boldwood who go the extra mile to make sure this book has left the nest in as near a perfect a state as it is possible to be.

My team of ARC readers are my cheerleaders, and help with promotion of the book, alongside making sure their reviews are ready to go on launch day. A brilliant team! And I have to mention my beta reading team of Marnie Harrison, Alyson Read, Nicki Murphy, Tina Jackson and Denise Cutler. Where would I be without the five of you?

My next thank you is for a special lady, Vic Dolan, who won the chance to have her name in one of my books. Here it is, Vic! Happy reading.

And on to my author friends, without whom I wouldn't even get through the day. Valerie Keogh, Judith Baker, you make me smile. Constantly. A big shout out to other members of the writing community for their support – Susan Hunter, Diana Wilkinson, Mandy James, Patricia Dixon and Keri Beevis. It would be a lonely job without your invaluable support with assorted queries, and your listening ears.

And finally thank you to my family, too many to name, but you all know who you are. Love to you all.

Anita Waller

Sheffield, UK, 2023

MORE FROM ANITA WALLER

We hope you enjoyed reading *The Couple Across the Street*. If you did, please leave a review.

If you'd like to gift a copy, this book is also available as an ebook, hardback, large print, digital audio download and audiobook CD.

Sign up to Anita Waller's mailing list for news, competitions and updates on future books.

https://bit.ly/AnitaWallerNews

Explore more gripping psychological thrillers from Anita Waller...

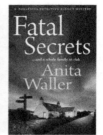

ABOUT THE AUTHOR

Anita Waller is the author of many bestselling psychological thrillers and the Kat and Mouse crime series. She lives in Sheffield, which continues to be the setting of many of her thrillers, and was first published by Bloodhound at the age of sixty-nine.

Visit Anita Waller's website: https://www.anitawaller.co.uk

Follow Anita on social media:

twitter.com/anitamayw
facebook.com/anita.m.waller
instagram.com/anitawallerauthor

Boldwœd

Boldwood Books is an award-winning fiction publishing company seeking out the best stories from around the world.

Find out more at www.boldwoodbooks.com

Join our reader community for brilliant books, competitions and offers!

Follow us
@BoldwoodBooks
@BookandTonic

Sign up to our weekly deals newsletter

https://bit.ly/BoldwoodBNewsletter

THE

Murder

LIST

THE MURDER LIST IS A NEWSLETTER DEDICATED TO SPINE-CHILLING FICTION AND GRIPPING PAGE-TURNERS!

SIGN UP TO MAKE SURE YOU'RE ON OUR HIT LIST FOR EXCLUSIVE DEALS, AUTHOR CONTENT, AND COMPETITIONS.

SIGN UP TO OUR NEWSLETTER

BIT.LY/THEMURDERLISTNEWS